"You don't have much of a sense of humor, lady," Jed taunted.

Tara refused to rise to the bait. "Not when it comes to you I don't. For three years I've watched how you operate—disarm your intended victims with your charm—"

"Intended victims? Now wait just a minute," Jed protested. "I—"

"Well, I don't find you charming," Tara interrupted. "I find you superficial, predictable, and manipulative."

"Why not add homicidal to your list? That's how I'm feeling toward you right now."

A peculiar surge of excitement rushed through her, emboldening her in a strange new way. "I'm so scared," she jeered, her dark eyes bright with challenge. She wondered vaguely what had gotten into her.

Jed stared, floored by her response. "I wonder if you realize just how badly you're asking for it, baby?"

"That old line?" Tara dismissed him with a shrug. "No one could accuse you of originality."

Jed moved toward her with the swiftness of a cat about to pounce on its prey. But Tara quickly and easily stepped out of his reach.

Jed frowned. It was the first time he'd tried that lunge and missed. Then it hit him. He'd made a sexual move on Tara Brady, the one woman in the world he didn't dare want. But he couldn't deny the hot flash of desire that surged through him. . . .

WHAT ARE *LOVESWEPT* ROMANCES?

They are stories of true romance and touching emotion. We believe those two very important ingredients are constants in our highly sensual and very believable stories in the *LOVESWEPT* line. Our goal is to give you, the reader, stories of consistently high quality that may sometimes make you laugh, sometimes make you cry, but are always fresh and creative and contain many delightful surprises within their pages.

Most romance fans read an enormous number of books. Those they truly love, they keep. Others may be traded with friends and soon forgotten. We hope that each *LOVESWEPT* romance will be a treasure—a "keeper." We will always try to publish

LOVE STORIES YOU'LL NEVER FORGET
BY AUTHORS YOU'LL ALWAYS REMEMBER

The Editors

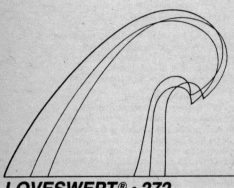

LOVESWEPT® • 272

Barbara Boswell
And Tara, Too

BANTAM BOOKS
TORONTO • NEW YORK • LONDON • SYDNEY • AUCKLAND

AND TARA, TOO

A Bantam Book / August 1988

*If you would be interested in receiving protective vinyl
covers for your Loveswept books, please write to this address
for information:*

Loveswept
Bantam Books
P.O. Box 985
Hicksville, NY 11802

ISBN 0-553-21917-0

Published simultaneously in the United States and Canada

PRINTED IN THE UNITED STATES OF AMERICA

O   0 9 8 7 6 5 4 3 2 1

One

Tara Brady noticed the sleek, low-slung black sports car parked in front of her apartment building the moment she turned the corner onto her street. She couldn't identify the make of the car, but guessed that it was imported and wildly expensive, the kind of car which inevitably drew attention from admiring passersby. Unfortunately, it was also parked in the space where she always parked, and she had a trunkful of groceries to unload. A quick glance up and down the street revealed no other available parking places. She frowned. It was either double-park in the street or lug eight bags of groceries from the nearest available space, which was probably halfway across town.

Tara chose to double-park. She was lifting the first of the bags from the trunk when a tall, lithe, platinum blonde rushed out of the building, calling her name. It was Katherine Cann—"I'm Kayci. That's K-a-y-c-i" —Tara's upstairs neighbor in the renovated old house.

"Isn't it a beauty, Tara?" Kayci asked breathlessly. She was wearing a tight leather miniskirt and thigh-high stockings, the tops of which showed when she bent over—which she seemed to do with predictable regularity. Her narrow high-heeled shoes added length and shapeliness to her legs. "And you should see who drives it!" she said dramatically.

"I take it you're referring to that alien intruder parked in my space," Tara said dryly, offering the woman a paper sack. Tara was well aware that Kayci Cann was not given to neighborly gestures like helping to carry groceries and wasn't surprised when she completely ignored the bag.

With an inward smile, Tara hoisted it onto her hip and grabbed two more light bags. She headed toward the front door, Kayci trailing her.

"It's a Lamborghini Countach!" Kayci paused to lovingly stroke the shiny black hood of the car. "One of the newest, most expensive cars on the market this year! And, Tara, the owner is moving into our building! He's taking the empty downstairs apartment, right across from yours!"

Kayci always spoke with breathless urgency, as if she were reading dialogue written in italics and punctuated with exclamation points. Tara resisted the urge to make a comeback in the same style. She knew it would sail right over Kayci's head, anyway.

"I haven't met the guy yet," Kayci prattled on, "but I saw him come into the building with the landlord. He's got a body to die for, Tara! Six feet two inches of muscled masculinity. Tanned, broad shoulders, long legs. Great face, too!"

"Sounds a lot like the Ken doll my little sisters used to play with," Tara remarked.

Kayci giggled. "Well, I'll play Barbie to his Ken any day."

There were two apartments downstairs and two upstairs in the building, and Tara headed to hers, the first floor on the left. She set down her bags on the mat and was groping for her key when the door to the apartment on the right swung open.

"It's him!" Kayci whispered before letting out a delighted little gasp. "He's coming out!"

Tara turned impassive brown eyes to her new neighbor's door and waited. Jed Ramsey stepped out into the small hallway. He was wearing a blue chambray shirt, the sleeves rolled to his elbows, a pair of faded jeans which conformed all too faithfully to the virile outlines of his body, and a well-worn pair of scuffed leather boots.

Tara's jaw tightened. Like all the other Ramseys, Jed was good-looking, and he knew it. Some people claimed that he was the most handsome of the four Ramsey brothers. He wore his dark, sable-brown hair a bit longer than his more conservative brothers and it gave him a slightly disreputable look.

And he *was* disreputable, Tara knew. Those beautiful light gray-blue eyes of his, screened by thick, dark lashes, always seemed to hold a sexually speculative rakish gleam. His mouth was well shaped and frankly sensual. Whether twisted into a derisive smile or a sullen scowl, the two expressions he most often wore, his mouth was always compellingly sexy.

He radiated an intense and dangerous sexuality which women found challenging and irresistible. Not Tara, though. She knew too much about him and the Ramsey family. Forceful, dominating and ruthless might attract and excite others, but not her. She knew enough to keep her distance from him.

Kayci, however, did not share her antipathy. "Well, hello, neighbor," she said in a manner so blatantly seductive that under normal circumstances Tara would've been hard pressed not to grin. But the threat of Jed Ramsey was not a normal circumstance.

"What are you doing here?" Tara demanded, frowning at Jed.

"Moving in, baby-face," was his laconic reply. "Any objections?"

Tara scowled. "Plenty! What are you Ramseys up to now?"

"Paranoid, isn't she?" Jed directed his characteristic sardonic smile at Kayci, who was gazing at him with admiring, limpid blue eyes.

"She's a reporter for a radio station," Kayci explained,

as if that bit of information explained Tara's uncon-
cealed hostility.

"I'm well aware of that," drawled Jed. "It caused quite
a furor within our respective families when little Tara
announced that she'd been hired by a radio station
way up north in Pittsburgh, Pennsylvania."

Tara grimaced. Furor was putting it mildly. Neither
her family nor Jed's had wanted her to move so far
from Houston. Hers because they would miss her dread-
fully, his because they had plans for her—a fate she'd
been determined to escape.

Kayci was not pleased that Jed's attention had been
diverted from her. Seeking to recapture it, she thrust
her ample chest forward and cooed, "I'm Kayci Cann.
That's K-a-y-c-i. I live in the apartment upstairs right
above you, and I'd like to personally welcome you to our
building."

Jed's dark, thick brows lifted and he gave a slow,
sexy smile. "I'm Jed Ramsey, and I can't think of anyone I'd rather have above me than you, K-a-y-c-i."

Tara rolled her eyes. Obviously, his lines hadn't im-
proved any, she thought waspishly. She stooped to
pick up her groceries.

Jed followed her into her apartment, pausing to gaze
around the living room which she'd furnished in shades
of blue and yellow. "Your place looks good," he remarked. "Not at all what I expected."

Kayci followed them, appearing somewhat bewildered.
Tara put the bags on the kitchen counter and started
back out to her car for more.

"Aren't you going to ask me what I'd expected?"
prompted Jed, tramping along after her. Kayci followed
him.

Tara heaved an exaggerated sigh. "I know I'll probably regret this, but what did you expect my apartment
to look like?"

Jed's pale blue-gray eyes gleamed. "I thought everything would be done in baby pink with white lace and
ruffles. Girlish and sweet, just like you."

As much as she would've liked to counter with a

lecorating slur of her own—something about black
eather and chains and nasty-boy studs—Tara let his
emark pass. She refused to be drawn into a verbal
slugfest with a Ramsey. It might be their favorite sport,
but it wasn't hers.

The three of them reached her car, a somewhat dented
teal blue Mercury Cougar. She had just the slightest
problem with depth perception and the Cougar bore
the evidence of it. After firmly plunking three of the
heaviest grocery bags into Jed's arms, she managed to
unload one onto Kayci, leaving just one more to carry
herself. They all trudged back into the apartment in
silence.

"If you'll excuse me, I have to find a place to park my
car," Tara said, flicking a disapproving glance at Jed.
"Yours is in my parking space."

Jed was entirely unrepentant. "A car like mine has to
be kept within sight. Yours will be undisturbed anywhere."

"Thanks a lot," Tara grumbled. She could always
insist that he move his Lamborghini, of course, but
she knew how the Ramseys adored their cars. Jed
undoubtedly had a personal relationship with his. Her
car did not engage her emotions; furthermore, she
suspected that no self-respecting car thief would bother
to steal it.

The sky was overcast as she trudged back to her
apartment, six and a half blocks west of the parking
space she'd found. Tara made it inside just moments
before the clouds burst to drench the city with a late-
afternoon October shower. Jed and Kayci were still
ensconced in her apartment, sitting on opposite kitchen
counters while the groceries sat untouched between
them.

"Time for you to go home, Jed," said Tara. It was
more of an order than a suggestion. She didn't want
him around. He was too strong, too powerful. He was
intensely sexual and his presence disturbed her. It
always had. And *that* disturbed her. He shouldn't af-
fect her at all. She ought to be indifferent to him. He

certainly wasn't her type. She liked nice, quiet, friendly, nonthreatening men. Hardly an apt description of Jed Ramsey.

"I think I'll stay here," Jed replied, his gray eyes taunting her.

"Why do I have the strangest feeling that you two know each other awfully well?" Kayci wondered aloud. "And that you don't like each other awfully much?"

Jed chuckled. "Hey, is this girl perceptive or what?"

Tara cast him a cool glance, then turned to Kayci. "You're right, Kayci, Jed and I do know each other—way too well. We met four years ago when my family moved from West Virginia to Houston, Texas, where his family lives."

"Thus beginning a series of Brady—Ramsey entanglements," Jed added. "My two older brothers are married to her two older sisters."

"Rad to Erin and Slade to Shavonne," Tara clarified.

Kayci was already looking bored. "So you're what we call 'kissin' kin' down home in South Carolina." Her Southern drawl became startlingly more pronounced as she sidled closer to Jed.

"No." Tara shook her head. "We're what is called no relation at all." She turned to Jed. "Nor are we ever going to be, Jed Ramsey, so if you're here because your father has offered you some spectacular bribe to marry me, you can just forget it."

"Marry you?" gasped Kayci, her blue eyes widening.

"You have delusions of grandeur, kitten," Jed drawled. "I wouldn't marry you if my father offered to make me chairman of the board of Ramsey and Sons and threw in a fire-engine-red Rolls Royce Corniche convertible as added incentive. I'm here in Pittsburgh strictly on business."

"And that's why you moved into the apartment next to mine, when there are any number of places in the city where you could stay?" Tara asked archly.

"Tara, have you lost your mind?" demanded Kayci. "Why would a man like Jed—a man who drives a Lamborghini Countach!—want to marry you? And on the off chance that he did, why in the world would you refuse?"

Tara concentrated on unpacking her groceries and putting them away. "It's a long story, Kayci."

Kayci made a face. "I hate long stories!"

"I know you do, so I won't bore you with it," Tara promised. It was times like these when she found it difficult to believe that Kayci was almost twenty-eight years old, nearly five years older than she.

"Tara and I share a mutual aversion," Jed interjected blithely, his eyes roving wolfishly over Kayci's voluptuous figure.

Tara had seen him look at hundreds of women in just that way during the four seemingly interminable years that she had known him. His practiced, seductive gaze, brimming with machismo, had always annoyed her, but right now it infuriated her. Kayci didn't seem to mind, however. She was studying him just as intently and with just as much undisguised sexual hunger.

Tara viewed the two of them with open disgust. What could be worse than being stuck in her own kitchen watching the two of them practice their moves on each other?

"I can't believe that cute little Tara shares a mutual aversion with anybody," Kayci cooed. "She's so sweet! Everybody likes her and she likes everybody."

Tara frowned. How had Kayci managed to make those innocuous words sound so insulting? "Well, I don't like Jed Ramsey and he doesn't like me."

"It's nothing personal," Jed explained easily. "It's just that cute little Tara and I, through no fault of our own, have been thrust into a very awkward situation. Things have worked out so well between her sisters and my brothers—you know, marriage and kids and all—that both our families have it in their heads that the two of us should get together."

He took a strand of Kayci's platinum hair between his fingers and rubbed it in the most suggestive way. "The third-born Ramsey brother marries the third-born Brady sister. Like it's destined or something."

"How creepy," Kayci said and yawned.

"To say the least," Tara agreed. "The last person in the world I'd marry is Jed Ramsey. You see, it *is* personal on my part. I've disliked him from the moment I met him."

She shivered, remembering that traumatic initial meeting. "Even though the Ramseys have more money than they know what to do with, they tried to cheat my sisters and me out of an inheritance we'd received from Augusta Ramsey, one of their relatives. I'll never forget the first time my sisters and I met the Ramsey family. They were angry and insulting. They shouted and threw things and nearly scared us out of our wits."

She didn't add that she and her two younger sisters, Colleen and Megan, had been so frightened and hurt by the hostility directed toward them that they had cried. But it was true, and Tara would never forget it.

"Scaring little girls! That was mean of you, Jed," Kayci admonished in a flirty tone that completely belied her words.

Tara burned. "Jed Ramsey is probably the meanest of the bunch—and if you know the Ramseys, that's saying a lot. They've perfected meanness to state-of-the-art standards."

"You're exaggerating," Jed protested. Her descriptions of his family were beginning to get to him, and he wasn't sure why. Certainly, he'd heard worse said about the Ramseys—he'd even said far worse to his family members' faces! But this . . .

An uncomfortable and unfamiliar feeling of shame crept through him. He remembered that first Brady—Ramsey meeting quite well. And it had gone exactly as Tara described. The Ramseys had been intimidating and unfriendly and yes, mean, to the Brady sisters. His brother Slade had been the only one to champion the girls, to stand up for them and prevent the rest of the Ramseys from wresting their inheritance from them. And the three youngest Brady sisters, teenagers Tara, Colleen, and Megan, had cried. If he tried, he could summon up a picture in his mind of the three tearful and trembling young girls. It was not an image he cared to dwell on. Jed Ramsey liked to think well of himself, and he was aware that it was hardly to his credit that he'd made three defenseless little sisters cry.

He frowned and shifted uncomfortably. "Anyway, that's all in the past," he said and wondered whom he was trying to convince. Kayci? Tara? Himself? "I mean, Shavonne and Erin are happily married to Slade and Rad and Mom and Dad are crazy about all five of the Brady sisters. The Ramseys and the Bradys are just like one big, happy family now."

"One big, happy family?" Tara repeated incredulously.

"Well, it's true. I'm fond of your sisters," Jed insisted. Though he'd never given it a previous moment's thought, he decided that he really was fond of the Bradys. His sisters-in-law, Shavonne and Erin, were loving wives and mothers and had made his older brothers very happy. Yes, he genuinely liked them. As for the younger girls . . . he thought of nineteen-year-old Megan and twenty-year-old Colleen, both students at the University of Texas in Austin. They were pretty and sweet and he had come to view them benignly, as something akin to favorite cousins or nieces.

And Tara? It was a little different with her, he realized. For a while, he'd thought of her in the same vein as the two youngest girls, as just a cute kid. She was nine years younger than he, and light-years removed from him in experience and interests. But after Erin married Rad, forming the second Brady—Ramsey alliance, the families had started making all those jokes—which he wasn't sure were jokes at all—about him and Tara getting together. It was then that he'd begun to feel actively hostile toward her.

But she had always been hostile toward him, he realized with a start. Thinking back, he couldn't remember a single time when Tara Brady had ever had a friendly smile or word for him. The realization astonished him.

And unleashed a flood of perceptions. Jed thought

back to all those Ramsey—Brady family celebrations and holidays spent together and realized that Tara had never really mixed with his family at all. She'd been polite, had replied when spoken to, but essentially had kept her distance from the Ramseys. She invariably stuck close to her sisters, and to her small nieces and nephew, whom she doubtless considered more Brady than Ramsey.

"Don't you like my family?" Jed was flabbergasted. When the Ramseys had decided to bury the hatchet and accept the Bradys, while reluctantly leaving their inheritance intact, he knew that it had never occurred to any Ramsey that their positive feelings wouldn't be reciprocated in full by each and every Brady. It was amazing to hear that Tara Brady retained her own impressions and opinions of the Ramseys. Unfavorable ones.

"I like your brother Slade," Tara admitted. "And I've come to like Rad, too. He's changed a lot since he married Erin. He's so loving with her and the children that he hardly seems like the overwhelming, overbearing ogre he used to be."

"Overwhelming, overbearing ogre?" Jed yelped. "Is that how you see me, too?"

"No, you're a shark," Tara replied. "The people-eating kind. Your arrival should be preceded by tuba music."

Kayci looked confused. "Huh? I don't get it."

"Shark. Tuba music. Like in *Jaws*," Jed explained impatiently. His tolerance for Kayci Cann abruptly ended. "Look, don't you have somewhere you have to be, Kayci?"

"You don't have to leave, Kayci," Tara interjected quickly.

"Are you afraid to be alone with me?" asked Jed, his eyes sliding over her. "You needn't be. You're extremely cute, but you're way too young for me. And I promise that I'm not here to carry out some nefarious marital scheme of my father's. I do not—repeat do not—want to get married for a long, long time. That's one of the reasons why I'm here in Pittsburgh: to keep my neck free from the matrimonial noose."

"Are you fleeing a paternity suit or something?" Tara asked severely.

Jed grinned. "Sorry to disappoint you, honey, but I'm very, very careful. No woman is ever going to land me that way."

Tara rolled her eyes heavenward. "I can't think why any woman in her right mind would want to."

"I can," Kayci put in eagerly. "He's obviously rich. His Lamborghini Countach says it all."

"Later, Kayci." Jed placed his hand on Kayci's back and pushed her toward the door. "Good-bye, Kayci. Don't call us, we'll call you." As soon as she was in the hallway, he pulled the door closed behind her. He turned with a grin to find Tara glowering at him across the sun-filled living room.

"That was very rude," she scolded.

"Don't try to tell me that K-a-y-c-i is a friend of yours. Sweet little things like you aren't good buddies with opportunistic action girls like Ms. Cann."

Tara frowned. True, she and Kayci weren't exactly friends. "We're neighbors who are friendly," she decided.

"At Kayci's convenience. Like when she wants to borrow something or needs an audience."

Tara's frown deepened. He was exactly right. "Kayci does have some tales to tell," she said thoughtfully. "She's been all over the world. She says she was at a party with Prince Andrew, before he married Fergie, of course. She's skiied in Aspen and Vail and gone to parties in New York and Miami and Las Vegas. She's even cruised on some Arab sheik's yacht and gone to the Cannes Film Festival."

"Mmm, the usual party-girl circuit. I know the type."

"I'm sure," Tara said dryly. "She seemed to recognize your type, too. You two honed right in on each other."

Jed shrugged. "A year ago I might've taken her up on what she was so obviously offering. Now . . ."

"If you're going to try to tell me that you're searching

for depth and commitment in a meaningful relationship, save your breath. I'll never believe you."

"Smart girl," he said. "Depth and commitment in a meaningful relationship? It's enough to make me lose my lunch."

"Well, you'd better watch out because your father is determined to see it happen to you," Tara informed him. "Worst of all, he's decided that I'm the one to teach you, quote, the joys of wedded bliss, unquote. The thought is enough to make *me* lose my lunch."

"Joys of wedded bliss?" Jed hooted. "C'mon, Dad didn't really dredge up that corny old cliché, did he?" He flopped down onto her blue-and-yellow flowered sofa and propped his feet up on the hexagonal coffee table.

Tara nodded her head vigorously. "Yes, he did, the last time I was in Houston. It was over Memorial Day weekend and he cornered me during the barbecue and told me I was his ideal choice of a wife for you."

Jed surveyed her lazily. "I suppose I can follow the old man's reasoning. You're pretty and bright and your two sisters have proven themselves to be sweet, supportive, and fertile Ramsey wives."

"And, perhaps most important of all, my trust fund from Augusta Ramsey consists of shares of Ramsey stock and your father would like to keep it all in the family," Tara concluded wryly. "He said that he and your mother were both hoping to see the two of us married and benefiting from joys of wedded bliss by the end of this year. I told him I'd rather go over Niagara Falls in a cardboard box than marry you."

"Good for you!" Jed laughed. "You've always been the most outspoken Brady sister, haven't you?"

Tara silently admitted she was relieved that he wasn't insulted by her outright rejection of him. She knew he had an enormous ego and was well aware of how cutting and cruel he could be when he chose. It irked her to realize that Jed Ramsey still scared her a little, but it was true.

"Well, your message came through loud and clear to Dad," Jed continued, "because he hasn't mentiond you to me at all lately, except to say that you're seriously involved with a guy here in Pittsburgh. What's his name? I've forgotten."

Oh no! Tara thought in horror. What was the old saw about weaving a tangled web when practicing to deceive? It seemed that she'd just been caught up in it. She swallowed. "His name is Chad Cherrington."

At least that was the name she'd given Quentin Ramsey during a phone call in an attempt to discourage him from promoting her as a bridal candidate for Jed. She'd known she couldn't simply demur. Quentin Ramsey didn't take no for an answer. Nor would he have been satisfied with an ordinary young Pittsburgher as her suitor. She had to come up with someone with wealth and position.

And so she had invented Chadleigh Winston Cherrington, son of Alexander J. Cherrington, also a figment of her imagination. The names had a certain panache, she'd thought. They sounded like the shoe magnates she'd decided they were. Quentin Ramsey had bought the story. He'd even asked if Cherrington shoes were carried by any of the stores in the Ramsey malls. Tara had said she thought maybe they were.

"Cherrington," Jed nodded his recognition. "They're in shoes, Dad said. A good solid company, he said. Congratulations, Tara. You've landed a winner. Everybody back home is looking forward to meeting this guy."

Tara groaned inwardly. She'd considered the creation of Chad a brainstorm at the time and Quentin had seemed grudgingly impressed with her new suitor's credentials. She had thought that would be the end of it, that the senior Ramseys would turn their attentions elsewhere in their quest for an eligible bride for their third son. But it seemed that the specter of the mythical Chad W. Cherrington had returned to haunt her.

"When Dad suggested I take on this project here in Pittsburgh, I immediately suspected him of plotting to throw you and me together," Jed admitted. "But when

I heard that you were practically engaged to a Cherrington, I knew it was safe for me to come."

"And take the apartment across the hall from mine?" Tara asked suspiciously. She neither liked nor trusted Quentin Ramsey. If Jed were a metaphorical shark, then his father was one of those mythical, fire-breathing sea serpents.

"Dad had nothing to do with me taking this apartment. Your sister Shavonne told me you'd mentioned to her that your neighbors were moving out of their apartment and she suggested I contact the landlord about renting it. She raved about the size of the rooms, the location, and the neighborhood. I told her she should consider becoming a real estate agent. She certainly sold me on the place. I rented it sight unseen."

"Great," Tara muttered. "I'll have to be sure and thank Shavonne for that."

"Don't look so disgruntled," Jed said. "You're safe from the threat of wedded bliss with me because I have no intention of marrying anyone anytime soon." He heaved a deep sigh. "As I said earlier, that's another reason why I've temporarily left Houston. I'm sick of being pursued by the avidly marriage-minded there. I can relax here. I know you're involved with someone else and have no designs on me."

"I wouldn't have designs on you even if I wasn't involved with someone else," Tara assured him. Her curiosity got the better of her and she couldn't resist asking, "Which avidly marriage-minded woman are you escaping from now?"

"Several, but one in particular. Carling Templeton. I've known her for a number of years, but only started dating her recently."

"Senator Templeton's daughter?"

He nodded. "Suddenly darling Carling has decided that being single is passé. She's twenty-seven years old and wants a wedding ring. After surveying the market in Washington and Houston, she's decided that I meet her requirements for a husband."

Tara laughed. "And you're so scared that you left town!"

"It's not funny," Jed said sourly. "The pressure I've been under from Carling is intolerable. To make matters worse, her father is a good friend of Dad's. Suppose those two were to join forces with Carling and turn up the heat? I decided to get out of sight before that happened."

"I've seen pictures of Carling Templeton," Tara said thoughtfully. "She's gorgeous. Sophisticated. Glamorous. She sure doesn't look like a suffocating, determined-to-trap-a-man type to me."

"When a woman wants to get married, she gets desperate." Jed grimaced. "And when she gets desperate, she becomes the suffocating, determined-to-trap-a-man type. Believe me, I know what I'm talking about."

"Men!" Tara shook her head. "From what I've observed, a man feels the strongest romantic desire for a woman when he can't have her. He's the most actively attentive when he's unsure of her feelings for him. As long as she's distant, he'll pursue her. His passion is linked with his uncertainty. But the moment the woman says she loves him and he feels sure of her—wham! End of romantic fervor. The man backs off, drops her, or flees in terror."

"I'm not fleeing in terror, I'm merely avoiding an awkward, inconvenient situation," Jed insisted. "But I admit you've made some interesting points. Is that how you hooked Chad Cherrington? By being manipulative and acting hard to get?"

"Chad is another story entirely," Tara said with what she hoped was an enigmatic smile. Was he ever! "Anyway, I don't like games and romantic strategies. I'm not desperate to get married, and I've never fantasized about some big, strong man who would come along and take care of me."

"Never?" Jed demanded skeptically. "Knowing what I do about women, I find that hard to believe."

"Well, it's true. Caring men have always been nonexistent in my life and you don't miss what you've never had. You probably know something about the Brady family history—our father abandoned the family when I was four years old and left Mama with sole responsibility for us. After she died, Shavonne was named our legal guardian and we all pitched in to help her with work and expenses. We Brady sisters learned early to depend on ourselves and it's a lesson I've never *un*learned."

"Maybe that's why Chad Cherrington is so hot to marry you," Jed said, "because you aren't desperate to marry him."

So now Chad was hot to marry her? Tara almost smiled. But she wasn't about to correct his illusion. This was the longest conversation she'd ever had with Jed Ramsey, and the first time she'd ever been alone with him. It was tolerable only because Jed thought her already involved with another man.

"So when do I get to meet him?" Jed asked, picking up two framed photographs which rested on the nearby end table. One was of Slade and Shavonne and their two small daughters, Robin and Rachel. The other picture showed Rad and Erin with their children, Carrie Beth, Courtney, and Connor. He smiled slightly at the photographs and put them back down.

"M—meet Chad?" Tara's dark brown eyes widened. She gulped. "Well, he's not here now, he—he's away. Out of the country. He's in the Soviet Union," she threw in hastily. That was certainly far enough away. And would keep him conveniently incommunicado, too. "His company is hoping to—uh—to introduce a line of aerobic shoes over there."

She wondered if it sounded as absurd to him as it did to her. Apparently not. Jed nodded his head. "Interesting. What does he think the chances are of closing the deal?"

"Oh, um, good. Very good, I hear." She might as well make Chad successful in the family business. "But that's Chad for you. He could sell snow to Eskimos."

"Smooth talker, huh?" Jed studied her thoughtfully. She looked much younger than her age, more like a high-school girl than the working reporter he knew she was.

And, as he'd told her earlier, she was cute. Small-boned and delicate, just a little over five feet three with big, wide-set brown eyes, an upturned nose, and a sweet mouth with lips that were pink and full and expressive. All the Brady sisters were blond, the shades varying. Tara's hair was a rich strawberry blond, a stunning contrast with her dark eyes. It was shoulder length and she wore it in a ponytail that bounced when she moved. Her bangs were upswept, which somehow created the effect of making her eyes appear even larger than they were. Jed's gaze lowered to her figure. Her loose-fitting, oversize pink-and-gray sweat suit rendered her virtually shapeless.

"Stop staring at me like that," Tara commanded suddenly.

"Like what?"

"Like a shark sizing up a possible snack." She'd watched his beautiful, brooding eyes sweep over her, devoid of the bold sexuality and arrogant male confidence which brimmed in those hot looks he normally directed toward his potential conquests. Not that she had any inclination or desire to be one, heaven forbid. Still, it was insulting to be sized up and rejected. Sexual sharks, like their marine counterparts, were supposed to be indiscriminately voracious.

"I was just wondering if smooth-talking Chad has talked his way into your bed yet," Jed said, continuing to study her speculatively. "Maybe you're no longer a little innocent?"

Two

Tara blushed. "You have no business asking that question, Jed Ramsey!"

He stared at her. Those big velvety brown eyes of hers seemed to fill her small face, and the pink flush on her cheeks emphasized her ivory-smooth complexion. And her mouth . . .

Jed was thoroughly taken aback by the renegade thought that jumped into his head. He was *not* interested in finding out if her mouth was as soft and sensuous and kissable as it looked, he told himself firmly.

"But I'm not ashamed to admit that Chad and I aren't sleeping together."

Tara's voice broke into his sensual reverie. He shifted in his seat, disconcerted to realize that he was semi-aroused. From speculating about kissing Tara Brady? No, he insisted to himself, that was impossible. His eyes darted to her and he watched her pace the rug in front of the window. The soft knit material didn't conceal quite so much now. He saw the definite outline of small, full breasts and a pertly rounded derriere.

"I made a promise to myself a long time ago that I would wait until I was married to have sex," Tara continued, talking as she paced. "And that's what I'm going to do."

"Saving yourself for marriage, huh? How does Chad feel about your vow of virginity?" He was beginning to feel definitely uncomfortable. There was a distinct bulge against the fly of his jeans and it was growing harder. If she were to glance down at him, the tempting little virgin would get quite an eyeful.

"Chad respects my wishes," Tara replied grandly. "He's sensitive and thoughtful and caring." Chad was her creation and she could make him as noble as she wished, couldn't she?

Jed watched her with brooding blue-gray eyes. Her ponytail swung and her hips swayed saucily as she walked. He swallowed, his mouth suddenly dry. She was not a tempting little virgin, he decided. The phrase itself was an oxymoron.

She stopped pacing to stand on tiptoe, her back toward him, and adjust one of the slats of the bright yellow window shutters. Her top rode up a little, exposing a band of smooth white skin. It looked silky, warm, and untouched by the sun, or by a man.

Jed bolted upright in his seat. It disturbed him that he had suddenly, inexplicably become sexually aware of Tara Brady. He'd never gone for the sweet, sincere, and inexperienced type. In fact, he and his brother Rad used to joke that the "Sadder But Wiser Girl" of the tongue-in-cheek show tune perfectly described their tastes in women. Until Rad had lost his head over sweet, sincere and inexperienced Erin Brady . . . who'd turned out to be everything that Rad had ever wanted, in bed and out.

Abruptly, he rose to his feet. "Have you ever thought that there's another reason why Sir Chad is so willing to respect your wishes? Maybe the guy is a sterile, bloodless automaton without an ounce of passion in him. Or maybe he's a wimp, happy to let a woman call all the shots." His voice rose as he warmed to his subject. He felt an irresistible urge to quarrel with her. "Or maybe he's as scared of sex as you are!"

Tara cast a nervous glance at him. Their brief truce appeared to be over. Jed had turned back into his aggressive, intimidating Ramsey self, and she was eager to put distance between them. "Since the subject of Chad and me appears to annoy you so much, why don't you leave?" she asked with a coolness she didn't feel.

"You're throwing me out?" Jed was clearly astounded at the idea. And not at all pleased. Ramsey's were accustomed to leaving on their own terms, not anybody else's.

Tara had the uncomfortable sensation of having pulled a sleeping tiger's tail, and having him awaken with a growl. She gulped. "You don't want to be here, anyway," she reminded him. "Think how much I get on your nerves."

Well, that was certainly true, Jed thought testily. So why did he feel like staying? And why, why couldn't he keep his gaze from straying to her mouth where his eyes feasted on the soft pink fullness of her lips?

The telephone rang and Jed was as grateful as Tara for the interruption. She hurried into her bedroom to answer the phone while Jed stayed in the living room, moodily listening to her conversation.

"Leslie, hi!" she said happily. "Of course, you're still invited for dinner tonight. Come anytime—in fact, why don't you come now? I'm not doing anything."

Jed winced. That was the unkindest cut of all. His company had never been dismissed as "not anything" in his entire life. Scowling, he stormed from her apartment across the hall into his own.

Ten minutes passed, then fifteen. Restless and out of sorts, he began to pace the floor of his sleekly furnished apartment. One of the many advantages of being a Ramsey involved ordering a secretary to call a decorator, long distance, and arrange for an apartment to be completely furnished within days. But Jed was neither appreciative nor aware of the tastefully appointed room. He was irritable and restless and unspeakably bored.

It occurred to him that this was possibly the first

Saturday night since he'd reached his teens that he didn't have plans—plans that included a beautiful, sexy female. He briefly considered going upstairs to Kayci Cann's apartment where he was sure of a welcome, but he instantly dismissed the idea. She was too easy, too available. He wanted—What did he want? He paused to think about the answer to that question, but not for long. Jed Ramsey was not given to introspection. He preferred action to thoughts.

Besides, he was too busy sulking over his dilemma. Here he was, stuck with nothing to do on a gloomy October Saturday night—in Pittsburgh of all places! He had wasted too much time with that obnoxious little pest across the hall. He ought to have spent that time making plans for tonight.

Even *she* had plans for tonight. The thought galled him. With her girlfriend Leslie, whose company she preferred to his. He didn't want to admit it, but that galled him even more.

He wondered what Tara's friend looked like. Maybe this Leslie was pretty and sexy and, given a choice, would rather spend Saturday night with a man like Jed Ramsey instead of boring little Tara Brady. His lips twisted into a smug smile. Of course, she would! What woman wouldn't?

He ambled across the hall and pushed the buzzer. Posing casually against the doorjamb, he folded his arms and waited, an expectant gleam lighting his eyes. The door opened. And Jed's jaw dropped comically at the sight of the young man who stood in the doorway.

"Who is it, Leslie?" Tara's melodious voice sounded from the kitchen.

"You're Leslie?" Jed managed to find his voice. Sweet, loyal little Tara had a date? His previous perceptions abruptly shifted in disorienting kaleidoscope fashion. While the inestimable Chad was thousands of miles away, attempting to sell aerobic shoes to the Soviets, she was cheating on him with this tall, gangly guy who was dressed in clothes that looked as if they'd been purchased at a rummage sale.

"Uh, hi. I guess you must be Jed Ramsey, the new talent," said the younger man, awkwardly shifting from one foot to another. "I'm Leslie Polk. I live in the apartment above Tara's."

Tara joined them at that moment, a mixing bowl and wooden spoon in hand. Her eyes widened at the sight of Jed. "Oh, it's you," she said with all the enthusiasm of an ancient Egyptian facing another plague.

Jed thought back to the receptions he'd received at various women's doors throughout the years. They'd never varied much; he could count on the woman's pleased, seductive smile, her throaty hello and flush of sexual anticipation. Tara Brady looked at him as if he were a roach and she was fresh out of bug spray.

A spurt of indignation tore through him. "While the cat's away the mouse will play, eh, Tara?" Most insulting of all was that she had chosen this awkward young dope in favor of him! "How will the noble Chad react when he hears that you've been cheating on him?"

He watched Tara and Leslie exchange uneasy glances and his blood boiled. His eyes swept over the younger man, Leslie Polk. *Leslie!* What kind of a name was that for a guy? He was about six feet four and much too thin for his height. His hair was a dull ash color which had been hacked rather than cut and was plagued by unruly cowlicks. A truly pathetic specimen, Jed silently pronounced, whom Tara had chosen over him!

"Uh, Tara isn't cheating on Chad," Leslie Polk stammered. "You see, he's in the Middle East buying—"

"You mean, he's in the Soviet Union, selling, Leslie," Tara corrected him quickly, and Leslie flushed scarlet.

"Oh! Oh, yes," he said nervously. "I always get those non-NATO countries mixed up. Anyway, Tara invited me to dinner. She's my best friend," he added, giving her a grateful smile. "She's helping me with Melissa."

"Who's Melissa?" Jed demanded. Whatever his initial impression, he was suddenly convinced beyond a doubt that there was no romance here. He could tell by the way Tara looked at Leslie, with the kind of exasperated fondness one might display toward a favorite but inept cousin. He felt unaccountably satisfied, though once again, his nonintrospective nature didn't require an explanation.

"You don't have to answer him, Leslie," Tara interjected. "It's none of his business."

"I don't mind, Tara. I like to talk about Melissa." Leslie turned his big, sheepdog-like eyes to Jed. "Melissa is the girl I work with. I—I'd give my right arm to go with her."

There was something about the young man's wistful sincerity that caused Jed to reject the sarcastic response he'd originally planned to make, and which Tara clearly expected him to make. She was clutching her mixing bowl and glowering at him, her dark eyes fierce. Jed had no doubt that she was prepared to leap to Leslie's defense should the need arise.

He surprised himself as well as Tara by replying matter-of-factly, "Well, maybe I can help, Les. I've had my share of success with the ladies."

"Leslie doesn't need your help," put in Tara. "He's making fine progress on his own."

"Not entirely on my own, Tara," Leslie said modestly. "If it wasn't for you, I'd never have had the courage to make the first move."

The poor schlemiel was getting help from Tara "no-bed-till-wed" Brady. Jed gave his head a shake. Some courtship that would turn out to be. "What move did you make?" he asked, curious in spite of himself.

"Well, Melissa and I always bring our lunches to work," Leslie volunteered eagerly, his big eyes lighting. "We sit and eat in the lab, but we've never talked about anything else but our projects. So Tara suggested that I bring a pack of Twinkies in my lunch—there are two cakes in the package—and offer one to Melissa. You know, say I'm too full to eat them both. An—an ice-breaker, Tara called it. So I did it and it worked! Melissa took the Twinkie and we talked about food preservatives for at least ten mintues."

Jed stared at him in disbelief. "That was your big

move?" he asked incredulously. "You offered the babe a Twinkie?"

"Melissa is not a babe," Tara protested. "She's shy and reserved and—"

"How long have you worked with the girl, Les?" Jed interrupted.

"Almost a year," Leslie murmured. "We're doctoral fellows working on a research project at CMU, that's Carnegie—Mellon University, and—"

"Leslie is brilliant," Tara put in and Leslie blushed and looked at the ground. "And Melissa is his intellectual equal."

"Melissa has no equal when it comes to molecular biology," Leslie said proudly.

"Two repressed, introverted scientific geniuses being advised by an inhibited virgin," Jed said, rolling his eyes. "No wonder it's taken nearly a year to work up enough courage to share a pack of Twinkies. I can see that some emergency intervention is essential here. Les—that's what you're to think of yourself from now on, Les, not Leslie—I'm going to take over as your adviser."

"Forget it, Jed," Tara countered sharply. "The last thing a sweet, sensitive man like Leslie needs is advice from a Ramsey."

Jed ignored her and turned his full attention to Leslie. "How old are you, Les?" he asked. "How old is Melissa?"

"We're both twenty-four," Leslie said. "We graduated from college the same year."

"*Summa cum laude*," Tara added. "Right now they're both working on a federally funded energy program, run by the university. And neither of them needs any so-called help from you, Jed Ramsey."

Jed laid a fraternal hand on Leslie's shoulder. "Les, I'm certainly not a science whiz, but it seems to me that if it takes one year to offer a Twinkie to a woman, it's going to be at least a decade before you get around to taking her on a date. Do you really want to wait that long?"

Leslie looked distressed. "Well, I—"

"How would you feel about having a date with her tonight, Les?" Jed asked, his voice enticingly smooth.

"T—tonight?" Leslie gasped.

He looked so eager, so hopeful that Tara's heart ached. She felt quite protective toward Leslie. They'd been neighbors for nearly three months before he'd stopped looking at the ground and choking out a mumbled hello in response to her own cheery greeting. She'd made it her goal to break through the barrier of his crippling shyness and befriend him, and in the months since, their friendship had blossomed. He was finally at ease with her and had even confided in her about his hopeless passion for the unattainable Melissa—who sounded as desperately bashful as Leslie himself.

"May I speak to you a moment, Jed?" Tara said tightly. It was a demand, not a request.

Jed shrugged and followed her into the kitchen.

"Let's get something straight right now, Jed Ramsey," she said in a low fierce voice. "I don't know what you're up to, but I'm not going to stand by and let you use Leslie and Melissa for your own amusement. I'll do whatever I have to do if—"

"Are you trying to threaten me?" Jed cut in. The idea seemed to entertain him greatly. She shot him a ferocious glare.

"I'm not the irredeemable reprobate you seem to think I am," he continued lightly. "I do have an occasional humanitarian impulse, and our hapless neighbor has inspired this one. I can help him win his lady biologist far quicker and easier than you can, Tara. And I intend to do just that."

He strolled out of the kitchen, Tara trailing him. "Les, I want you to give Melissa a call," he said. "Tell her that your neighbors are having an impromptu party and you'd like her to join you."

"Call Melissa?" Leslie echoed, paling. "Oh, I—I couldn't. It—I—She—"

Jed ignored him. "What's her last name? I'll get her number from directory assistance."

"It's Minger. Melissa Minger." Leslie trailed him into the bedroom where Jed picked up the phone. "But I—I really don't think—"

Tara followed them, adding her own protests about Jed's high-handedness.

Jed requested the number and dialed it, ignoring them both. All three of them heard a young woman's voice on the line say a tentative "Hello?"

Jed held out the receiver to Leslie who stood immobilized, as if he'd been turned to stone. He'd gone so still and white, Tara wondered if he was still breathing.

Shrugging, Jed took over. "Melissa? This is Jed Ramsey. I'm a friend and neighbor of Les Polk's. A few of us here in our apartment building are getting together for a little party tonight and we'd like you to come."

Leslie uttered a strangled sound and closed his eyes. They snapped open when he heard Jed say, "Great. Come on over as soon as you can. And dress casually. Directions?" He offered Leslie the receiver, again to no avail. The younger man seemed incapable of both speech and movement. "I'm new to these parts, Melissa," Jed drawled into the phone. "I'll have to turn you over to Tara here, our resident travel director."

He thrust the receiver at Tara. She took it and proceeded to give directions to the apartment building. "Melissa said she'll be here within the hour," Tara reported to the dazed Leslie.

"W—what am I going to do? What'll I—" He gulped. "What'll I say to her?"

Jed clapped him heartily on the back. "Not to worry, Les. Tara and I will be here. We'll pick up the slack. Now, let's get you into something a little more . . ." he searched for the word, then abandoned the search. "Do you have a pair of jeans? A sweatshirt, maybe? CMU sweatshirt?"

Leslie nodded. "Go put them on and come right back," Jed ordered. He took his arm and walked him to the door. "Now stay calm and keep cool. Everything is going to work out, Les. I promise you."

He was smiling as he turned around to face Tara. "Y'know, it does have its rewards—being a nice guy, helping others. Sure beats doing nothing on a Saturday night. So . . . what are we having for dinner?"

She gritted her teeth. "Lasagna. And salad and garlic bread."

"Nix the garlic bread, honey. Very quelling to close-ups."

She fixed him with a withering glare, which had no discernible effect whatsoever upon him.

"What about dessert?" he continued. He snapped his fingers. "I've got it—you and Melissa will be dessert. We'll dim the lights and then pair off. Since Les and Missy are the novices here, we'll let them have the bedroom and you and I will take the couch." He paused to guffaw at the improbable scenario he'd conjured up. "Then we'll—"

"I'm making brownies for dessert," Tara interrupted quickly, glancing down at the mixing bowl of batter she was holding. She was unnerved by the odd rush of heat that flared in her belly at the thought of herself lying on the couch with Jed Ramsey. He'd been joking, of course; she knew that. Obviously, he found high hilarity imagining the two of them making love. She should, too. Barring that, she should at least feel acute distaste. Why didn't she?

"Brownies, huh?" Jed stuck his finger into the batter and tasted it. "Well, that's right in keeping with your Twinkie advice. You seem to view rich, cakelike desserts as aphrodisiacs."

She bit her lip to keep from smiling. She knew very well how Jed Ramsey operated. She hadn't been observing him for the past four years for nothing. First, he disarmed his intended conquests with his smiles and glib little asides, then he moved on to sexual innuendoes, and—

Tara caught the direction of her thoughts and instantly put a brake on them. None of this applied to her because she was *not* one of his intended conquests, she assured herself.

She quickly turned and headed back into the kitchen. Jed followed her, aware that he was unwelcome and not caring. He couldn't seem to leave her alone. Nor could he stop baiting her.

"So now I know the way to score with you," he continued, watching her pour the brownie batter into a rectangular baking pan. "Take you into a bakery. You'd be all over me after a dozen cookies. And if I were to throw in a couple of eclairs—"

"Jed, if you're trying to be funny—"

"Then I'm succeeding. Because you're trying awfully hard not to laugh." He caught her chin in his hand and tilted her head up, making her eyes meet his.

He was right, she was trying very hard not to laugh.

Jed liked the sparkle of humor in her eyes, the cute dimple in her cheek. When she finally relented and permitted herself to chuckle, he felt as if he were being propelled into the stratosphere.

"It all stands to reason that a wedding cake would be the ultimate turn-on for you," he continued. Her smiles were inspiring him to new heights. "All that symbolism combined with tiers of butter-cream frosting." He didn't care how far he had to extend his metaphors as long as she kept looking at him that way. He moved closer to her. Their bodies brushed lightly.

Tara stared at him with wide, upturned dark eyes. He was so close to her. Too close. The heady male scent of him filled her nostrils. His hard, masculine heat warmed her. He stroked the curve of her neck with long, lazy fingers. She caught her breath as hot little ripples of sensation seared her. Her legs felt oddly like rubber. It was scary, and it was thrilling. She'd never had such a purely physical reaction to a man's nearness before. Her hands began to shake and she lost her grip on the mixing bowl. It clattered into the sink and broke into pieces. She jumped. And abruptly pulled away from him.

"G—good thing I got most of the batter into the baking pan," she said breathlessly, her gaze riveted on the remains of the bowl. She was flushed. "I, uh, I can really be a klutz sometimes."

Jed stared at her. He knew exactly what was going on with her; he was too experienced not to recognize arousal in a woman. Little Tara? So turned on by him that she couldn't hang onto her brownie batter? A slow smile crossed his face. He decided that he liked the idea. "You weren't being klutzy," he assured her in a sexy, smoky voice. "I'm getting to you, aren't I?"

Waves of embarrassment crashed over her. He knew! She was horrified. After all she'd said about not liking him, not finding him attractive, he must be relishing her unexpected, uncontrolled response to him. And now he was rubbing it in, laughing at her!

"You're getting to me, all right," she said, pulling herself together. "The way ipecac syrup gets to me." She'd been striving for a cool, snappy comeback. If only her voice hadn't quavered, if only her breath hadn't caught in her throat, she might've pulled it off.

"Nice try, honey, but I know differently." Jed moved toward her with the swiftness of a cat about to pounce on its prey. But Tara was faster. She quickly stepped out of his reach.

Jed frowned. This was the first time he had executed that particular lunge and missed. And then the full realization of his actions struck him. He had made a sexual move on Tara Brady! For his inevitable follow-up to that particular pantherlike lunge was a passionate, possessive kiss. Had he managed to capture Tara, he would have kissed her. *He wanted to kiss her!* The thought left him reeling.

Tara was equally stunned by the wild and dangerous feelings coursing through her. All her life she had been cautious and careful and restrained, yet the one time she got too close to Jed Ramsey . . . She swallowed hard. He made her feel reckless and daring. He made her long to take chances. Oh, she had been so right to avoid him for so long.

For several moments, they stared at each other, caught in a maelstrom of confusion.

Leslie reappeared in jeans and a sweatshirt. "Is this okay?" he asked anxiously.

Jed tore his gaze away from Tara and cleared his throat. "A definite improvement, Les." He felt as if he were emerging from a trance.

Tara felt her head clear and she purposefully fixed her eyes on Leslie. "Maybe I ought to change clothes, too," she said, "If this is supposed to be a party, I should look as if—"

"—you aren't about to clean out the garage," Jed finished bluntly.

Tara threw him a glance.

Leslie saw and gave a quiet chuckle. "Did you two ever, uh, go together?" he asked curiously.

"No!" Tara and Jed chorused the emphatic denial.

"Leslie, where would you get an idea like that?" Tara demanded, aghast.

He shrugged diffidently. "It's just that you two fight like lovers. Like on TV, where the couples are always snapping at each other to diffuse the sexual tension between them."

"Leslie, it's nothing like that between Jed and me!"

"Stick to biological research, Les," Jed advised. "You're definitely out of your league when it comes to making human behavioral analyses."

Tara scurried into her bedroom to change clothes. Fight like lovers, she thought. Ha! Russia would reinstate the czar, the pope would become a Moonie, and Queen Elizabeth would abdicate to seek fame and fortune as a rock star before she and Jed Ramsey ever became lovers.

She snatched a denim miniskirt from its hangar and stepped into it, then topped it with a blue and white striped cotton shirt. She thought of Kayci and the sheer stockings and high heels she'd worn with her mini and immediately pulled on white socks and sneakers. No one was going to accuse her of trying to attract Jed Ramsey, she decided grimly, and gave her ponytail a quick flick of the brush.

Back in the kitchen, she busied herself with the

dinner preparations while Jed and Leslie talked in the living room. At least, Jed talked. Amidst the din of kitchen noises, Tara could hear his deep, distinct masculine tones. If Leslie spoke at all, it must have been in a whisper.

When the buzzer rang, signaling Melissa's arrival, she hurried to join the two men in the living room. Leslie was beginning to shake. Jed gave him an encouraging, fraternal shove. "Answer the door, Les. And say exactly what I told you to say. What we rehearsed."

Three

Tara marched over to Jed as Leslie trudged slowly to the door. "What did you tell him to say?" she demanded in a whisper. "If it's one of your phony smooth-operator lines, so help me, Jed Ramsey, I'll—" She abruptly lapsed into silence as Leslie opened the door.

"That's his dream girl?" Jed stared incredulously at the very tall, very thin, very plain young woman who stood in the doorway. She wore black jeans and a black turtleneck sweater and the darkness seemed to drain the color from her already pale skin. Her straight, dark hair was parted in the middle and hung nearly to her waist. "She looks like an apparition, like the specter of death or something."

Tara elbowed him sharply in the ribs. "Will you please shut up and smile? She's shy, maybe even shyer than Leslie. We have to look welcoming."

"Hi, Melissa." Leslie's voice was nervous and low.

Tara held her breath, praying he wouldn't say something sleazy. Lord only knew what would happen with Ramsey supplying the dialogue.

"I'm so glad you could come over tonight, Melissa," Leslie said. "I'm sorry it was on such short notice, but my friends and I just threw this little party together at the last minute." The words were spoken in a rush, without a single pause for air.

"See." Jed nudged Tara. "I can be appropriate when the occasion demands. Les remembered everything, but I wish he didn't sound as if he were reading from cue cards."

Tara allowed herself to relax a little. Her face was beginning to hurt from the warm, welcoming smile she was determinedly displaying. Since Leslie seemed to have exhausted his supply of words—or run out of breath—she stepped forward to introduce herself.

"And this is Jed Ramsey," she added, nodding at him while she silently willed him not to dazzle Melissa with the full force of his charm. How could poor Leslie compete with a man as attractive and exciting as Jed Ramsey? she thought worriedly. She'd been watching women fall at his feet for the past four years.

To her relieved amazement, Jed merely offered his hand to shake and said quietly, "Pleased to meet you, Melissa." Melissa was not bowled over by him. In fact, she hardly seemed to notice him. She was staring intently— longingly?—at Leslie.

For the first time since Jed had forced this "impromptu party" on her, Tara allowed herself to hope that perhaps it wouldn't be an unmitigated disaster, after all. At least the attraction between Leslie and Melissa appeared to be mutual. If only they could break through their defensive walls of reserve.

But neither Leslie nor Melissa relaxed during dinner. Both concentrated strictly on their plates, not daring to look up, let alone talk. It was up to Tara and Jed to keep awkward silence at bay. That meant talking to each other, while maintaining a pretense that the other couple was actually involved in the conversation.

"Jed works for his family's mall development and management company," Tara told the couple, neither of whom acknowledged her in any way. "His father, Quentin Ramsey, is founder and chairman of the board of Ramsey and Sons. His older brother Rad is president of the company, and another brother, Slade, is a vice-president, as is Jed himself. And I guess there's a place in management being readied for Ricky, the youngest, who'll graduate from college next June."

No response from Leslie or Melissa. Tara caught Jed's eye and sent him a silent message. He jumped in to take over. "You bet there's a place for Ricky." Silence. Jed cleared his throat. "Er, Ramsey and Sons has built more than a hundred and twenty-five shopping centers and office complexes in thirty states."

More silence.

It was Tara's turn. "Uh, Jed, before Melissa arrived, you were about to tell Leslie and me what project you're working on here in Pittsburgh." It wasn't true, but at least it was a viable topic. "We'd like to hear all about it."

Jed's lips twisted into a smile. He was aware that Leslie and Melissa were too panicked to comprehend a word that was being said, and Tara's lack of interest in anything that concerned him was well documented. But he had to give her points for gamely carrying things along. Since this party had been his idea, she could've rightfully left him to sink all on his own.

"Are any of you famliar with the Southland Mall?" he asked.

Melissa and Leslie said nothing. Tara nodded politely. "I've been there. It's southeast of the city. The Simon Company just built a brand-new mall less than two miles away from the Southland Mall."

"I know. And the new mall is drawing business from our mall." Jed grimaced. "To be honest, it's not merely drawing business away—it's murdering the Southland Mall. Sales have dropped over eighty percent since the new mall opened. I'm here to see if Southland can be turned around."

"And if it can't?" asked Tara.

"I'll make a full report and Ramsey and Sons will try to unload it as quickly as possible."

"I'll save you a lot of time and trouble. The Southland Mall is dead," Tara said bluntly. "Trying to resuscitate it would be a hopeless waste of time and money. You might as well sell it and go right back to Houston because the new mall is superior in every way."

"Anxious to be rid of me, are you?" Jed chuckled.

"Sorry, honey, it's not quite that easy. The Southland Mall happens to be a sentimental favorite of my father's. It was the first covered mall built by Ramsey and Sons, a revolutionary concept when it opened twenty-seven years ago. Of course, the 'Sons' part of the company was strictly nominal in those days. My brothers and I were just kids. But Dad had big dreams for his company, and the Southland Mall launched his career. He doesn't want to let it go without trying to save it."

"That doesn't sound like your father," Tara said, grimacing at the thought of Quentin Ramsey. "He's the epitome of the pragmatic, unsentimental businessman."

"Dad does have his soft spots," Jed said. "His family—wife, kids, grandchildren."

"And the Southland Mall," Tara added sardonically.

Jed nodded. "I have an idea that might turn the place around: Turn it into a discount-store mall. Bring in the outlets and the chains that sell brand-name merchandise at discount prices." He leaned forward, an eager expression on his face. "It'll be a first for the company, since Ramsey and Sons has always gone with the concept of building new, high-tech, high-class malls. This will target an entirely different segment of the buying public, the retired and the lower-income customer. What do you think?"

"I think it's a great idea," Tara admitted. "But I don't believe your father will agree. The words 'discount' and 'lower income' probably make him break out in hives. He'll opt to sell the mall rather than alter the exalted Ramsey image."

"Tara, Dad is looking for a creative solution and I've come up with one. It's going to work. I know it."

Tara shrugged. "Who can argue with all that Ramsey confidence?" she murmured. She paused to take a bite of food. So did Jed. A shroud of silence fell, and they both remembered that Leslie and Melissa were still there, as silent as ever.

The prospect of trying to drag them into conversation was daunting. "I'll start clearing the table," Tara announced, hopping to her feet. She was eager to escape for a bit. "You three just stay put. I'll take care of the dishes."

Jed stood up. "Nonsense, sweetie. I insist on helping." He grabbed the empty wine bottle and followed her into the kitchen.

Tara turned on the faucet and began to scrape the plates. "Go on back with the others, Jed. I'll stay and—"

"Oh, no, you don't. I need a break as much as you do." He dropped onto the bright yellow stool and ran his hand through his hair. "I'm exhausted. I've never had to work so hard on a date in my life."

"I know what you mean. My most difficult interview pales in comparison to making conversation with Leslie and Melissa."

Jed groaned. "Haven't those two mastered *any* small talk? I mean, couldn't one of them at least make a comment on the weather or something? It's raining. That's a point of interest worth noting, isn't it?"

Tara nodded. "You and I noted it about ten times apiece."

He grinned. "Yeah, I guess we did, didn't we? But, hey, it's not easy to entertain the dead. I think we kept the old conversational ball rolling pretty well."

"I think so, too." She put down a plate and glanced over at him. He smiled at her.

Her heart jumped in her chest. She'd seen his practiced, sexy smile and its effect on his potential conquests; she'd seen his sardonic smile and its intimidating effect on his targets; but she'd never seen him smile like this. This was a genuinely warm smile, a friendly smile, a we're-in-this-together smile. A slow heat suffused her cheeks. Confused, she quickly turned back to the dishes.

Her thoughts tumbled through her mind. And they were all of Jed. His behavior had been shockingly out of character since Melissa's arrival. He had actually been nice, and helpful. She still found it difficult to believe that she and Jed Ramsey could ever be allied in any cause, but they'd definitely been allies during the ordeal that had been dinner.

Jed watched her work at the sink. He wanted to commiserate with her some more, but she seemed disinclined to talk and he was tired of working at conversation.

"So, what comes next?" he asked. It occurred to him that he could leave any time he wanted and wondered why he didn't. He'd never spent an evening like this one in his life. Leslie Polk and Melissa Minger were veritable strangers to him, and catatonic ones at that. The prospect of spending a few more hours in their dull company was paralyzing. He didn't owe it to them, and he certainly didn't owe it to Tara. He frowned. What was he doing here?

"We could have the brownies," Tara answered his question, unaware of his mental machinations. "And then—then—" She glanced at the kitchen clock and groaned. "It's only eight-thirty. What *are* we going to do for the rest of the evening?"

Tell her you don't intend to hang around and find out, one part of his brain advised. *Tell her that you're taking off to look for a little action.* He didn't have to look far, he reminded himself. K-a-y-c-i, the action girl herself, was just upstairs.

He stood up. At that moment, Tara turned off the faucet. The ensuing silence in the apartment was almost palpable.

"They're not saying a word to each other out there," Tara murmured glumly. "It must be terrible to be so self-conscious and insecure." She gazed up at Jed, her big, velvet brown eyes filled with compassion and concern.

Suddenly, he couldn't seem to breathe. He felt as if he'd been literally kicked in the gut. He didn't move. He couldn't. Somehow, he had been rendered as catatonically still as the hapless Leslie Polk in the presence of Melissa.

Impulsively, Tara caught his hand and gave it a tug. "Come on, we've left them by themselves for too long. They just aren't ready for it. They can't handle it."

And to his utter astonishment, Jed allowed her to

drag him back to the small dining area where Leslie and Melissa sat stiffly in miserable silence. He sat down at the table, bewildered by the turn of events. He was supposed to have been out that door, seeking action with an action girl. What on earth was he doing at this table discussing the merits of brownies with nuts versus brownies without with Tara Brady while Leslie and Melissa, ever silent, stared on?

When the dessert was finished, the four of them returned to the kitchen to finish up the dishes. The activity ended all too soon, leaving the rest of the evening looming ahead of them.

"Why don't we move across the hall to my apartment and watch a flick on the VCR?" suggested Jed, and silently congratulated himself for coming up with the idea. It was an ingenious way of making the interminable silence work for them.

"As long as its not an X-rated porno movie," Tara said, fixing him with a forbidding look. Poor Leslie and Melissa would probably expire of embarrassment at the first glance of one.

What a goody-goody little stiff she was, Jed thought resentfully, and abandoned his plans to show *Cave Women in Chains*. The opening scene alone would've been a hilarious icebreaker. He didn't like Tara Brady at all, he reaffirmed. He was only enduring the evening for his friend Les's sake. After all, he'd always been a fraternal-type guy, willing to help out a buddy in the ongoing battle of the sexes.

The alternate movie he chose, *Attack of the Killer Tomatoes*, was so classically terrible that even Melissa and Leslie unbent enough to laugh. The pitcher of frozen blackberry daiquiris Jed whipped up was undeniably an aid as well. By the end of the movie—and the pitcher of drinks—the inhibited couple wasn't quite so inhibited.

"We're all going to have to get together again soon," Leslie said jovially. He was sitting just a cushion away from Melissa on the long sectional sofa. They'd begun at opposite ends of it.

"Yes," agreed Melissa in that low, quiet voice of hers.

"How about two weeks from today?" Leslie suggested. "My cousin is having a party. It's formal. His parties always are. The last party he gave was written up in the *Post-Gazette's* Seen column—you know, the society column."

"The Seen column, huh?" Jed echoed, looking amused. He caught Tara's eye and she grinned.

Leslie didn't notice; he was too busy making plans. "My cousin invited me to his party and told me to bring some friends along. The more the merrier, he said. Would you come? All—all three of you?"

"Oh, I—I don't know," Melissa said hesitantly, twisting her fingers in nervous agitation.

Tara suppressed a groan. For Leslie to have issued the invitation at all was a milestone for him. If Melissa turned him down, he would be so crushed, he'd probably never attempt another overture. She looked at Jed and knew he was thinking the same thing. He made a gun out of his fingers and pointed it to his head.

Tara sighed. As much as she didn't want to, they were going to have to take over again. "Of course we'll come, Leslie. We can all go together in my car, if you don't mind being a little squashed. We'll pick you up. Okay, Melissa?"

Melissa managed a smile. "If you're sure."

"We're sure," said Tara.

Leslie beamed. "You'll like my cousin's house, Jed. It's an old place up in the Point Breeze section of the city. The Seen columnist referred to it as a swankenda."

"*Swankenda?*" Jed choked back a laugh and managed to answer with a straight face. "Much as I'd like to party in a genuine swankenda, I'm afraid I'll have to pass, Les. Chad will undoubtedly be back by then and Tara will take him."

He assured himself that he was relieved to be spared another evening with Tara Brady. Furthermore, a party thrown by Leslie Polk's cousin promised to be hopelessly dull, even if it was being held in a Pittsburgh-styled swankenda. It would probably be attended by genius types, discussing the theory of relativity or something equally serious. Within two weeks, he most certainly would have a date with the type of gorgeous, glamorous woman he preferred. Not an indiscriminately available one like Kayci Cann or an infuriating, irritating, bossy, virginal one like Tara Brady.

"Tara, didn't you tell me that Chad is supposed to go to China when he finishes up in Russia?" Leslie asked, a teasing gleam in his eye. "To sell, uh, whatever it is he sells to the Chinese?"

"I think you've had a little too much blackberry daiquiri, Leslie," Tara said dampeningly.

"But Chad definitely isn't going to be here," Leslie insisted with surprising tenacity. "You and Jed have to go with us, Tara. We make a great foursome." He turned boldly to Melissa. "Don't we, Melissa?"

Melissa gave him a shy smile, her eyes downcast. "Yes," she replied in a whisper.

"Well, I'll, uh, think about it," Jed said vaguely. He had no intention of going but couldn't bring himself to dash Leslie's hopes just yet.

Leslie and Melissa exchanged shy, furtive smiles. Tara released the breath she'd been holding. Jed frowned at his empty glass and wished for another round of blackberry daiquiris.

"Thank you for not giving Leslie an outright refusal to the party in front of Melissa," Tara said to Jed later, after both Leslie and Melissa had departed. The two of them were standing in the small hallway between their apartments. "They have two whole weeks to get used to the idea of going to the party together. By then, they won't need us along to bolster their courage."

"Well, I hope you're right, because I'm not going to that party. I refuse to be a stand-in for the winsome Chad again. Tonight was enough."

"I wholeheartedly agree." Instead of going into her apartment, Tara headed to the wide front door of the building.

"Where are you going?" asked Jed, before he could stop himself. Not that he cared, he added quickly to himself.

"Out to my car. I forgot to bring in my library books when I was unloading the groceries this afternoon."

"What are you going to do with library books?"

She tossed him a dry smile. "Read them." She walked out of the building into the night.

A moment later, Jed was by her side. "I know you're going to read them." He'd gritted out the words. "But why now? It's late, and your car is parked miles from here."

"Six and a half blocks, to be exact. And I want them because I happen to like to read in bed."

"I could make some lewd remark about a virgin not having—or knowing—anything better to do in bed than read, but I won't. You're too easy a target."

"Thank you for your restraint," Tara retorted.

They tramped along the sidewalk, side by side. It was drizzling cold drops, and a strong gust of wind sent piles of fallen leaves flying around their feet. "It was seventy-eight degrees in Houston today," Jed said gloomily. "Warm, sunny, dry, and here we are in the frozen north."

Tara's eyes danced. "Go back inside, you poor, delicate southern magnolia. You don't have to come with me."

"Oh, sure. And let you walk by yourself for six and a half blocks along a deserted city street at midnight?"

"It's a residential area. I'll be perfectly safe."

"Famous last words. No, I'll come with you, even if it means coming down with a freaking case of pneumonia. If you were to get attacked by some maniac out here, both your family and mine would be on my case forever for not looking out for you."

"Your gallantry takes my breath away. You're a regular knight in shining armor." She cast him an amused glance. "A shivering one, though."

Jed jammed his hands into the pockets of his jeans and fought a smile.

They reached her car and Tara got her books from the backseat. Jed didn't offer to carry them. His knightly instincts extended only so far. They were approaching the apartment building when a gray Oldsmobile braked to a stop with a squeal of tires in front of the building. A middle-aged man in a beige trench coat climbed out. He had a shock of dark hair, tipped with silver. Though Tara and Jed were near enough to see him, he did not see them.

"I know who he is," whispered Tara. "That's Senator Saxon, Glenn Saxon. He's running for reelection in November. I've been assigned to cover his speeches when he campaigns here in Pittsburgh."

The senator proceeded to lope toward their apartment building and the Oldsmobile drove off. "I wonder what he's doing here?"

"Could he have come to see you?" Jed asked. "With an exclusive scoop or something?"

She shook her head. "He doesn't know me at all. I'm just one of a crowd of reporters assigned to cover his city appearances. A lowly junior reporter, at that."

"Well, I don't know him either, and it's a safe bet that he's not here to see Les at this hour." Jed's lips twisted into at sardonic smile. "That leaves just one other occupant in the building."

Tara gaped at him. "Kayci? Jed, do you think he's here to see her?"

"Bingo. Give the lady her prize."

"But Senator Saxon is married. He and his wife have four children!"

"He's not the first politician to cheat on his wife, Tara."

"But he particularly stresses his family-man image. His speeches are full of references to his 'fulfilling partnership' with his wife. Yes, he used that exact phrase just the other day. And he's always talking about how he's raising his kids with 'good old-fashioned values and morality.' That's another direct quote."

"Yet another hypocritical slimeball." Jed grimaced. "It's enough to make you gag."

Tara cast him a curious glance. "I'd've thought he'd be a hero to you, knowing your views on commitment and loyalty and fidelity."

"Well, maybe you're not quite the expert on my views that you'd like to believe you are, Miss Brady. I happen to believe that loyalty and fidelity are inviolate requisites in marriage. I take commitment very seriously. When I marry, it's going to be forever—that's why I'm in no hurry to do it."

His declaration astonished her. "I suppose you're making sense," she conceded. "In your own peculiar Ramsey way, of course."

"I'm glad you understand," Jed said dryly. "In your own peculiar Brady way, that is."

Tara surprised herself—and him—by laughing. He joined in her laughter, inexplicably pleased with her response.

The light drizzle abruptly accelerated to a cold, steady downpour. Jed's big hand closed around her elbow. "Come on, let's get out of the rain."

They ran to the building, entering just in time to hear the door to an upstairs apartment creak open.

"Why, hello there, Glenn-o," sounded the high girlish voice of Kayci Cann. There was a low rumbled response and then Kayci again, loud and clear. "Oooh, yes!" A millisecond later, the door was firmly and audibly closed.

Tara and Jed exchanged glances. "Glenn-o?" Jed echoed sardonically.

"He's really there, with her," Tara whispered, her big brown eyes troubled. "Jed, what am I going to do?"

"Why should you do anything?" Jed asked with a shrug. "Granted, the senator and the action girl are an unsavory pair, but what happens behind closed doors has nothing to do with you, Tara."

"But it does! I'm a reporter, remember? And this is news . . ." She frowned. "Isn't it?"

"Sure. If you work for a scandal sheet. But the last I heard, you worked for a radio station."

"Jed, we both know that reporting the—uh—clandestine activities of a political candidate isn't solely the province of scandal sheets. Even the most respected big city dailies do it."

"True." He heaved a sigh. "But those stories have involved presidential candidates, where the man's character is inseparable from his role as a leader. I don't know where the right to privacy and the right to know begin and end in other cases."

"I don't either." She looked at him, her dark eyes wide. "I want to do the right thing, Jed. But I'm not sure what the right thing is."

An icy draft whipped through the cracks of the door and she shivered. "It's too cold to stand out here talking," Jed observed. He took her arm. "Come to my place."

She went with him, too preoccupied with the subject of Kayci and Senator Saxon even to give a thought to all those tales she'd heard back in Houston about Jed Ramsey and the happenings behind his closed doors. She'd heard it said that no "nice girl" ever spent time alone with Jed at his place and emerged with her reputation intact, but the thought didn't cross her mind as she trailed him inside his apartment.

It crossed Jed's, however, the moment he saw her gracefully settle herself on the long, comfortable sectional sofa. She crossed her legs and his eyes immediately focused on them. Even those schoolgirl socks and shoes didn't disguise the shapeliness of her calves. The short denim skirt provided him with a tantalizing view of her thighs, which were slender, but alluringly rounded. He had a reputation as a "leg man," and she had great legs.

He swallowed hard. A hot flash of desire surged through him. How long would it take for him to have her stretched out on those cushions under him? The thought jumped unbidden into his mind. He imagined the short, tight skirt riding up her thighs as she opened those shapely legs to him. . . .

Was he going crazy? he wondered with a jolt. This was the one woman in the world whom he didn't dare become sexually involved with. Not with all those family ties between them. If he were to take her to bed, he would be supplying her with the ammunition to trap him. All she would have to do would be to go crying to her sisters and his brothers, to his parents, and he might as well put on the old ball and chain and throw away the key. His family could—and would—make his life miserable until he married the girl.

Who claimed that she didn't want to marry him. He thought of her fast and heated response to him in the kitchen earlier. She might not want to marry him, but he turned her on. An intriguing thought, he mused, with intriguing possibilities.

"Do you agree, Jed?"

Her voice catapulted him out of his sexual reverie. He stared at her, uncomprehending. He'd been so busy contemplating the delights of her body, and then mentally reviewing the consequences, that he hadn't heard a word she'd said.

"It doesn't matter whether I agree or not," he said, trying to cover his lapse of attention. "You're the reporter and you have to decide."

"You're right." Tara sighed. "And I guess what it boils down to is whether or not Glenn Saxon's fling—or whatever he has going with Kayci—has any effect on his career as a senator. Do you think that it does?"

"I don't know." He couldn't seem to think clearly. His brain felt clouded with erotic thoughts and desires that he had no business having. He sank down on the sofa beside her. His loins felt heavy and full and he remembered that this was not the first time today that he'd had this reaction to her.

Damn, maybe he was cracking up. From lack of sex? He wondered if it were possible. For the truth was that in the past six months, his sex life had slowed considerably. Missing was the real, hungry drive of desire, and though he was adept at performing despite that lack, lately he just hadn't felt it worth the effort.

But tonight . . . He stared down into Tara's soft dark eyes, and saw her flick the tip of her tongue over the pink fullness of her lips in a worried little gesture. Tonight desire, driving, real and intense, flooded him.

A thump sounded from above. And then another and another in a hard, pounding rhythm. Tara's eyes flew to Jed's face. "W—What do you suppose they're doing up there?" She knew, of course, but felt the need to make some comment, however trivial. Sitting there, listening in silence, was more than a little embarrassing.

"It's a safe bet that they're not moving furniture," Jed drawled. *Or sitting chastely on the sofa, pretending to talk.*

"This is all so sordid," Tara exclaimed. "I wish we'd never seen him come in. Jed, do you suppose that he's in love with Kayci? That maybe he wants to divorce his wife and marry her but doesn't dare because—"

"Hey, let's not weave a plot of romantic tragedy around Glenn-o and his good-time girl. You don't have to be in love to make love, Tara." His whole body was aching with the throbbing evidence of that fact, he added grimly to himself.

"It's just so shallow and meaningless," Tara lamented.

"Yeah," he agreed. And if only they could follow Kayci and the senator's lead and indulge in some shallow, meaningless and deliciously hot sex on this cold, rainy Saturday night.

Well, why couldn't they? he silently demanded. He wanted her and he'd been raised on the principle that what a Ramsey wants, a Ramsey gets. She was naive and inexperienced. It should be easy for an acknowledged master like himself to sexually entice her. After all, he'd managed to get her hot and bothered enough to drop a bowl in her kitchen.

He debated on how and when to make his move. Obliterated in the heat of his lust with his pledge to keep his distance from Tara Brady. It wasn't as if she were after him, he reminded himself again. She already had a man chomping at the bit to marry her, and she'd made no secret of her aversion to marrying a Ramsey. Why, he'd actually be doing her a favor, he decided. Being deflowered by the sexually acclaimed

Jed Ramsey had to be more exciting, more satisfying—and infinitely less awkward—than being introduced to sex by the fumbling, virginal Chad Cherrington. For Jed had conveniently decided that the unseen Chad must be exactly that.

With deliberate smoothness, he turned toward her and slid his arm over the back of the sofa. "Tara," he said in the husky, sexy tones which had turned many a woman's bones to water.

Tara was too engrossed in thought to notice. "Maybe I should keep quiet about it for a while," she mused aloud. "Think how hurt his family would be if they found out. As you said, there is a line between a public figure's right to privacy and the public's right to know."

Jed inched closer at the same moment that Tara turned her head toward him. She looked at him in that direct way of hers, her dark eyes shining.

Jed remained frozen in position, while a sensation akin to electricity rippled through him.

"I'm glad you were here tonight, Jed," Tara said, and she smiled warmly.

"You are?" Hardly the dazzlingly smooth reply this situation called for, but it was all he could manage. His mouth was dry, his body taut and thick. He drew in a sharp breath.

Tara nodded, her soft brown eyes alight with sincerity. "You're worldly and sophisticated and you helped me put this situation with Kayci and Senator Saxon in the proper perspective."

"I did?" he croaked. Lord, he sounded about as suave as Les Polk with Melissa. He berated himself. What was the matter with him? He'd never been undone by a smile or a pair of pretty dark eyes. He tried to rally himself. He wanted her and he was going to have her. It was definitely time to pounce.

"Mm-hm. Heaven only knows what would've happened if Leslie and I had stumbled onto this nasty little secret together." Her beautiful eyes were earnest and full of trust.

Jed didn't pounce. He sat and stared and listened to

her. He simply couldn't bring himself to turn that trusting admiration—the first time he'd ever seen it in her eyes—into anything else. Not even arousal.

"Les and I probably would've made a citizen's arrest or something," Tara continued, a wry grin lighting her face, "and totally disgraced ourselves, wrecked the senator's career, and hurt his family. It's much better this way." Her smile faded. "Isn't it?" Uncertainty flickered in her big velvet eyes.

Jed groaned. "Yeah, baby. Sure. It's much better this way." Better that he keep his sexual distance, better that she keep her virginity.

Tara stood up. "Thanks again, Jed." She gave him a quick little wave and headed for the door. " 'Night."

This was not going the way he'd planned. Jed watched her, his eyes on her cute little fanny, the swingy ponytail. The thumping noises upstairs intensified and he swore that he heard frenzied moans.

Tara left his apartment, as chaste as when she'd entered. He frowned fiercely, wondering what had gone wrong. It was Virgins 1, Rakes 0, he conceded grimly, and prepared to spend a restless, difficult night.

Four

Jed glanced at his watch for perhaps the tenth time that hour. Where could she be at 11:03 on a Sunday morning? For lack of anything better to do, he tramped across the hall and rapped on Tara's apartment door, calling her name. There was no answer. He'd been pounding on her door since he had awakened ninety minutes ago, and the response had been the same. None. She wasn't home.

"Will you *please* keep the noise down?" A hoarse, sleep-filled voice whined from the landing. "How's a person supposed to get any sleep with the racket you're making?"

Jed glanced up to see Kayci Cann standing above him, her hair impossibly tangled, her face puffy, her eyes deeply shadowed. Not even the sheer coral negligee could detract from the ravaging effects of too much action the night before.

Jed thought of the midnight visit from the married senator, that devoted family man, and his lips curved into a cynical smile. "Had a really hot date last night, huh?"

"So what if I did?" Kayci snapped. "It's not my fault that you didn't, so don't take it out on me." She stormed back into her apartment, giving her door a mighty slam.

Jed scowled. He considered stomping up the stairs and leaning on her doorbell or bouncing a basketball against her front door or playing his stereo at full volume, then decided against all three. As fractious and quarrelsome as he was feeling this morning, he knew that his fight wasn't with Kayci Cann. He glowered balefully at the door of Tara's apartment. Her empty apartment. Not for anything would he admit that his foul mood had begun the moment that he'd found out she wasn't at home.

He was drinking yet another cup of coffee and staring moodily out the window at the rainy gray sky when Tara and Leslie Polk turned the corner into his field of vision. Jed sat up straight and peered through the glass pane. Tara and Leslie were sharing an umbrella and appeared deeply involved in conversation as they walked together.

Jed was stunned by the rush of pleasure which surged through him at the sight of her. She was wearing a mint green jacket and skirt and her bright ponytail swung from side to side as she moved her head. She was animated, alternately smiling and serious, her expressions visually enhancing her words.

Impulsively, Jed headed toward the door. And then he caught himself. Here he was, standing in a room alone, grinning like an idiot and about to go charging out to—to do what? he asked himself. To say hello to Tara Brady? Was he crazy?

He made himself wait a full ten minutes after he heard their footsteps on the stairs and the opening and closing of both Tara's and Leslie's apartment doors before he simulated a casual saunter across the hall.

Tara opened the door on his second knock. "Jed." The sudden, sharp somersaulting of her heart was like nothing she had ever experienced before. "Hi." Her voice was a mere whisper, her smile shy and uncertain.

Jed settled himself against the doorjamb and thrust his hands deep into the pockets of his jeans. He didn't trust himself to speak. The way she was looking at him sent his senses spinning. Those beautiful eyes . . . that tremulous little smile . . . the husky softness of her voice.

Was this what had happened to his brothers? he wondered with growing alarm. Erin Brady had batted her big, dark eyes and—wham!—Rad Ramsey was ensnared? Shavonne Brady had tilted her head and smiled shyly and—zap!—Slade Ramsey was caught? The Ramsey brothers seemed to fall like bowling pins under the alluring charms of the Brady sisters. And yet knowing all of this, here he stood, gazing down at Tara Brady, his body coming alive, every sensory nerve sharpened, every muscle taut with need.

But he couldn't have her. He'd reviewed the situation last night in the shower. The proverbial cold shower, which he'd often made jokes about but had never had to resort to . . . until last night when Tara had left him with an acute case of— No, he wasn't going to think about it anymore, Jed promised himself. He'd put the insanity of last night behind him. He was not going to pursue Tara Brady. She was a danger to his freedom and to his mental health, not to mention his physical well-being.

All he wanted with her was a quick, hot affair, and he knew she was not an advocate of passion on the run. To get anywhere with Tara Brady would involve extensive time and effort. Long conversations and countless dates. A sexual progression staged with maddening slowness, beginning with elementary hand-holding. Courtship in the old-fashioned sense of the word. He knew how the game was played. That's why he'd always opted out of it in the past. If guys like Chad Cherrington wanted to invest their energies in such a frustrating endeavor, that was their choice, but count Jed Ramsey out.

So why had he been in such a frenzy to see her this morning? And what was he doing at her door? He panicked. It took him almost a full minute to come up with something. "I wanted to know if—uh—if Les likes football. I have tickets to the Oilers–Steelers game at

Three Rivers Stadium today. I wondered if he wanted to go with me."

"Why don't you ask him?" Tara suggested. She looked slightly bewildered.

And no wonder. Jed stifled a groan. Here was suave, cool, Jed Ramsey, behaving like a self-conscious junior high school student. "I thought I'd save myself a flight of stairs by asking you first. I'll go up and ask him now." Weak, but somewhat face-saving, he hoped. He started up the stairs.

"Jed?"

He turned at the sound of her voice.

"Around here, it's called the Steelers—Oilers game. Just so you'll know."

He smiled reluctantly. "That's going to take some getting used to. The Oilers always come first to a true-blue Houstoner." He felt Tara's eyes upon him as he bounded up the stairs, taking two at a time.

Leslie didn't come to the door until Jed rang the buzzer twice and knocked three times. He appeared at his door at the same moment that Kayci Cann flung open her door.

"Dammit, I asked you to keep quiet!" she shrieked. "Now I'm *telling* you! I'm trying to sleep!"

"But it's almost noon, Kayci," Leslie pointed out. "Tara and I have already been to church and back."

Kayci replied with a bloodcurdling scream and slammed the door. "Was it something I said?" Leslie asked dryly.

Jed grinned. "I have tickets to the Oil . . . the Steelers—Oilers game today, Les. Care to go?"

"I'd really like to, but I can't. I promised my folks I'd visit them this afternoon." Leslie looked disappointed, then brightened. "I know, why don't you ask Tara? She's a real football nut. She'd love to go."

"Tara Brady likes football?" Jed gave a disbelieving hoot. "Come on, Les, I know her sisters. They're my sisters-in-law, remember? Neither one of them has the slightest interest in football. They didn't even watch the Super Bowl," he added, still somewhat shocked by this lapse. And by his brothers' indulgent forgiveness of it.

"Well, Tara likes it," Leslie replied with a shrug. "The Steelers, and the local college teams—Pitt, Penn State, West Virginia—she follows them all."

Jed didn't believe him. He decided to test her so-called knowledge of football with a few pertinent questions, just to watch her flub them. It would be good for a few laughs, he assured himself.

Tara correctly answered every question he threw at her. They stood on opposite sides of her open door as he grilled her. "Les can't go to the game this afternoon," he blurted out after she'd correctly named which teams were currently leading in each division of the NFL. "Do you want to go?"

"Was this some kind of test I had to pass before you'd go to the game with me?" Her brown eyes gleamed with humor.

Jed flashed an unrepentant grin. "When I go to a football game, I like to watch it. I don't want some bubble-head cooing, 'Ooh, why are they kicking the ball?' when it's fourth down and twenty-seven yards to go."

Tara laughed. "I don't blame you." She glanced at her watch. "The kickoff is at one. We'd better hurry if we want to get there on time. Give me just five minutes to change clothes."

"You don't need to change. You look fine." Better than fine, he silently added. She looked adorable, appealing, alluring. . . . He gave his head a shake. And those were only the A's. He had a feeling he could work his way through the alphabet in complimentary adjectives describing the charms of Tara Brady.

"Believe me, we both need to change," Tara assured him. "Into warmer clothes. Three Rivers Stadium isn't the climate-controlled Astrodome. When the wind and rain come whipping through there, you get chilled to the bone. And we won't be in a box like the one Ramsey and Sons has in Houston. We'll be in the stands."

"Freezing in the wind and getting soaked in the rain?" Jed frowned at the prospect.

"We Steeler fans are hardy," Tara boasted. "When Vinnie and I went to the Steelers—Browns game two weeks ago, it was pouring rain, not just drizzling like it is today. It went into overtime and everybody stayed till the bitter end."

The drizzling rain had escalated to pouring by the time they arrived at Three Rivers Stadium, dressed in several layers of clothing, plus raincoats. Jed cast a longing glance up at the heated, enclosed corporate boxes as they climbed to their two seats in the open stands.

Tara had come prepared for the weather. She dried off their seats with the towel she'd brought, then plunked down a vinyl cushion on each seat. Jed was forced to huddle under her black-and-gold umbrella stamped with the Steeler logo. It was either that or sit unprotected in the now driving rain. He glanced glumly at the wet field and mud-drenched players and wondered if they, like himself, were questioning their sanity for being here.

Tara pulled out a small transistor radio and a set of headphones and tuned right in to the game. A gust of wind sent rain splashing into their faces. Jed moaned. He tried to tell himself that he was soaking up local color, watching the game under the same challenging conditions as all these stalwart natives, that all he had to do was to concentrate on what was happening on the playing field to forget his physical misery. That strategy appeared to work for Tara. She seemed oblivious to the adverse weather.

But it wasn't working for him. He still felt cold and wet and the game being played on the muddy field seemed irrelevant compared to his discomfort. He stole a glance at Tara, who was watching the field with rapt attention. He tried to imagine his sister Vanessa, five years his junior—fastidious, imperious, impeccable Vanessa—willingly getting drenched in the rain to watch a football game. He couldn't.

"Why are you smiling?" Tara asked, casting a puzzled glance at him. She removed her headphones. "The Oilers were just intercepted."

Jed's gaze flew to the field. He hadn't even noticed! "I was just trying to imagine Vanessa sitting here in this downpour," he confessed a little sheepishly.

"Your sister Vanessa? Out in this?" Tara looked incredulous. "My imagination doesn't extend that far."

"She's mellowed since she married Linc last year," Jed said loyally. "He's had a very humanizing effect on her."

"She does seem to be crazy about Linc," Tara acknowledged. "But I still find your sister incredibly intimidating. She's not exactly the kind of woman other women can pal around with."

"And you are, of course."

Tara arched her brows. "Uh-oh, I forgot the cardinal rule: Only Ramseys are allowed to speak in anything but glowing terms about other Ramseys. But, yes, as one of five sisters, I do find it easy to get along with other women."

"And other men," he said, his words sounding as if they'd been growled. He was suddenly, extraordinarily aware of her nearness. Huddled together under the umbrella as they were, their shoulders were touching, their faces close. He could smell the scent of her perfume. It was as sensuous and elusive as she was. He inhaled deeply and arousal shuddered through him.

She was so close to him. He could feel the heat emanating from her body, feel her small, soft frame against him. His senses were full of her. He could think of nothing else. Her presence did what the football game hadn't, making him impervious to the wind, rain, and cold. Tension, frustration, and desire coursed through him, so intermingled that he couldn't begin to separate one from the other.

"Oh yes, you have lots of male friends, don't you?" He knew he was deliberately needling her. He felt an irresistible urge to fight with her, about anything, about everything. "In addition to your idyllic romance with the worthy Chad, you have dinner and go to church with Les Polk, you go to football games with Vinnie—" He broke off with a scowl. "Who the hell is Vinnie, anyway?"

"Vince Krajack. He works at the station with me." Tara frowned right back at him.

"Doesn't Chad mind your spending all your time with other guys?" Part of him knew that he was lashing out at her to diffuse the explosive urges which roiled within him. The other part clung stubbornly to the fallacy that he was running interference for the unseen Chad. That he had to preserve that romance for the sake of his own freedom. "It can't be good for your relationship."

"Oh, you're a fine one to be offering advice on relationships. Have you ever had one that lasted longer than ten minutes?"

She was pleased with the hyperbole. Jed was not. "We're talking about you and Chad, not me. Are you running around on him behind his back? Where was he two weeks ago, when you and this Vinnie character went to the game?"

"Will you stop interrogating me like some sort of FBI agent! I haven't done anything wrong. Chad trusts me implicitly. He doesn't—uh—care for football so he doesn't mind if I go to games with someone else. He prefers the symphony and the ballet, performances at the Benedum Center and Heinz Hall," she added grandly. Good old Chad, she thought with a secret smile. She was turning him into the cultured, sensitive embodiment of every woman's dream.

"Chad is a twerp," Jed proclaimed crossly. "And he's asking for trouble by letting a girl like you run around with any man you please."

Tara sat up very straight. "A girl like me?" she repeated softly, dangerously. "Explain exactly what you mean by 'a girl like me.'"

"Cute. Smart." Jed snapped the words at her. "Fun to be with." He swallowed. "Pretty." And swallowed again. "Sexy." He was breathing heavily, and the blood was thundering in his head. The world seemed to be careening around him.

Tara's heart was thumping, but she masked her emotions to stare at him with impassive brown eyes. "I've always suspected that you considered women fungible. This proves it."

How could they be so out of sync? Jed wondered wildly. He was on fire for her and she was gazing at him with the detached interest of a scientist viewing an odd specimen. And using words he'd never heard before. "Fungible?" he echoed hoarsely. "What does that mean?"

"It means being replaceable by another equivalent thing. Something freely exchangeable. Coins are fungible. Grains of wheat are fungible. People are not—at least they're not supposed to be." She paused, her dark eyes meeting and holding his light ones. "But to you, all women are exchangeable and interchangeable. Fungible."

"I do not think women are fungible!" Jed protested indignantly.

"You do. You gave yourself away when you said that you think I'm pretty and sexy and all those other things. A fungible compliment for a fungible woman. This is me you're talking to, Jed. Tara Brady. I happen to know what you really think of me."

"And what's that?"

"You think I'm boring. And bland. And naive and tiresome. Shall I go on? I know the list by heart. You've recited it often enough."

He resented her patronizing air. He wanted to obliterate her cool composure, to watch the expression on her face dissolve into passion as he aroused her, to see her serious brown eyes flame into hot velvet pools of desire. He vaguely recalled that he had his reasons for keeping Tara Brady at a distance. That he'd been fighting against becoming interested in her for a long time. That a third Brady—Ramsey union was one too many, a downright bad idea.

But somehow it all seemed irrelevant in comparison

to the primitive sexual hunger raging through him. He couldn't wait another moment to touch her. He moved suddenly, catching Tara completely off guard. Cupping her chin in one big hand, he tilted her head back and lowered his head to hers.

She made a startled, inarticulate sound of protest and tried to jerk away, but he was too quick for her. His mouth came down hard on hers. For a split second, she was too stunned to murmur or move, or even breathe. Her eyes were wide open and she saw the black-and-gold umbrella above them, saw the raindrops hit the fabric and roll down. She saw Jed's face, his eyes tightly closed, his brows drawn together. She'd never kissed anyone with her eyes open before; the thought skittered across her mind. It was very strange, seeing a face from this angle.

Jed lifted his mouth slightly from hers. It was a shock to meet her wide, amazed brown eyes. Her self-possession enraged him. He had always been the cool one, the master of his passion, orchestrating his affairs for his own convenience.

But inexplicably, without warning, the tables had been turned. It was not convenient to burn with need in the soaking stands of a football arena with fifty-nine thousand screaming fans in attendance. He was confounded. Confused. And furious with himself and with her. For the first time in his life, he'd lost his head and his self-control. And Tara Brady, the cause of it all, appeared completely unmoved.

"Kiss me back, dammit," he rasped.

Tara gazed into his eyes. Her mind wasn't as clear as it ought to be, she thought worriedly. Muddled thoughts and impressions tumbled through it. Like the way his eyes held unexpected shades of cobalt blue, which seemed to blend into the gunmetal gray color if one stared long enough. And the intense, hot look he was giving her made her feel breathless. No man had ever gazed at her with such burning ardency, such focused sexual attention. And when that man was Jed Ramsey . . .

She should run, not walk, away from him because he was dangerous and she knew it. She had watched and learned for the past four years. She knew more about him than he ever suspected. When a woman aroused his interest, he would pursue her, pulling out all the stops until his quarry surrendered to him. And then, inevitably, he lost interest and moved on to someone else. She'd seen the pattern repeated time and time again, with woman after woman. Cautious, observant Tara did not dare to become yet another participant in the latest round of his game.

"I don't want to kiss you," she said, steeling herself against the delicious surge of heat in her abdomen.

It was the first time in his life that Jed Ramsey had ever heard those words. He was momentarily astounded. And then incensed. "Well, then I'll have to make you want to, won't I?"

Now she'd done it! Tara scolded herself. She had challenged him and no self-respecting Ramsey turned away from a challenge. Worse, she'd appeared uninterested and unavailable. Wasn't that a sure-fire way to intrigue a man, especially one who was accustomed to having women throw themselves at him?

She decided that Jed Ramsey must be living, breathing proof of her mother's bitter invective: Men only want what they can't have. Well, if her mother were to be believed, the antidote for Jed's sudden and unexpected desire for her would be to stop resisting, to let him think she wanted him, too. To kiss him without further struggle. She decided to give it a try.

When his mouth opened over hers, she didn't pull away or try to fight him in any way. She felt the probing of his tongue against her closed lips and responded by parting them slightly. He emitted a groan and thrust his tongue deep into the warmth of her mouth. Angling his head, he sealed their mouths in a searing kiss.

It was like nothing she had ever experienced. Tara's eyes fluttered shut as his tongue rubbed against hers. A hot, heady pleasure exploded within her, filling her with heat. His arm was around her, her head wedged against his shoulder while his hand cupped her neck, his long fingers stroking the smooth, sensitive skin. She felt surrounded by him, overwhelmed by his taste and his touch.

And she wanted more. She wanted to get closer to him. His masculine heat and hardness beckoned and tantalized. Her arm crept slowly around his neck as she strained toward him. She murmured a small, soft sound as he held her tighter and deepened the kiss.

Her breasts felt full and firm, the nipples almost painfully hard. Even the soft material of her bra felt abrasive against them. Swirls of sensation ribboned down her middle, her belly, and knotted tightly between her legs.

The armrest between their seats dug into her ribs, but she was unaware of any discomfort. Her fingers, wrapped around the handle of the umbrella, reflexively loosened their grip and neither one noticed when the stem slid between them, bringing the umbrella to rest on top of their heads.

They were both panting and breathless when Jed slowly lifted his head. Tara stared at him, her heartbeat drumming in her ears. His blue-gray eyes were heavy lidded with passion, his mouth moist from kissing her. She lay against him, submissive and pliant, her lips pink and swollen, her pupils dilated, darkening her eyes to velvety blackness. Her pulse was throbbing, her body tingling and aching with pleasure, and the need for more.

So now she knew, she thought dazedly. These feelings Jed had aroused with his passionate kiss were what all the songs and books and movies were about. She'd comprehended the words and meanings, of course, but until now she had never actually experienced them for herself. And there was an incredible difference between understanding desire and passion intellectually and feeling them physically and emotionally.

Her scattered thoughts jumped to her two older sisters and their first physical encounters with the brothers Ramsey. Were these intense, thrilling feelings what had given them the nerve to risk relationships with men who could break their hearts? Or make them happier than they'd ever been in their lives?

Why, it was like a crapshoot! Tara thought with dismay. Shavonne and Erin had lucked out, but their mother hadn't. She had to eke out an existence with five small children and a million regrets. Tara shivered. The odds in this game were too dismal to contemplate.

She thought of her mother again. Jerilyn Brady, so pretty and so hurt and mixed up. Jerilyn Brady had never had any trouble attracting men, but keeping them had been another matter. *No*, Tara decided for perhaps the fifty-thousandth time. *That's not going to be me.*

Jed reached up to lift the umbrella from their heads. He smiled and her heart turned over. It was a warm, intimate smile that made her want to snuggle closer and cling to him. To raise her lips to his and kiss him again and again. The sweet longings unnerved her. It was a crapshoot, she reminded herself, and the dice were loaded—against her.

"Let's get out of here," Jed said huskily and reached for her hand. He clasped it in his, interlocking their fingers in a possessive lover's gesture.

"Jed, no." Tara pulled her hand from his. A terrifying mixture of anxiety and anticipation bubbled within her. If they left now, it would be to continue what they'd begun here. His voice, his eyes, his body language confirmed it. Did she dare take up the emotional and sexual challenge posed by Jed Ramsey?

Her mother's woeful face appeared vividly in her mind's eye. "*I was so sure he loved me, Tara,*" she heard Jerilyn Brady's melancholy tones echo in her brain. "*He wanted me so much. But then he took all my love and left me, just like all the others.*"

The pronoun 'he' was a substitute for a long list of male names, but the end results were always the same. The pathos of her mother's love life could have served as lyrics for a sorrowful country-western song. Tara shivered again. Wanting was not loving. She had figured that one out years ago. Her poor mother never had.

"No," she repeated with conviction.

"No?" Jed looked astounded, as if he'd never heard the word before.

He probably didn't hear it very often, and never from women, Tara decided grimly. She squared her shoulders and sat up very straight, forcing herself to meet his eyes. "What just happened," her voice faltered and she drew in a steadying breath, "was a mistake, Jed. I told you I didn't want to kiss you and I meant it."

"Like hell!" Jed cursed explosively, his voice low but no less fierce in its intensity. "You wanted it as much as I did, baby. You went up in flames when I kissed you. Don't bother to deny it."

Tara shook her head. "It's just that I got caught in my own trap. I knew resisting would only provoke you more so I decided to go along with you. I thought you'd lose interest. I never dreamed that it, that I—" She gulped. "I thought—hoped!—we'd both be bored."

"Bored?" echoed Jed incredulously. "Bored?"

She nodded.

"Are you often bored when a man kisses you?"

She thought back to the kisses she'd received over the years. There hadn't been many, by her choice. "Well, yes," she admitted. She preferred friendship to romance and when a man tried to cross the boundary between, she generally found his overtures awkward, rather embarrassing, and yes, on the boring side. But she hadn't been bored one whit when Jed kissed her. And that disturbed her more than she was willing to confess.

"Poor Chad," Jed said, his lips twisting into at sardonic sneer. "No wonder the poor sucker was so eager to hawk his shoes in Russia. The woman he wants to marry finds him sexually boring."

Oh no, she'd forgotten all about Chad! "I'm not bored when Chad kisses me, of course," she interjected hastily. "That goes without saying. I meant I find it, uh,

boring when someone I'm not interested in—someone
like you—kisses me."

"You weren't bored with me, honey," Jed said roughly.
He thought about her impassioned response to him
and the flame still smoldering within him flared higher.
When was the last time he had been so aroused, so
moved by a single kiss? He couldn't remember. And
that worried him.

"It's all wrong, Jed." Her voice was quiet but firm.

"Don't I know it!" He gave a self-mocking laugh. Everything about their first kiss was wrong, from the
inappropriate setting to the abysmal weather to his
wild reaction at the touch of her soft young mouth. He
knew he should be relieved that she was being so sensible about the whole thing. What if she had lost her
head and given into him completely? What if she'd let
him take her to his apartment to explore this surprising and exciting passion which had flamed between
them?

His carefree bachelor days would be winding to a
close, that's what, he told himself severely. A girl like
Tara Brady would inevitably confuse sex and love and
if they were having sex, she would convince herself
that she was in love with him. And the entire Ramsey
—Brady tribe would hound him to the ends of the
earth until he slipped that gold wedding band on her
finger.

As the rain splashed down on him—she wasn't sharing her umbrella with him anymore—he tried to tell
himself how lucky he was to be here with Tara Brady at
this moment instead of in bed with her. Except he
didn't feel lucky or relieved, he felt cold and wet, and so
hard that his whole body ached with the force of his
need. And his imagination was running rampant. In
his mind's eye, he kept seeing images of Tara and
himself lying naked on his bed, their bodies inter-
twined. . . .

He was jolted out of his erotic daydream by the sudden roaring of the crowd. The mass of Pittsburgh fans,
including Tara, jumped to their feet screaming and

cheering as a Steeler running-back penetrated Houston's defensive line and crossed the goal line to score a touchdown. It happened twice more during the first half. The Oilers' luck seemed to be paralleling his, Jed thought wryly. Neither could score.

The announcer's voice boomed over the loudspeakers to announce the halftime festivities, including a special appearance by Senator Glenn Saxon who was attending the game with his two young sons. The senator was on hand to present a humanitarian award to one of the retired Steeler players on behalf of his work with handicapped children.

Tara and Jed watched Glenn Saxon stride onto the field, an umbrella held over his head by a solicitous aide. "Wonder if that's the Oldsmobile-driving stooge who dropped Glenn-o off last night?" Jed muttered caustically.

"And picked him up afterward," added Tara in a whisper. "I heard him leave last night, did you? It was a couple of hours after we said good night."

Jed frowned. "Yeah, I heard him leave, too. The bastard was whistling!" Considering the aroused, uncomfortable and frustrated state he'd been in last night, he had thoroughly resented the other man's tuneful self-satisfaction.

They sat in silence as Glenn Saxon took the opportunity to expound on his views of good old-fashioned virtue and values—and to lambaste the blackguards who did not abide by them.

"Well, that does it for me." Jed stood up. "I can take the rain and the Oilers' fumbling and even your sexually rejecting me, but I can't hack Glenn-o's hypocritical spiel."

Tara stood up too. "In light of what we saw and heard last night, it is sickening," she agreed.

"Want to get some coffee and something to eat? I'll treat if you'll let me back under your umbrella."

His wry, crooked grin sent a surge of warmth rushing through her. "It's a deal." Taking a step closer, giving him a tentative, guarded smile, she held the umbrella over his head.

Maybe they could be friends, she thought hopefully. Maybe now that he'd made his obligatory pass and gotten it out of his system, he could relate to her as a person and not as one of his fungible sexual conquests.

She had the most appealing smile he'd ever seen, Jed thought, gazing down at her. And its effect on him was alarming. It made him almost light-headed with pleasure. He took her arm and guided her toward the crowded refreshment stands. It felt good to touch her, even in such an impersonal, practical way. He wanted her, he admitted to himself. He would never have believed that he could lust after the sweet young woman whom his parents had handpicked as a wife for him, but somehow it had happened.

Well, marriage was out of the question, but they definitely were going to have an affair, Jed promised himself. And then they would part company. He would return to Houston a footloose and fun-loving bachelor and Tara would return to her safe and boring zombie consort, Chad Cherrington.

A happy ending for the third Ramsey son and the third Brady sister, even if it wasn't the one their families had scripted for them.

Five

Tara was at her desk in the small WQQW newsroom shortly before nine Monday morning. Vince Krajack and Bob Fusco, the other two reporters on the Double Q news team arrived a few minutes later, commiserating about the Steelers' unexpected loss in the fourth quarter yesterday afternoon.

"They just rolled over and died out there!" howled Vince. "Three interceptions that resulted in three touchdowns for Houston! That's criminal!"

"I was there with a devout Oilers' fan," Tara put in. "He gloated the whole way home."

"A classic example of adding insult to injury," Bob said with a grin. "Who is he, Tara? A new boyfriend?"

Tara shook her head. "I'm not sure how to describe my relationship with Jed Ramsey. Neighbor? Family friend? Unrelated relation? One thing he is *not* and never will be is my 'boyfriend.' New or otherwise."

They weren't even on speaking terms this morning. After the game yesterday, Jed had been at his most charming when he'd asked her to have dinner with him.

She'd declined his offer. Cold and wet from hours in the rain, shaken by the volatile emotions stirred by his kiss, she wanted only to soak in a hot bath, to eat leftover lasagna for dinner, and to spend the evening reading. She wanted to relax in peace and quiet, something she knew she never could do in Jed Ramsey's irritating, challenging, fascinating, disturbing company.

Jed's charm had rapidly evaporated when she told him of her plans. Ramseys did not take kindly to being thwarted, Jed least of all. "You're telling me that you'd rather take a bath and wash your hair than be with me?" He'd been indignant, and highly offended. "That's the excuse women give to avoid clods and dolts. Nobody has ever used it on me!"

Except Tara. She'd stuck to her guns and they'd parted as less than friends. When they'd met in the hall this morning while leaving their respective apartments, Jed's response to her polite good morning had been a glowering silence.

Christine Logston, the station's news director, joined them to make the day's assignments. Bob drew the county courthouse for a highly publicized ongoing murder trial, Vince the USX Building for the latest round of labor negotiations being conducted there.

"Tara, I'd like you to go to the William Penn Hotel for Glenn Saxon's news conference. It's scheduled for ten o'clock in the lobby," Christine concluded.

Tara stared blindly at her notebook. Last week, she wouldn't have given a second thought to covering the senator's news conference. Now it seemed as if their paths were ominously fated to cross. And try as she might, she couldn't dismiss Glenn Saxon's late Saturday night visit to Kayci Cann. Was it relevant to his reelection campaign? Jed didn't think so, but he'd admitted that he wasn't sure. As for her own opinion . . .

She needed to talk to someone in the news business about the situation, Tara decided. She waited until Bob and Vince had departed to approach Christine. "Can I talk to you a few minutes, Christine? It's about Senator Saxon."

Christine Logston was something of a mentor to Tara. She had been the one to hire Tara after hearing the audition tape she'd sent from her school radio station.

There were few women in radio news in Pittsburgh and Christine, as news director, had been immensely supportive of Tara.

Christine smiled at her. "I wonder if you've been hearing the same rumors about him that I have."

Tara stared at her. Maybe this was going to be easier than she thought. "What have you heard?" she asked deferentially.

"That after Glenn wins reelection to the senate next month, he's going to announce his intention of running for president." Christine's eyes lighted with enthusiasm. "Of course the presidential election is a full year away, but Glenn has commissioned some private polls that turned up encouraging results. Bradford Lipton looks unbeatable and it's always difficult to defeat an incumbent, of course, but Glenn appears to be his party's strongest candidate against Lipton and his party."

Tara attempted to breathe. It wasn't easy. "Saxon is thinking of running for president?" she managed weakly.

"I'm personally excited because Glenn is an old college friend of my husband's. They've always kept in touch—in fact, Jim had lunch with Glenn last month. We're both ready to campaign for him. As a card-carrying member of NOW, I want a candidate who respects women as equals."

"And you think Senator Saxon does?" Tara asked carefully. "Respect women, that is."

"Oh yes. He and his wife have a model marriage." Christine beamed. "You see, Glenn appreciates women as thinking individuals whom he respects on an equal intellectual plane."

Tara found herself wishing that Jed were here. She knew he would have something to say about Glenn Saxon's appreciation of women as thinking individuals and his propensity toward the likes of Kayci Cann. Nor had their illicit midnight tryst been conducted on anything remotely resembling an intellectual plane, equal or otherwise.

Tara mocked herself for her naïveté. She'd hoped it wouldn't be hard to tell Christine about Saxon and Kayci. After listening to the glowing testimonial, it was impossible! But if the man was planning to run for president and his popularity was based on the image of him as a devoted husband and family man, a feminist whose attitudes toward women were exemplary and nonexploitative, an image that was false—Tara's head swam with the implications.

"I guess I'd better get down to Saxon's headquarters," was all she could think to say. She gathered her materials—tape recorder, pad and pencils—and stuffed them into her oversize bag.

"If you get a chance, say hello to Glenn for me," Christine called after her.

Tara suppressed a groan.

The rest of the day proceeded at its usual hectic pace. After attending the news conference—where she didn't pass on Christine's cheery hello to the senator—Tara went back to the station to check the details of several other breaking stories via telephone. She had discovered that her presence wasn't always required at the scene and she could gather a wealth of information about certain events from a few well-placed phone calls.

She pulled out her lunch, eating the tuna salad sandwich on rye and orange she'd brought, between calls and writing up her stories. Two months ago she'd been given the additional duties of afternoon anchor which meant compiling the days' events into a six-minute broadcast and reporting the latest news three times during the P.M. drive-time slot at four, five, and six o'clock.

The Lamborghini Countach was not parked in front of the apartment building when she arrived there shortly before seven, and Tara quickly pulled her car into the empty spot. She was totally nonplussed to find Jed standing in the small hallway between their apartments.

"I didn't think you were around," she said, striving to sound nonchalant. Her heartbeat had taken off at a terrific rate at the sight of him, but she wasn't about to betray any signs of—what? What exactly was she feeling? she wondered. Nervous? No, not really. Excited? She swallowed. That was it, all right. "Your car isn't," she added, purposefully turning her full attention to finding her doorkey in her purse.

"I talked Mr. Safran, down the street, into renting me his garage. That's where my car is."

"And where is Mr. Safran's car?"

Jed shrugged. "Parked along the street, I guess."

Tara rolled her eyes. "There's a Ramsey solution for you." She turned the key in the lock.

"Hey, I offered him a more than generous sum that he was more than willing to accept."

Tara opened the door, conflict raging within her. Should she invite Jed in? She knew it wasn't wise to be alone with him, not after the pass he'd made yesterday. And yet a peculiar exhilaration bubbled through her veins at the forbidden prospect. And fizzled flat at the thought of him leaving. She paused on the threshold, immobilized by her internal civil war.

"I hope you don't think I was waiting for you," he said, his gaze affixed to her back. She'd worn her hair down today and it lay soft and silky over her shoulders. His gaze lowered to her legs, slim and shapely in low-heeled blue pumps. He cleared his throat. "I just happened to be leaving my apartment when you walked in."

A blatant falsehood. He'd turned his car radio to WQQW on his way back from the Southland Mall in time to catch her five-o'clock broadcast. The sound of her voice, cool, crisp and professional, had had the strangest effect on him. He'd been unable to keep himself from grinning ear to ear. She was good! He'd beamed with vicarious pride. Back in his apartment, he'd tuned in for her six-o'clock broadcast as well. He couldn't stop thinking about her, and provocative memories of that tempestuous kiss they'd shared yesterday whirled obsessively through his head. Desire, fierce and sharp, coiled through him.

He forgot that he was furious with her for turning

down a dinner date with him to wash her hair. He wanted her. As soon as the news report was finished, he'd begun to wait for her to come home. And she'd caught him in the act. Lucky for him, she didn't know that, though, and he certainly had no intention of telling her.

"Why would I think you were waiting for me?" Tara's common sense reasserted itself. She would not invite Jed Ramsey inside. "You weren't even speaking to me the last time I saw you," she added, entering her apartment.

He followed her, not bothering to wait for the invitation she'd decided against. "I don't take kindly to being buzzed off, Tara. And that's what you did to me last night."

The door swung shut behind them, closing the two of them inside. She turned swiftly and nearly collided with him. A growing heat suffused her. Suddenly, the room seemed cozily private and she was awkwardly aware that they were very much alone. In a determined effort to appear natural, she slipped off her blue-and-gray jacket and dropped it on a chair.

Jed came closer and she immediately took several quick steps backward.

He arched his brows, his slate-colored eyes mocking her. "I see your hair is nice and clean. But was it really worth forgoing an evening with me to wash it?"

She did not care for that unholy glimmer in his eyes. Setting her jaw, she forced herself to face him squarely. "Yes," she interjected. "It really was."

He gave a short laugh. "I don't think I want to believe you." One giant stride brought him directly in front of her. He caught both her hands in one swift grip and stroked his thumbs over the pulse points at her wrists. "Your pulse is racing, Tara. Does that mean you're scared of me?"

"No!" she denied hotly, realizing too late that she'd taken the bait he'd so craftily dangled.

"No? Then it must be something else." One big hand

slid to her waist and anchored her against the lower half of his body. "Excitement?"

She felt the virile thrust of his hips against hers. Her wide brown eyes flew to his face. "Jed," she began, her mouth suddenly dry.

"Or arousal?" he continued smoothly. He lowered his head and sensuously nipped at her earlobe. "Both, perhaps?" He rubbed suggestively against her and smiled when she audibly caught her breath.

"Don't." Her voice quavered. His lips had moved to her neck to nibble along the soft, sensitive curve.

"Why not?" His other hand moved with deliberate slowness along her ribcage to pause just below her breast. "You know you want me to."

She shook her head, the denial trapped in her throat. The way he was looking at her made her feel weak. It was both unnerving and thrilling to be the focus of the intense sexuality burning in his gaze. A sensuous little shudder tingled along her spine.

He extended his thumb to lazily caress her nipple, which was hard and tight beneath the soft layers of her clothing. Tara tried and failed to suppress the soft little moan that escaped from her throat.

"You like it," he murmured, brushing her lips lightly, sensuously, with his. He shifted slightly and thrust his thigh between hers.

She instinctively arched into his masculine warmth and hardness. Oh, he was right, she thought dizzily. She did like it. It felt so good when he touched her. A swell of hot pleasure flooded her, making her feel weak and warm and soft. Her eyelids drifted shut. His tongue and lips continued to play with hers and she responded with shy, sensuous little kisses of her own.

She wasn't aware that he'd unfastened the buttons of her blue silk blouse until she felt his hand slip beneath her wispy bra and cup her bare breast. She felt her nipple throb against his palm as he rubbed it into a taut little point of sensual fire. His other hand kneaded the rounded firmness of her buttock, making her moan and move against him in a primal feminine rhythm.

For several blazing moments, Tara thought she would faint from the wild forces raging within her. Hot flames ripped through her, emanating from the deep, secret place where Jed's thigh was pressed between hers.

"Oh, baby, I want you so much," he rasped in a voice so intimate and sexually stimulating that she shuddered with desire. A throbbing anticipation drummed within her, heightened by his confident expertise.

When his mouth came down on hers, she clung to him, responding to his ardent, compelling technique. She moaned as his tongue masterfully penetrated the moist warmth of her mouth. Reflexively, her arms crept round his neck and she fitted herself to him, her feminine softness pressing intimately against the corresponding masculine planes of his body. She felt both a hunger and an emptiness she had never before experienced. Her fingers tangled in the thickness of his dark hair and she savored its coarse texture, so different from the silken softness of her own golden strands.

His mouth hot and hard on hers, his hands holding her firmly against the unyielding length of him, Jed lowered her body to the sofa, laying her full length along the cushions. He came down on top of her, his solid weight pressing her in place.

He lifted his head, momentarily freeing her mouth, and Tara's eyes opened languidly to see him staring down at her, his gray eyes dark and smoldering fiercely with arousal and desire and—determination.

"It's going to be so good between us, baby," he murmured huskily. "It's what we both want, what we both need. I promise you won't regret it."

She stared into his eyes. It was the fierce determination burning in them which reawakened her caution. It was so very Ramsey. She'd long observed that every member of the Ramsey family had been blessed—or was it cursed?—with a relentless tenacity. None of them would give up until what they wanted was theirs. Whatever a Ramsey wants, a Ramsey gets was the family credo and was quoted often, both jovially and seriously.

Nobody said no to a Ramsey.

But she had. Tara tensed at the realization. Nobody said no to Ramsey and made it stick, she silently amended. Jed was about to make sure of that. He had, however, not reckoned with the exceptionally strong will of Tara Brady. "Jed, I can't. I won't. This is wrong." She placed her hands on his chest and tried to push him off her.

Her words barely penetrated the steamy, sensual fog which engulfed him. But when she repeatedly turned her face away from him to avoid his mouth and began to pummel at his chest with small, tight fists, it slowly dawned on him that something was amiss.

He stared down at her with passion-glazed eyes. "What's the matter, baby?"

The hot sweetness of sexual arousal burgeoned achingly in Tara's body, almost making her abandon her fight and sink into sublime submission. Almost. However, she happened to possess a toughness and a tenacity equal to any Ramsey's. "Let me up, Jed," she insisted.

"What?" Jed's voice squeaked. Shock waves reverberated through him like the aftershocks following an earthquake. He could hardly comprehend what was happening. Only moments before, Tara had lain pliant and responsive beneath him. Now her slender body was totally rigid and the drowsy passion in her eyes had been replaced by a combative glitter.

His body pulsed and ached with unquenched desire. Remembering the past few nights' misery of frustration, he was not averse to a little pleading. "Baby, baby, please. I'll—"

"My name is Tara," she said coolly, her resolution growing stronger. Using all her strength, she gave him a hard, swift shove. She caught him totally off guard and was able to slip from beneath him, landing on her knees on the floor beside the couch.

"It's a good idea to remember the name of the person

you're attempting to make love with," she added with asperity as she rose to her feet. "Instead of using fungible nomenclature."

Jed felt dazed. He'd plunged too far, too fast from the hot sweet heavens of arousal and anticipation to the bitter depths of rejection. He wanted to beg her to come back to him, he wanted to swear at her, to grab a handful of her beautiful blond hair and drag her into his arms, to crush her beneath him.

Slowly, he pulled himself to a sitting position. *"Fungible nomenclature?"* His voice sounded muddled and thick to his own ears. Where did she come up with this stuff? he wondered dazedly. His eyes followed Tara's lithe figure as she paced back and forth like a restless tigress. She was clearly in a state of agitation. Her face was flushed, and her hands trembled as she tried to rebutton her blouse.

"I—I admit it's more my fault than yours," she said in a choked voice. But the way he'd made her feel . . . Tara quivered. She'd never felt that way before, so wildly alive, so totally overwhelmed by the voluptuous pleasure flooding her body.

"Fault?" Jed echoed, watching her as one mesmerized. His eyes were riveted to the ivory lace of her bra, still visible as she struggled with the buttons of her blouse. He remembered the soft, slick feel of the material against his fingers, the incredible warm softness of her breasts beneath. He barely managed to suppress a groan of longing. "Sweetheart, no one is at fault here. We want each other, we want to make love. It's normal and natural and—"

"And it's wrong," Tara interjected. "Jed, we don't love each other. Most of the time we don't even like each other."

Paradoxically, her statement provoked a rebellion within him, and startlingly reframed his perspective. "I like you well enough, I suppose," he admitted grudgingly.

"That's not enough for me. And even if we loved each other, I'd still say no. We're not married and—"

"You don't have to be married to make love!" Jed interrupted, aghast at the concept.

Tara heaved a weary sigh. "Jed, I've told you how I feel about premarital sex. I don't believe in it. Especially not for me."

"Sure, I heard you say it, but I didn't think you actually *meant* it!" He found it unfathomable. That she would deny them both the pleasure of sexual fulfillment because it was contrary to her beliefs! "This is crazy! I feel like I'm caught in a time warp, trapped in the fifties during the Eisenhower administration. Good girls don't put out. They make men marry them for it. Help! Quick, transport me back to the eighties."

Tara tucked her blouse back into the waistband of her gray-and-blue pleated skirt, her fingers shaking as violently as her knees. "On Saturday night you said it was wrong for Senator Saxon to be with Kayci. Well, it's just as wrong for you and me—"

"There's an enormous difference between our situation and theirs, Tara!" Jed stood up, his expression an almost comical portrait in exasperation. "For one, Saxon is married. In addition, he's a public official who trades on his upstanding-and-devoted-family-man image to garner votes. And—"

"He's going to run for president," Tara blurted out. "My boss told me today. Her husband is a friend of Saxon's and they're both staunch supporters of his."

"Saxon is going to run for president?" Jed repeated, momentarily diverted. He gave a low whistle. "Can this mean that Kayci has a crack at becoming first lady?" he asked, his tongue firmly in cheek.

Tara's dark eyes met his and she smiled hesitantly.

He had to steel himself against the effects of her smile. After all, he was defending modern sexual ethics here. A position which conveniently happened to coincide with his own interests.

"Forget Kayci and Saxon, we're talking about you and me," he persisted. "You want me, Tara. Don't bother to deny it. And don't give me any crap about your undying love and fidelity to that dullard Chad

Cherrington. He doesn't make you feel what I do, you don't want him, and—"

"Jed, I may as well tell you the truth about Chad right now," Tara cut in. This would send him packing, as nothing else would. She drew a deep breath and looked at the floor. "He doesn't exist."

It took a few moments for her words to fully register. And then, "He doesn't exist?" Jed was staggered. "There is no Chad?"

"I made him up to discourage your father from trying to get you and me together," Tara confessed, daring to lift her eyes. He was staring at her, agape. "And it was working. He'd stopped calling to tell me what a great husband you'd be. And you admitted that he stopped nagging you about me, too. I never thought you'd show up in Pittsburgh," she added, a little nervously. "And I *really* never thought that you'd, that I'd—" She gulped. "That there would ever be anything physical between us."

"Why, you conniving little liar!" That she had gone to such lengths to keep him away from her left him flabbergasted, and irked him beyond measure. "And just what did you plan to tell our families when they started asking about your wedding plans?"

Tara shrugged. "I hadn't thought that far ahead. But all I'd have had to say was that Chad and I broke up. I figured by then your folks would have found someone else for you."

"But what about me? I'm here in Pittsburgh, right across the hall from you. What were you going to tell me when I kept asking about Chad?" His mouth tightened. "Or did you plan to keep him safely out of the country pitching shoes forever?"

The conversation was bordering on the surrealistic. Tara stared at him, nonplussed. "Something like that, I guess. I don't know. I didn't think you'd be around very long."

"Well, you were mistaken, Tara. I'm not going anywhere. My father and I had a long distance telephone conference this afternoon and decided that I should stick around and flesh out my ideas for the Southland Mall. That means I'll be right next door. And I'm not going to leave you alone, baby. Now that I know how hot you are for me, it's just a matter of time before I have you in my bed begging me for it. And then, then . . ." His voice trailed off as he imagined the ecstasy of his body embedded snugly in hers. It was exhilarating, it was irresistible, it was downright scary. He had never wanted another woman as badly as he wanted Tara Brady.

"You want to go to bed with me, even though you're furious with me and don't love me and only quote, like me well enough, you suppose, unquote," Tara said flatly.

Put that way, it seemed ridiculous, but he wasn't about to concede her point. Or admit to anything else. "Correct," he replied.

"That's the stupidest thing I've ever heard." It took every bit of her self-control to appear calm and composed before him, for her heart was slamming against her ribs. She'd been shocked at her impassioned response to him and to her uncharacteristic loss of control in his arms. What if he were to do as he threatened and increase his attentions? To wear down her resistance with his kisses and caresses?

A shiver tingled along her spine. Her belief in no sex until marriage had never been put to the test before. Could she hold out against an experienced, determined man like Jed Ramsey? Tara thought of him cold-bloodedly pursuing her for the twin purposes of salvaging his ego and quenching his lust. She imagined him making love to her and then discharging her in triumph. That was the way he had it planned.

Her dark eyes glittered. What Jed Ramsey didn't know was that the Brady sisters possessed a sense of self-preservation as strong as the Ramseys' sense of entitlement. He didn't know about all those long talks with her mother late at night. Oh yes, Tara assured herself, taking all of those factors into consideration, she could most certainly withstand sexual pressure from Jed Ramsey.

She tilted her head, all her pride and dignity inherent in her bearing. "I'll never let you use me, Jed Ramsey. I'll sleep with you on our wedding night or not at all." And then her lips twitched into a sudden, irrepressible smile. "And since I know for a fact that you'd rather face a firing squad than marry me, I don't have much to worry about, do I?"

Jed stared at her. He felt cast adrift in totally unfamiliar seas. "Well, we'll just see about that, won't we?" he mumbled. A thoroughly inadequate response, he knew. The situation called for a forceful, intimidatingly sexy comeback and he'd scraped by with a banal one.

Which Tara was fully aware of. Her dark eyes gleamed.

"Careful, little girl," he said, recovering himself. His voice was a silky growl. "You're not used to playing these games and now you're in a match with a grand master. You're bound to lose."

"While you're tossing out trite metaphorical advice, don't forget to add that I'm playing with fire and am likely to get burned." She hadn't meant to issue a sexual challenge, but she had.

And Jed reacted to it at once. "We're both going to go up in flames," he promised, reaching for her again.

Tara stepped away, eluding him. She was so tempted to go back into his arms, it was alarming. She sought to distract him, and herself. "No more, Jed. I'm starved and I want to eat dinner now."

Jed took her withdrawal with good grace. "I make it a point never to seduce a woman with an empty stomach," he said dryly. "Grab your jacket and let's go."

"Go where?"

"Out to eat. You said you were hungry."

She wasn't sure what to make of this odd turn of events. "You're taking me to dinner?"

"I have to eat, too." Jed shrugged. "I'll drive to the restaurant, but you're paying for your own meal, honey. I have no intention of trying to court you. My sole goal is to get you into bed, not to make you fall in love with me."

She stared at him warily. "I have no intention of falling in love—or into bed—with you."

"You want me," Jed drawled. His lazy smile exuded masculine confidence. "And you'll sleep with me, eventually. It's inevitable."

"No!" Tara insisted, but her stomach lurched convulsively. The telephone rang and she welcomed the diversion. She hurried to answer it with the sense of being temporarily rescued.

"Shavonne!" she cried at the sound of her sister's voice. "Oh, I'm so glad you called." Gladder than Shavonne would ever know, she silently added.

Jed's ears perked. Would Tara tell her sister what was going on between them? he wondered. And what would happen if she did?

"Oh yes, Jed moved in across the hall," Tara continued on the line. "I don't expect to see much of him. You know how it is. We get along about as well as Iran and Iraq. How are the kids?"

Jed frowned. Perversely, he was piqued that she'd dismissed him so summarily.

And then: "Shavonne, are you serious? Megan? *Our* Megan? *And Ricky Ramsey?*"

Jed gave up the pretense that he wasn't eavesdropping and strode into the bedroom. "What's going on?" he demanded. "What about Ricky?"

Tara glanced up at him. "Shavonne, hold on a second, okay?" She covered the mouthpiece and whispered to Jed, "Some startling developments from the home front. My little sister Megan and your little brother Ricky have decided that they're in love."

"That's impossible. Ricky considers both Colleen and Megan hopelessly square. His tastes have always run to fast, flashy girls."

Tara shrugged. "Well, it seems he's changed his

mind. Apparently, Ricky and Megan started seeing each other after he got kicked out of the university last year and—"

"He didn't get kicked out, he was asked to leave for a year," Jed inserted quickly. "I never did understand why. Okay, so he had a one-point-one average and there were a few fraternity high jinks, but—"

Tara eyed him archly. "Please spare me the boys-will-be-boys philosophy. According to Shavonne, Megan went to see Ricky when she was on spring break last year to express her sympathy about his being 'asked to leave' school, and that's when their romance began. They kept it a secret because they didn't want either family involved. Ricky was allowed to return to the campus this fall and now—brace yourself—this afternoon they told the family they want to get married. As soon as possible."

Six

"She must be pregnant," Jed said for perhaps the tenth time. "Megan has to be pregnant, and she and Ricky are in a panic and feel they have no other choice but to get married immediately."

He picked up a slice of pizza, raised it to his mouth, then set it back down again. After the long, emotional phone call with her sisters, they'd decided against going out to eat and ordered a pizza to be delivered instead. They were sitting at the table in Tara's apartment, eating it. At least Tara was. Jed seemed to have lost his appetite completely.

"How could Rick have been so careless?" he lamented. "I've been warning him for years about the hazards of not taking precautions."

"Megan says she isn't pregnant and I believe her," said Tara. "She says they want to get married because they love each other and want to be together." She reached for another slice of pizza. "Megan feels that it isn't right to make love unless a couple is married and Ricky agrees with her."

"How can he possibly agree with her? Ricky lost his virginity at the age of fourteen, Tara!"

Tara shrugged. "Megan says Ricky told her that she is the first and only girl he's ever loved. I'm sure his feelings have changed his ideas about a lot of things. She wouldn't lie about being pregnant. Why can't you believe that?"

"I'm supposed to believe that two healthy, normal, attractive college kids are insisting that they have to be married to sleep together? Give me a break, Tara. The only person in the world who holds that bizarre notion in this day and age is *you*!"

Tara drew a long sip of soda through her straw and said nothing.

"You can't possibly think it's okay for them to get married!" Jed pressed. "They're just kids, for heaven's sake!"

"Megan is young but she's mature," countered Tara. "We all had to grow up early, especially after Mama died. But I think both our families are reacting too strongly to the whole situation. Have they forgotten one of the most basic tenets of psychology? There's nothing like fierce family opposition to more deeply unite a young couple."

"You're suggesting that we should stand by and let those two kids make the biggest mistake of their lives?" Jed demanded. "Ricky isn't ready for marriage. The thought of my kid brother as somebody's husband is ludicrous!"

"I think Megan and Ricky should make their own decisions about marriage," Tara replied calmly. "Not be coerced by either family."

"And if they decide to marry?"

"Then they'll marry." She met his gaze steadily. "I think that you, of all people, should champion your brother's right to make his own choices, Jed. Remember, your parents were as determined for you to marry me as they are for Ricky not to marry Megan."

"You're always drawing parallels between cases that don't apply," Jed muttered. "Megan and Ricky have nothing to do with you and me."

"To me, interference is interference," replied Tara, picking the pieces of pepperoni from his discarded pizza slice and carefully arranging them on her own.

"Damn, you're obstinate!" Jed stood up, frowning. "There's no use trying to reason with you!"

Tara hid a smile. "I love the Ramsey definition of reasoning with someone. It means browbeating anyone with an opposing viewpoint into seeing things the Ramsey way."

"Obstinate *and* argumentative," amended Jed.

"I guess you'd prefer it if I simply smiled and simpered and agreed with everything you said," Tara said dryly.

"As a matter of fact, I would."

She laughed. "Well, at least, you're honest. A woman knows exactly what she has to do to please you."

"And you have no intention of doing it," he said, watching her intently. "You don't want to please me."

"Nope," Tara agreed equably.

The notion rankled, and challenged. Jed Ramsey was accustomed to women going out of their way to accommodate him, to please him, to do and say what he wanted them to do and say. He'd come to expect it. And yet . . . And yet, he felt a grudging admiration for Tara because she hung onto her own opinions even though they contradicted his. She didn't allow him to dominate her. Perversely, he respected her for not giving in to him!

It was crazy. He was beginning to wonder if *he* were crazy. Jed stared at her, his dark brows drawn together, his face a study of confusion. He was too preoccupied to respond to the knock on the door. Tara answered it, stuffing the last bite of pizza into her mouth.

"I'm glad you're both here," Leslie Polk said, a huge grin splitting his face. "I have terrific news."

"We could use some at this point," said Tara dryly. "What is it, Leslie? Something to do with Melissa?"

"We had dinner together tonight!" Leslie exulted. "She told me she wanted to repay me for Saturday and treated me to a Chinese dinner at the House of Lee."

"Oh, Leslie, how wonderful!" Tara exclaimed. "Did you have a good time?"

"The best," Leslie said happily. "And we talked about my cousin's party. Melissa said she'll drive. Her car is bigger than yours, Tara, and the four of us will fit more comfortably in it."

"You don't want Jed and me tagging along like a couple of chaperones, Leslie," Tara inserted swiftly. "You and Melissa will—"

"We want you to come with us!" insisted Leslie. "Melissa and I won't know anybody at the party but each other. My cousin doesn't count. He'll be too busy with his other guests to have any time for us."

"I guess I'll have to stand in for Chad again," Jed said, flashing a sudden sly smile. "Say, Les, have you heard the latest on our intrepid traveling shoe salesman?"

Leslie froze. "Uh, no, I haven't." His eyes darted to Tara. "What is it?"

"Chad won't be returning from Russia," Jed told him. "Seems he fell madly in love with a ballerina there and decided to defect. Poor Tara." Jed mocked her with his eyes, his voice, his smile. "She's heartbroken."

"As you've probably guessed, I told him the truth about Chad, Leslie," Tara said, casting a dark glance at Jed. "He's still sulking about it. His enormous ego can't accept the fact that I'd go to such lengths to keep him away from me."

Leslie stared thoughtfully from Jed to Tara. "Since you invented Chad to keep the two of you apart, does this mean that you two are going to get together?"

Tara grimaced. "No," she stated emphatically.

"Oh, yes," Jed replied with maddening confidence. "The only variables are when and whose bed—hers or mine."

"You wish." Tara tossed their paper plates into the pizza box and began to crumple it.

"I know," Jed taunted.

Leslie looked uneasy. "There seem to be a lot of undercurrents in this room tonight."

"More like a riptide," agreed Jed, casting Tara a baiting glance. She chose to ignore it.

There was a sharp rap at the door. "I'll get that," Les offered swiftly and rushed to the door, obviously glad of the reprieve.

Tara attempted to stuff the pizza box into the trash. Jed watched her. "Looks like we'll be seen at the swankenda together, after all," he remarked drolly. He allowed himself to admit that he was looking forward to it. Since he'd announced his intentions of sexually pressuring her, she might have felt obliged to keep away from him. Now she had no choice, at least on that one night. "We can't let good old Les down," he added righteously.

"No, we can't," Tara agreed. She continued to try to fit the awkward-sized box into the already overfilled can, not trusting herself to look at Jed. Because, heaven help her, she was glad for an excuse to go to that party with him. Though he'd bluntly stated his dishonorable intentions toward her, though she knew she'd have to spend the evening fending off his advances—and fighting her own traitorous responses to him—she wanted to be with him.

The pizza box fell out onto the floor and Tara heaved an exasperated impatient sigh.

"Allow me," Jed said with mock gallantry and proceeded to successfully dispose of the box. "And now . . ." He turned and backed her against the wall, placing his hands on either side of her head.

"Jed, I don't think this is a good idea." Her words emerged in a breathless gulp. She laid her hands on his chest, ostensibly to shove him away, but when she felt the hard warmth of him beneath her fingers, her original purpose was forgotten. Her arms slid slowly, steadily upward and twined around his neck.

"I think it's a damn good one," he whispered huskily, leaning into her, irrevocably trapping her between him and the wall.

His lips feathered the soft curve of her neck. Tara's lashes fluttered shut as his body sensually impacted with hers. She felt the hard strength of his chest pressing against the softness of her breasts. When he angled his hips into the notch of her thighs, a wild flash of heat surged through her.

He cupped her chin with one big hand and tilted her head up. And then his mouth took hers in a deep, hot kiss. She made a small, soft sound and clung to him.

Leslie returned at that moment with Kayci Cann in tow. "Oh my," she exclaimed with a girlish giggle. "Leslie, honey, you should've warned me."

Tara jerked her mouth away from Jed's, her face flushed with embarrassment. She tried to wriggle away from him, but he clamped his hands around her waist, securing her to him.

"I just hate to break up this cozy little scene," Kayci twittered.

"Then don't," Jed said gruffly. He wanted to be alone with Tara with an intensity bordering on desperation.

Kayci, poured into a short, tight black dress and startlingly high heels, slinked to Jed's side and laid her hand on his forearm. "Jeddie, will you do me a great big favor?" she asked in a wheedling tone, her fingers kneading seductively.

Jed frowned. He could remember the time when a woman with Kayci's eye-popping figure and utter willingness could make him drop whatever he was doing to serve her in any way. Now he wanted to brush her off like an irksome gnat. "Probably not," he replied frankly.

Kayci chose to ignore his answer. "I need a ride to a friend of a friend's house and I have to leave now. Will you take me, Jed?" She batted her thick, artificial midnight-black eyelashes. "Pretty please? I'll return the favor any way you want me to, any time you say."

Jed's frown deepened. It was strange to realize that no matter what payoff she might offer as incentive, he simply wasn't interested. "You have a car," he reminded her. "You can drive yourself there."

"No, I can't!" For the first time, Kayci's voice held a note of genuine emotion.

Was it fear? wondered Tara, studying her. Or pain? The sharp stab of jealousy she'd felt at the sight of

Kayci touching Jed abated, allowing her to assess the situation more objectively.

"I need a ride," persisted Kayci. "I can't take my car."

Jed shrugged, looking impatient. "Then take a taxi. Or a bus."

Kayci turned imploring eyes to Leslie. "I can't drive you either," he said quickly, taking his lead from Jed.

Tara gazed thoughtfully at Kayci. Were those tears glistening in the other woman's eyes? Yes, definitely. "I'll drive you where you want to go, Kayci," she offered impulsively.

"Oh, Tara, thank you!" Kayci exclaimed. She seized Tara's shoulders to give her a pseudohug and kiss the air beside her cheek before rushing to the door.

Jed tightened his grip on Tara's waist, his voice rasping in her ear. "You are *not* going to drive that woman to some godforsaken place for a rendezvous that's undoubtedly illicit and cheap and—"

"Please, Tara, hurry. I have to get there as soon as possible," Kayci called over her shoulder. She was already out of the apartment and heading toward the building's entrance foyer.

Tara tried to pry his fingers loose, but Jed refused to release her. She raised her big brown eyes to him. "I have to go, Jed. Kayci looked ready to cry."

"She was faking it," Jed declared with a scowl. "All women use phony tears to get their own way."

"I don't." Tara tilted her chin proudly. "My sisters don't. And maybe Kayci doesn't, either."

"I can't believe you're such a naive little dope! Kayci Cann is a manipulative—"

"Kayci is my neighbor and she needs a favor," Tara said firmly.

Her tone brooked no argument. Reluctantly, Jed let her go. She was so unfailingly obstinate that he had no choice, he realized, and his temper flared. Giving in to another's will was not the course a Ramsey normally chose to follow.

"Okay, play Good Samaritan," he snapped as he watched her gather her purse and keys. "But don't expect me to bail you out of the trouble you're sure to find yourself in when—"

Her front door banged shut, cutting him off in midtirade. He turned to Leslie, who was standing behind him looking perplexed.

"Who gives a damn, anyway? If Tara Brady wants to waste her time chauffeuring that action-girl airhead all over the state, that's her prerogative. It's nothing to me. *She's* nothing to me. It's none of my business what little Miss Brady does or where she goes. I don't care."

"Oh," said Leslie. "I thought you did. Care about Tara, I mean."

"Well, I don't!"

"Let me in, Tara!' Jed demanded, his voice as insistent as his knock. "I know you're home because I saw your car parked out front."

Tara hurried to the door and opened it, not taking the time to put a robe over her candy-striped nightshirt, not even bothering to set down the cup of hot chocolate she'd been sipping.

Jed strode inside her apartment. "Answer me truthfully! Did you deliberately try to lose me in traffic?" he demanded.

She stared at him, uncomprehending, and he sighed. "I didn't think so. You didn't even know I was following you, did you?"

"When? Where?"

Jed kicked off his shoes and stretched out on the sofa. "Earlier tonight. When you took off with Kayci."

"You followed us?"

"Tried to." He had gritted out the two words. "But I lost you on the parkway, going into that nightmare of engineering design known as the Fort Pitt Tunnel. I've spent the last two and a half hours driving around lost. I thought I'd never get back here. This city is all hills and one-way streets and bridges, all of them taking me the wrong way. What's with this place? Haven't they ever heard of directional street signs? There aren't any around!"

"Everyone is always lamenting the lack of signs," Tara said, striving for a neutral tone. "And I once read that Pittsburgh is second only to Venice in the number of bridges it has."

"Well, I can believe it, because I crossed them all tonight." Jed sat up. "What happened, Tara?"

"With Kayci?" Tara caught her lower lip between her teeth. "I drove her to a big stone house in Mount Lebanon. That's a suburb in the South Hills. She told me she was meeting her boyfriend there, but that she wasn't allowed to tell me his name or to park her car anywhere in the vicinity. She was only allowed to come if she was dropped off. The gray Oldsmobile—the one we saw the senator get out of on Saturday night—was parked in the driveway, Jed."

"Did you see Saxon?" Jed asked grimly.

Tara nodded. "After I dropped Kayci off, I parked my car around the block and peeked in one of the windows of the house. Senator Saxon was there, all right. He had Kayci half undressed in the kitchen. It looked like they couldn't keep their hands off each other."

"You went sneaking around the house, spying in the windows?" Jed jumped to his feet. "You little idiot! I just knew you'd do something crazy. That's why I tried to follow you! Tara, this isn't just any man cheating on his wife, you know. This guy has plans, big plans. And if some nosy little girl happens to get in his way, he won't think twice about—"

"Jed, I think you've seen too many political espionage thrillers. Nobody was at the house but the senator and Kayci. My guess is that the place belongs to the man who drives the Oldsmobile and he was loaning it out to Saxon for the night." Tara drew a troubled sigh. "I left after a few minutes, then drove home. It was sleazy, but not dangerous."

Jed shook his head. "Damn, how did we get mixed up in this?" He stood up and crossed the room to stand in front of her. "I want you to promise me to stay out of it from now on, Tara. Keep your distance from Kayci. No more volunteering to drive her to trysts with the senator." His hands closed over her shoulders. "I can't understand why you did it, knowing how you feel about extramarital sex. You must've known where that bimbo was headed."

Tara stared at the ground. Her feet were bare, the nails painted a rose pink. "I felt sorry for her, Jed. Kayci seemed so desperate. Oh, she was trying not to show it, but I saw. I knew. She kind of reminded me of my mother tonight."

"Your mother?" Jed echoed, clearly appalled. *"Your mother?"*

Tara managed a sad little smile. "Poor Mama didn't have very good judgment when it came to men."

"Men?" Jed gave his head a shake. Damn, he was beginning to sound like a parrot.

Tara avoided his eyes. "There were other men in Mama's life, after our father left us."

Jed's eyes widened. "How many others?"

"Lots of men," she replied quietly.

"Lots of men." He swallowed. The thought that someone's mother . . . Tara's mother . . . with lots of men . . . "Men who paid her?" He knew it was a terrible question to ask. And worse to answer.

"Mamma never did it for money, it was always for love. She wouldn't sleep with any man she wasn't in love with," Tara replied, raising her eyes. There was no shame there, only compassion and understanding.

Jed said nothing, but her words seemed to boomerang in his head. Tara's mother had slept around. Why should that seem so wrong to him? he wondered, baffled by his reaction. Didn't he wholeheartedly endorse sleeping around? And he didn't even use being in love as an excuse for it.

Tara heaved a sigh. "Poor Mama couldn't seem to tell the difference between desire and love. She desperately needed a man's attention and approval. She was very pretty and when a man said he wanted her, she immediately thought it was true love."

"I know the type," Jed muttered. He stared at his shoes and shifted uneasily.

"And having five kids totally wrecked any chances she might've had for getting married again," Tara added. "A few of them told her that they weren't interested in taking on another man's litter, but Mama loved us too much to give us up."

Jed thought of the five Brady sisters. As young children, they'd been abandoned by their father and subsequently viewed as a burden by all those men their mother had fallen in love with. He was unprepared for the strange sadness which filled him at the thought. It spooked him. He didn't know why it should matter in the least to him, but somehow it did.

"I—I'm sorry," he mumbled. He knew it was inadequate, but he could think of nothing else to say. "It must have been terrible for you, growing up under those circumstances."

"Not really," Tara said calmly. "True, being poor was difficult at times, but there was always lots of laughter and fun in our home. Mama might've had bad luck with men, but she was a loving mother. I adored her. We all did."

Jed winced.

"Jed, it's true," Tara insisted. "We weren't pitiful, neglected waifs. We had Mama and each other—"

"And all your mother's men, coming and going. Mainly going," added Jed in a strangled tone.

"It wasn't like that," Tara hastened to assure him. "Mama was very, very discreet. She never had men to the house. She always met them in town. And she didn't start telling me about her boyfriends till I was at least nine or ten, old enough to understand. She tried to warn my sisters against being exploited by men, but she never went into specifics with them. Only with me."

"Why only with you, Tara?" Jed asked quietly.

"Mama didn't feel she could confide in Shavonne, not about men," Tara explained. "You see, from the time Shavonne was very young, she sort of took over for Mama in running the house and looking after us kids. She was smart and she worked hard and was so responsible and dependable, Mama was kind of in awe of her. How could she tell Shavonne about all her mistakes when Shavonne never seemed to make any mistakes? And Erin was so sweet and spacy that Mama knew she'd never understand. Colleen and Megan were too young. It seemed natural for Mama to turn to me. I already knew about her secret trips in the night. I was used to watching and listening."

Jed groaned. "So from age nine, you had to listen to . . ." His voice trailed off. At nine, his interests had been in sports, in trying to keep up with his older brothers, and in mercilessly teasing his kid sister. He couldn't have handled it if his mother had attempted to use him as a listening post for her sexual mistakes.

How would a child cope with such a role? he wondered, staring at Tara. He imagined her as a serious little blond girl, not much older than his niece Carrie Beth, imagined her trying to understand and make sense of her mother's confidences. He thought of her listening to herself and her sisters being referred to disparagingly as "another man's litter," and his heart clenched oddly.

"I guess that explains why you're in no hurry to hop into bed with a lover," he said slowly. He didn't have much practice with emotional analyses. He'd never cared to delve beyond the superficial, but suddenly he was struck with insight. And compassion. And an understanding he'd rarely felt for another.

"Tara, not all men are out to use women," he continued softly. "Just because your mother had a knack for attracting creeps doesn't mean that every guy you meet is going to try to use you and then dump you."

She stared at him, as startled as he by his statement. Jed flushed and forced a sheepish grin. "How's that for stepping out of character" he mocked himself. "Old love-em-and-leave-em Jed Ramsey offering reassurance to a sweet young thing . . . Now that's a new twist."

She didn't join in taunting him. "I don't judge all men by Mama's lovers," she replied, gazing at him with earnest brown eyes. "But I decided a long time ago that I'd never let anyone use me or mistreat me. I want to be in control of my own life, not buffeted about by the whims of others."

Jed nodded. "That's why you're so dead set against having sex without marriage," he concluded thoughtfully.

"I don't view marriage as some mystical, magical hold. After all, my father married my mother and ended up leaving anyway. What I want is an unbreakable, unshakeable commitment, and I think there's a better chance of achieving that in marriage. I don't ever want to be some man's sexual throwaway."

He nodded again. Her reasons for keeping away from sex until marriage were well thought out, he realized. She'd developed her own values, based on what she'd learned from her mother's unfortunate choices. He thought how much he wanted her, how he'd planned to seduce her and then leave her, and felt himself grow warm with shame.

It wouldn't be *right* to manipulate her into an affair based solely upon his desire for sexual gratification. It would be selfish; he would be no different from those men who had used and hurt her defenseless and lonely mother. It was a shock to realize that he was viewing those men through Tara's eyes, that he considered them cads and didn't want to be classed with them.

It was an even bigger shock to find himself thinking in terms of what was selfish and what was right. He'd never troubled himself with such bothersome concepts before. What was right had always been whatever he wanted at the time; the possibility of selfishness never entered into it. He didn't care as long as he got his way.

He cared now. And reprimanded himself sternly for his lustful intentions toward Tara. It wouldn't be fair to pursue her, and it would be wrong to talk her into bed, he concluded glumly. Unless he intended to marry her—and he didn't!—he had to do the decent thing and leave her alone. Jed scowled. Being wrong, selfish, and unfair had never held so much appeal as now.

"Jed, I've never told anyone about Mama," Tara said anxiously. She wondered what on earth had possessed her to confide in Jed Ramsey, of all people. What if he were to make some snide remarks to his brothers about their late mother-in-law's past? "Just you."

Just him? Jed was astonished. No one confided in him. His reputation of using whatever information he happened to gain to his own advantage made him a less than trustworthy confidant.

"I'd appreciate it if you wouldn't mention what I've told you to anyone," continued Tara. "I wouldn't want my sisters to know. They have their own memories of Mama and I'd hate for them to be hurt by something they might not understand."

"I won't say a word," Jed promised. Now that his amazement had subsided somewhat, he felt inordinately pleased that Tara had trusted him—out of all the Bradys and the Ramseys—with the information.

"Thanks." She was relieved. She smiled at him, those serious, velvety brown eyes of hers glowing.

He couldn't hold her gaze without wanting to take her into his arms, so he purposefully averted his eyes from hers. He knew he should focus on anything else in the room but found himself staring at her body, anyway. He tried not to notice the way the soft material of her nightshirt clung to the rounded firmness of her breasts. He tried not to wonder if she was wearing panties. She was no longer an object for his lust, he reminded himself. She had confided in him. She trusted him. He respected her strength and he understood her values. He suppressed a groan. He felt so damn noble. It was all so new to him, this placing someone else's welfare above his own wishes. He decided that he hated it, but felt compelled to do it, anyway. A most unnerving dilemma.

"Guess we'd better call it a night," he said, feigning a

nonchalance he did not feel. "Come on, walk me to the door."

She did.

She opened the door and they paused there, staring at each other. Tara gazed up at him, wanting him to take her in his arms, wanting him to kiss her good night. Tonight she'd seen a glimpse of the man beneath his devil-may-care facade. And he had been kind, and understanding, while remaining the most exciting, attractive man she'd ever known. And the sexiest. She swallowed hard.

"Good night, Jed," she murmured. They stared at each other for another long moment. " 'Night, Tara."

She watched him cross the hall to his own apartment. He paused at the door and raised his hand in a brief salute. She responded with a similar gesture. Then both disappeared behind their respective doors.

Seven

It was another cold and dreary rainy day. Tara used her umbrella as a shield against the wind as she trudged to the Allegheny County Courthouse to cover the city council meeting. She was decidedly damp and totally windblown by the time she reached the building nearly fifteen minutes later. Sighing a little, she watched several long black limousines pull up to the curb to discharge their passengers, the television reporters assigned to cover the meeting. There was no money in Double Q's small news budget for limousines to squire reporters. In weather like this, Tara dreamed of the day when she'd make the jump to television news and could arrive at the scene in a limo, dry and perfectly coiffed.

She recognized all the TV reporters—they had high visibility among the local news media—but she knew only one of them well. "Anne!" She hurried up to the attractive young woman emerging from one of the limos.

Pausing to open her own umbrella, Anne Linaberger greeted Tara with a smile. "Double Q won't even spring for a taxi, huh?" she guessed.

"Not even bus fare," Tara lamented. She knew that Anne knew all about the lack of travel amenities for radio reporters, for she had begun her career as one herself.

The two had met at the first city council meeting Tara had been assigned to cover, when her tape recorder had malfunctioned and failed to record the proceedings. Anne, perhaps remembering her own reportorial beginnings, had saved the day by offering Tara her own taped copy. They'd been friends ever since, and Tara considered Anne her professional role model.

"Do you have time for lunch after the meeting?" Tara asked as they dashed inside. "I need some advice. Professional advice," she added solemnly.

"Sure." Anne nodded. "Meet you at the New Deli as soon as the meeting is over." She hurried off to join the rest of the TV people.

Two hours later they were sharing a table at the New Deli, a popular delicatessen located near the courthouse. Tara had arrived first and was perusing the menu. "My treat," she insisted as Anne sat down.

"In exchange for my invaluable professional advice?" Anne asked wryly.

The waitress arrived and they gave their orders.

"Anne, what if a reporter knows something personal about a—a public official that might be damaging if it were to be made known," Tara began as soon as the waitress departed. "Something like—"

"A married politician cheating on his wife," Anne finished for her.

"That's exactly right," Tara exclaimed, impressed by her friend's powers of perception. "So what do you do? Keep it to yourself? Or expose it?"

Anne sighed. "You've just stumbled into one of the gray areas of journalistic ethics, Tara. There aren't any black or white answers to your question."

"I'll settle for a gray answer, then."

"Okay." Anne smiled. "I think it depends on who it is and the circumstances involved. I guess it doesn't get any grayer than that."

Their sandwiches and coffee arrived and they turned their attention to the food.

"It's Senator Glenn Saxon, Anne," Tara said, halfway through her turkey club. Her great, dark eyes were troubled. "The woman lives in my apartment building. I've seen them together."

"This isn't the first rumor I've heard about him, Tara. The man is a rake. He supposedly sleeps his way up and down the campaign trail, but the gossip has been contained so far. Like I said, it's a very gray area."

Tara frowned. "He's going to run for president, Anne."

"So I've heard. What's the country ever done to deserve *him*?" Anne finished her coffee and stood up. "I'd advise you to hang onto your information and do nothing, Tara . . . yet. Saxon seems so irresponsible and reckless that he's bound to cross the line from private indiscretion to public scandal. Then you'll have no trouble acting on your information."

Do nothing . . . yet. Tara pondered Anne's advice on her long, wet walk back to the station. Watch and wait. A sensible policy, though not an easy one to follow.

"The phone's been ringing off the hook for you," Bob Fusco announced as she entered the small newsroom. "Your sister Megan has been calling every fifteen minutes since nine o'clock. Apparently her boyfriend's family is using tyrannical oppression to keep the young lovers apart," he added. "Her words, not mine."

"Megan told you that?" Tara was astonished. "But she doesn't even know you."

"The girl is completely distraught and after I answered her fifth call, she felt like she knew me." Bob handed her the phone. "Call her, Tara. She's in her dorm room. She's cut all her morning classes. I gave her a sound lecture for that."

Megan, tearful and sobbing, was nearly incoherent over the phone. It took Tara several interpretative tries before she got the full story of the Ramseys' latest perfidy.

"They're making Ricky move out of his fraternity house and back home? They're withdrawing him from UT and having his credits transferred to the University of Houston? They've taken his car and intend to have him chauffeured around by one of their spies?" Tara repeated incredulously. "They being Quentin and Nola Ramsey, I presume?"

"Oh, Tara, it's awful," Megan wailed. "They're determined to break us up. I knew they were upset when we told them that we wanted to get married, but I never dreamed they'd go to such lengths to—to ruin our lives!" She burst into tears again.

"They're certainly taking a heavy-handed approach," Tara agreed. "Not that I'm particularly surprised. With every Ramsey firmly believing that what a Ramsey wants, a Ramsey gets, it's bound to get nasty when what they want happens to conflict."

"It's like being in prison!" Megan cried. "We have no freedom, no money—they closed out our checking accounts because they know we'll leave Texas to get away from them. They have us trapped, Tara!"

"The Ramseys can't close your bank account, Megan. Shavonne is your legal guardian and—"

"And Shavonne is married to one of *them*, Tara!" Megan's voice rose. "Who do you think handles our finances? If you guessed the Ramseys, you're exactly right. They took over from our own attorney, Sissy Timmons, last year, remember?" she added bitterly.

"I remember. I thought it was a bad idea at the time, but I let Shavonne talk me into it. Even so, Megan, I can't believe that Shavonne and Erin would stand by and let the Ramseys—"

"Shavonne and Erin say they're sorry I'm unhappy and think that Quentin is overreacting, but they feel the Ramseys have our best interests at heart," Megan interrupted, her voice trembling with emotion. "They think that we're way too young to get married and that we should date other people and have fun. *Fun?* How can Ricky and I have fun when we're miserable? When we only want to be together? When both our families have turned against us and are treating us like—like convicted criminals?"

"I'd say fun is a poor choice of a word," Tara agreed soothingly. But it was becoming increasingly difficult to remain calm. She was sorely disappointed with her two older sisters. How could they align themselves with the Ramseys at Megan's expense?

"Tara, you're our only hope." Megan's voice broke on a sob. "Colleen would help us and they know it, so they've cut off her funds, too."

"That's not fair!" Tara felt her temper rising. "Whatever the Ramseys choose to do with Ricky is their business, but when they start trying to control you and Colleen with their—"

"Gestapo tactics," suggested Bob Fusco, who was listening with unabashed interests from his desk next to hers.

"Gestapo tactics. The phrase fits perfectly," declared Tara. "How can I help, Megan?"

"We have to get away, Tara. Will you send us some money so we can elope?"

"Send you money to elope?" Tara repeated slowly. It occurred to her that although she deplored the senior Ramseys' actions, she, too, thought the couple, especially Megan, too young to marry. And under such volatile circumstances . . .

"Tara, please!" Megan pleaded.

She'd never heard such anguish in her younger sister's voice and it pained her. "Megan, if I send you money I want you to promise you'll use it to come here, to Pittsburgh. I want to see you. I want to talk to you before you do anything."

"Ricky and I will both come!" Megan exclaimed breathlessly. "Oh, Tara, I knew I could count on you! I told Ricky that there isn't a single Ramsey who could bully or outsmart you!"

"Megan, when you get here, I'm going to do my best to talk you out of rushing into marriage," Tara warned.

"We'll listen," Megan promised. "But when you realize how much Ricky and I love each other and how serious we are about getting married, you'll agree to be my maid of honor at our wedding."

Tara hung up with a groan.

• • •

"There seems to be a problem with your account, Miss Brady," the bank teller said carefully. "Until a thorough investigation has been made, any withdrawals are prohibited."

"What?" Tara grasped the cool marble ledge for support and stared at the impassive woman in the teller's cage. That the Ramseys were behind this timely "problem" which had frozen her funds was a foregone conclusion. But how? "I want to speak to the manager immediately!"

The teller was relieved to pass her along to one of the apologetic, placating bank officers who politely listened to her grievances. And patiently explained that until the "irregularities" discovered in her account were fully investigated, she would be unable to make any withdrawals. He was unable—or unwilling—to elaborate on the exact nature of the problem. Or to predict when it might be solved.

Tara endured the rest of the day in a haze of tightly controlled fury. Somehow she managed to write and file her stories, to do her drive-time news reports, to drive back to her apartment. Once there, she dialed her sister Shavonne's number, her hands shaking. She couldn't ever remember being so angry in her entire life. There was no answer. She tried Erin next.

"Erin," she said tautly when her sister's voice came over the line. "I want you to tell your—"

"Tara!" Erin sounded genuinely delighted to hear her voice. "This must be ESP. I was going to call you tonight. I have the most wonderful news, Tara. I just found out this afternoon that I'm going to have another baby."

Tara caught her breath. "You are?"

"Eight months from now. Oh, Tara, Rad is so thrilled, and so am I. We weren't sure if we could have another child and we wanted one badly. So this is just a dream come true for us."

Tara realized that she'd been successfully defused. She could hardly lash into her sister now. Anyway,

Erin was so gentle and sweet; she might be married to the eldest Ramsey son, but she wasn't the correct channel to use in dealing with them.

"I'm really happy for you, Erin," Tara conceded. "Uh, do you happen to know where Shavonne is now?" The adrenaline was still charging through her system. There was no reason to spare her oldest sister the severe tongue-lashing she'd been rehearsing since her fateful trip to the bank.

"Slade arranged for Shavonne and the children to go with him on his business trip to California," Erin said gaily. "They decided to make a little vacation of it. They left this morning and will be gone all week."

"Getting out of town, hmm?" Tara scowled at the phone. "Very sneaky. And so very Ramsey. All right, I'll go straight to the top—to Quentin Ramsey himself."

Talking to Quentin Ramsey was similar to dealing with an oil spill in a river, Tara decided twenty frustrating minutes later as she replaced the telephone receiver in its cradle. He was relentless and tenacious, his words slick, flowing over and around any clear statements, arguments or points, just as oil clogged and blocked everything in its path.

He knew nothing about any problems or irregularities in her checking account, Quentin claimed, and was sympathy personified as he listened to her rail on about the withdrawal prohibitions. She needn't worry about such mundane things as paying her rent, bills, et cetera, he'd promised with paternal assurance. All she had to do was forward any and all bills to Ramsey and Sons and everything would be paid. As for "getting-around-town cash"—why, he would see to it that a sum would be wired to her daily until the bank snafu was resolved. Tara knew that it would be a sum large enough to meet her needs, but too small to finance Megan and Ricky's escape. And she knew the "bank snafu" wouldn't end until Ricky Ramsey bowed to his parents' will and gave up his relationship with Megan.

Tara seethed. She was as effectively trapped as the thwarted young couple and Colleen and anyone else who'd ever attempted to oppose the indomitable Ramsey will.

The knock on her door temporarily diverted her from her homicidal thoughts. Temporarily. For when she opened the door, Jed Ramsey stood before her.

Her first impulse was to slam the door in his face. He was one of *them*, wasn't he? But before she could do so, Jed propelled himself inside. "You look like a pit bull ready to snap its jaws around somebody's throat," he remarked.

Tara glanced at him. "Coming from a Ramsey, I'll take that as a compliment."

Jed held up hands. "Hey, I've come in peace." He grinned at her. It felt as if it had been ages since he'd last seen her although it had been less than twenty-four hours. He'd spent a long time last night thinking about her and what she'd confided to him. He liked her more than he'd realized, he admitted to himself, for he still wanted to see her even though he had placed her sexually off-limits to himself. He'd spent much of to-day vowing to become the big brother she'd never had and was eager to try out his new role.

"I'd like the name of that pizza place we ordered from the other night," he continued. "I only had a bite or two of the pizza and I've been craving more ever since."

"It's Lucchino's." Her glower never wavered. "Good-bye."

He made no move to leave. "Have you had dinner yet? Care to go halves with me on a large pepperoni, mushroom, and onion pizza?"

"I can't afford to buy half a pizza," snapped Tara. She was burning with rage.

And he had the nerve to look bewildered and to add, "Okay, I'll spring for the whole thing and you can still have half. But you have to call and order it."

"No!" Tara's temper reached flash point and exploded. "I won't call and I won't accept any Ramsey's self-serving charity. I don't care if I have to panhandle in the streets, I refuse to take a dime from your despotic, arrogant, intrusive family!"

Jed arched his brows. "I have the feeling that this extends beyond my offer to pay for the pizza."

"You know it does! You're probably the one who went to the bank today and made the threats or bribes or whatever it is you Ramseys use to get your way. Well, it's not going to work, Jed Ramsey. I won't give up and—"

"I suppose it wouldn't do any good to interrupt your tirade to say that I don't know what in the hell you're talking about?"

That did it for Tara. She launched a verbal offensive worthy of any Ramsey, beginning with her outrage at the way Megan and Ricky were being treated and ending with her own passionate promises of revenge. And then, to her horror, she burst into tears.

"I'm not crying," she insisted. She wasn't. She couldn't be.

"And these aren't tears?" With his thumb, Jed traced the track of one teardrop along her cheek. He smiled slightly. "Maybe it's condensed steam, huh?"

"I'm steaming, all right. I've never been so mad in my life." She tried and failed to suppress the sob which escaped from her throat. "Dammit, I don't know what's wrong with me. I never cry when I'm angry. I seldom cry at all." She shot Jed a watery-eyed glare. "In fact, the last time I cried was when I thought my sisters' lives were endangered during that first disastrous meeting with your family."

Jed's lips twitched. "Thinking back on that meeting, they very well might have been. Tara." His hands closed over her upper arms—strictly in a big brotherly fashion, he assured himself. "I'm no armchair psychologist, but I think the reason you're crying isn't because you're furious with the Ramseys. It's because you're mightily ticked off at your two big sisters as well."

Tara sagged against him and closed her eyes. She

felt his arms close protectively, comfortingly around her, and suddenly the words and emotions poured out of her. "I've never felt this way toward them, Jed. It's awful. I love my sisters. We've been through so much together but today I just wanted to scream at both Erin and Shavonne. I wanted to tell them that I think they're traitors, that they've sold out to the Ramseys." She began to cry again.

"Hey, take it easy." Jed felt her body tremble with the force of her sobs and he held her tighter. "Every family has spats—hell, we Ramseys have world wars. There've been times when my brothers and sister and I have hated the sight of each other, but it doesn't last. The anger passes and everybody's friends again. It'll be like that for you, you'll see."

"But I can't stand being mad at my sisters," Tara whispered with a sad little sniff. "Oh, Jed, why are they acting this way? Taking the Ramseys' side? We Bradys have always stuck together but now . . ." Her voice trailed off and she buried her face against the crisp yellow cotton of his shirt.

She seemed so heartbroken. He didn't really understand why. Among the Ramsey siblings, fighting was as natural as breathing. But he wanted to soothe her, to ease her pain. "Honey, it's not a matter of taking sides," he attempted to explain. "Neither loyalty nor betrayal enters into it. Shavonne and Erin just don't think that Megan should get married now. They probably want her to experience all the fun and freedom they weren't able to have at her age. It's as simple as that."

"It's not simple!" Tara drew back and looked up at him with flashing brown eyes. "Slade and Rad agree with your father that Ricky shouldn't get married. So Shavonne and Erin are putting what Slade and Rad want above what Megan wants."

Jed heaved an exasperated sigh. "So? Shavonne and Erin are *married*, Tara. And one of the requirements for a successful marriage means putting your partner ahead of your own family." He shrugged sheepishly at her look of pure astonishment. "I happened to catch Oprah Winfrey's show a few days ago. It was all about successful marriages and that particular bit seemed to fit this situation."

"It does," she conceded softly. Her dark eyes locked with his gray-blue ones. "I just never expected to hear it from you."

He smiled and rubbed her back with his big hands. "Like I told you before, I can be appropriate when the occasion demands." His voice was deep, his tone intimate.

Tara was suddenly breathless. All at once, she was stunningly aware of their proximity and her whole body went taut as sensual sparks burned along her every nerve ending. Her emotions, already volatile and aroused, collided with the heated rush of sexual awareness sweeping over her.

Jed saw her eyes light with the glow of arousal, and watched her lips part under his gaze. A fierce spasm of desire shuddered through him. He'd never felt less brotherly toward anyone in his life. "Tara, I swear I had nothing to do with your problems at the bank," he said thickly. "I wasn't even aware of what Dad had done to break up Megan and Ricky until you told me tonight."

He took a deep breath. Her breasts were pressing against his chest and he could feel her nipples, tight and hard with arousal, sensuously butting him. "It's important to me that you believe me," he said raspily. He couldn't think why it should matter but somehow, it did.

"I believe you, Jed." She couldn't think why she should trust him but somehow, she did.

Jed's heart was banging like a war drum inside his chest as he lowered his head to hers. "I'm glad," he whispered huskily as his mouth nuzzled hers. He couldn't stop himself. His body was vibrating with a sweet anticipatory pleasure that was driving him out of his mind.

Her arms slid around his neck and her mouth opened beneath his. Jed crushed her against him and took her lips in a deep, wild kiss that went on and on, that grew deeper and wilder and blazed with unsuppressed passion.

His hands slipped to her bottom and enclosed the rounded firmness, lifting and holding her against his burgeoning heat. His blatant arousal triggered an even deeper, wilder response deep within her, and Tara moved sinuously against him, sighing softly as he groaned her name.

Her hands moved over the virile strength of his shoulders, of his back. And as her fingers continued their sensual exploration, Jed did some intimate exploring of his own. One big hand cupped her breast and slowly massaged it while his thigh moved between her legs, exerting an erotically rhythmic pressure. Tara clung to him in passionate response, lost in an intense world of pleasure.

It was a long, long time before they slowly drew apart. They stared at each other, breathless and shaking. "I feel like the top of my head has been blown off," Jed said hoarsely.

Tara said nothing. Standing within the circle of his arms, she gazed dazedly into his passion-clouded steel gray eyes. She felt too weak to speak.

"What are we going to do about this? About us?" Jed demanded, his voice thick and husky, his whole body throbbing with unslaked need.

"I was wondering the same thing," Tara panted through moist, kiss-swollen lips. She knew she needed him in a way that she had never before experienced. Did Jed feel this profound exigency, too? Reflexively, she reached out to trace the strong line of his jaw with her fingertips.

A fresh jolt of sensual shocks rocked him. His fingers threaded through her thick, blond hair and tightened around the silken strands. "Damn, I can't seem to be alone with you for ten minutes without wanting to—to—" he muttered a frankly sexual expletive.

Tara blushed.

It hit him with the force of a sledgehammer, that

blush of hers. For Jed Ramsey to be reduced to a stammering, trembling *celibate* by a soft-eyed, blushing virgin! The injustice of it sent him reeling. "You can't have it both ways, Tara!" he raged, railing against his fate. "You can't tell a man hands off, and then melt like butter whenever he puts his hands *on* you. You give off more conflicting signals than a—a—" he searched his mind for what type of person, place or thing gave off conflicting signals. His frustration was compounded when he failed to come up with a single example.

"Yesterday, you convinced me that you were committed to remaining, uh, chaste until you were married and I decided I respected your decision," he continued with an injured air. "I told myself that you and I could be friends, that I would be your big brother. I vowed that I wouldn't make any more attempts to seduce you. And you reward my good intentions by turning on like a nuclear generator when I try to comfort you."

"*You* decided. *You* vowed," Tara repeated slowly. The passion which had made her feel so languid and compliant just moments before suddenly joined forces with the pulsating sexual energy charging through her. The reaction was the emotional equivalent of that nuclear generator Jed had mentioned.

"Did it ever occur to you that *I* might have some say in whether or not we sleep together?" she demanded.

"No," he said frankly, shaking his head. "Because if I decided to really turn up the heat and seduce you, you wouldn't stand a chance. You'd be in bed with me before you could spell seduction."

His boundless male confidence touched a raw nerve. "Oh, would I?" she asked softly, dangerously, her dark eyes glittering. Her indignation grew. She'd already been raked over the coals by Quentin Ramsey today, and now here was Jed Ramsey adding insult to injury. Flaunting his power, insinuating that she was a mindless little dope who could be manipulated and controlled by his whims. It was the way every Ramsey viewed every Brady, she decided, fuming at the injustice of it all.

It was time for Tara Brady to even the score. Jed might think he had the upper hand with her, but . . . She thought of the way he had kissed her, of his instant, incendiary response to her, the yearning hunger in his voice as he moaned her name. And hadn't he just admitted that he couldn't be alone with her without wanting to . . .

No, Jed was not in control, however much he might wish. She held a power all her own—and she was going to use it. A warm, feminine satisfaction suffused her. She laid her hands on his chest and gazed up at him with sultry dark eyes. "Why don't you stop kidding yourself, Jed? Your feelings for me aren't the least bit brotherly and they never will be. You're well on your way to falling for me."

She braced herself for his explosive denial. Jed gaped at her and didn't say a word. Emboldened, Tara pressed on. "And if I decided to *really* turn up the heat, you wouldn't stand a chance. You'd be married to me before you could spell wedding ring."

Jed opened his mouth to speak. No words came out. Tara's wrath was promptly displaced by her sense of humor. She'd never seen anyone so comically stunned.

"But I've decided to give you a break," she said, grinning at him. "Let's call a truce. No seduction *or* wedding rings. Do we have a deal?"

Jed swallowed. Her earlier declaration was still ringing in his ears. God, she was right, he marveled silently. He was well on his way to falling for her. Falling hard. His pulses accelerated in a sudden, sharp leap.

He might be a Ramsey, and Ramseys might always win, but he'd met his Waterloo in this girl, he realized with dawning insight. Tara was not the naive little innocent he'd originally thought she was. She might be sexually inexperienced, but she'd spent her life observing and analyzing women and men and their fractured relationships. While he was blindly participating in the battle of the sexes, she'd been on the sidelines, taking notes and studying. He had an uneasy feeling that if came down to a test, she would prove the major strategist, after all.

"You know, you have all the makings of a world-class bitch," he murmured, his tone somewhat awed. "Oh, you're still too young yet, you haven't become sufficiently hardened, but given the proper circumstances, you could turn into one."

"Ah, another Ramsey compliment."

"It's not a compliment. I'd hate to see a compassionate, sweet girl like you turn into a cynical man-eating vixen. It could happen, you know."

"I can be saved by the love of a good man." Tara laughed up at him. She was delighted that she'd shaken his earlier, perverse, masculine complacency. "The love of a good husband," she amended teasingly. "Are you volunteering for the job?"

"No!" Jed snarled. It was the ideal time to make his exit, to leave without looking back. That would prove she'd read him all wrong, that he didn't care about her or what happened to her, that he wasn't already halfway in love with her.

Instead he lowered himself to the couch, pulling her down on his lap. "No, dammit!" he repeated. "I'm not!" With a groan, he tightened his arms around her and covered her mouth with his own.

Her slim body arched against him and she wound her arms around his neck, her lips parting for the hot penetration of his tongue. They kissed and kissed, the passion burning and building between them.

It was Jed who finally brought it to a halt. Slowly, reluctantly, he eased her from his lap and stood up. It hurt to walk, it hurt to think. "I'm too old for a virginal necking session, Tara. It's torture."

Tara sighed softly. She felt very desirable, very feminine, and very aroused. Sitting on Jed's lap, indulging in those passionate kisses, in the delicious light petting, was the most exciting and thrilling thing she'd ever experienced. She didn't want it to end. "But it's exquisite torture," she murmured huskily.

"For you, maybe. Not for me. I don't want to sample temptation. I want to give in to it." He jammed his hands deep into the pockets of his jeans. "You haven't changed your mind about going to bed with me, have you?" His voice rose on a hopeful note.

She shook her head and he muttered a curse.

"But I will call Lucchino's and order a large mushroom, pepperoni, and onion pizza," she offered softly.

"Some consolation prize," he grumbled.

She cast him a quick smile and rose to her feet.

It occurred to Jed, as he followed her to the phone, that no other woman in the entire world would dare to treat him this way. To arouse and then deny him. To expect him to respect her standards. Tara Brady had committed all those transgressions yet here he was, watching her with the same longing and intensity with which a hungry dog stares at a steak bone.

Tara bent her head to read the number from the telephone book and her hair fell over her shoulder, exposing the nape of her neck. It looked soft and vulnerable. Jed drew in a slow breath. He wanted to kiss her there. The visceral force of his desire shook him.

She ordered the pizza, then turned to find him staring at her. The dark intensity in his eyes had a wildly disturbing effect on her already sensitized body. Breathlessly, she averted her eyes. "They said they'll have the pizza here in half an hour," she said, her voice tremulous.

"Great." Jed sank down onto a chair and leaned his elbows on the table. His senses were rioting, his control on overload. He needed the mental equivalent of an icy shower. He searched his mind for one and came up with the marriage plans of the youngest Ramsey and the youngest Brady. "So what are you going to tell Megan? That you aren't going to be able to help her, after all?"

"I'm going to help her," Tara replied firmly. "I'll get a credit card and put the cost of the plane tickets on that. I've been deliberately avoiding getting credit cards because I didn't want the temptation of spending beyond

what I'm earning. But this is an emergency, so . . ."
She shrugged, her voice trailing off.

"You don't have to live on your salary," Jed reminded
her. "You have a trust fund that generates a monthly
income."

"I have it reinvested. I like knowing it's there if I
should really need it, but I want to make it on my
own."

"You're very independent," he observed and she nodded. He decided he approved; he even admired her for
it. "I can see why my family's, uh, tendency to try and
run things must be really hard for you to take."

Tendency to try and run things? That was mildly
understating the Ramseys' steamroller tactics of flat-
tening all and any opposition, thought Tara. But she
bit back the derisive retort. She didn't want to quarrel
with Jed. She sat down across the table from him. "It
does bother me," she said diplomatically.

"Well, it bothers me, too." Jed's tone was surpris-
ingly fierce. "I hate what's happening to my kid brother,
Tara. He doesn't deserve it—and neither does Megan."

Tara stared at him. An idea leaped to mind and her
eyes lit with sudden purpose. "Jed, how long does it
take for a credit card application to be approved?" she
asked casually.

"About a month, I'd guess, give or take a week or so."

"So Megan and Ricky have to endure at least a month
of Ramsey-style incarceration before I can help them.
It'll seem interminable to them, Jed. Who knows what
kind of desperation they might resort to?"

"Like the two of them sneaking off and getting her
pregnant?" Jed frowned thoughtfully.

"If they're allowed to decide when to marry, they'll at
least have the option of postponing babies for a few
years. Which I'm sure they would do." Tara leaned
forward, holding his gaze with hers. "You could help
them, Jed. You could put an end to this horrible situation tomorrow if you were to send them money—or
plane tickets to Pittsburgh."

"Tara, I can't do that!"

"You said you hate what's happened to Ricky. You said you admire independence," Tara interrupted swiftly, passionately. "Prove it by helping them." She reached over to grasp his hand.

Jed watched her slender fingers close around his palm.

"Please, Jed!" Her voice was soft but throbbed with urgency.

Jed thought how infuriated his parents would be if he were responsible for spiriting Ricky out of town. He thought of his sister and older brothers who would undoubtedly disapprove as well. It was so much easier to remain uninvolved, he reflected, for while he was sympathetic toward Ricky and Megan's plight, it really had no effect or bearing on his life.

But Tara was looking at him with pleading dark eyes, her hand was warm in his, forcing him away from the comfortable path of indifference. She would never remain uninvolved, he mused, recalling her match-making attempts with Leslie Polk and Melissa and her concern about Kayci Cann and the spurious Senator Saxon. Her little sister's unhappiness *did* have a direct effect on Tara's life; she took on Megan's pain and outrage as her own.

"I think those kids are nuts to think about marriage at their ages," Jed protested, knowing his resistance was weakening fast.

Tara's eyes sparkled beguilingly. "You think anyone is nuts to think about marriage at any age." Her thumb began to move in slow, concentric circles over his palm. "Won't you please help them, Jed?"

He deliberately pulled his hand away from her. Small charges of sensual electricity rippled through him. "Vamping a guy to get your way is fighting dirty, Tara," he said severely. "I should tell you to get lost right now."

"I'm sorry, Jed. I won't do it again." She looked and sounded utterly sincere.

Maybe she was, Jed thought grimly, for she had nothing to lose by that small concession to his pride. She'd already won and she had to know it. He heaved a deep sigh. "Give me Megan's university box number and I'll see that she receives two plane tickets and traveling expenses in the morning," he said gruffly.

Tara's face lit with joy. "You're wonderful, Jed!" she exclaimed exuberantly and launched herself from the chair onto his lap. "Would I be vamping you if I hugged you to express my thanks?" she asked innocently. But her eyes were devilishly agleam.

Jed's arms closed around her. "You're permitted to physically express your gratitude any way you want until the pizza arrives," he replied, opening his mouth over hers.

Eight

Whatever spell Tara Brady had cast upon him faded in the cold, clear light of morning. Jed woke up—alone, in his own bed, of course—and decided that he'd suffered a bout of temporary insanity last night when he'd agreed to finance Megan and Ricky's escape. His family was hardly a ruthless gang of terrorists holding the kids hostage, he reminded himself, though somehow Tara had made it seem that way.

He was totally disconcerted. Somehow she'd caught him at a weak moment and taken full advantage of him, he decided, though that very acknowledgment made him freeze. Jed Ramsey wasn't prone to weak moments. He'd always been the one to take advantage of the weak moments of others . . . until *she* had turned the tables on him. And now he was stuck with a promise he'd made to a baby-faced little temptress who'd sent him back to his own apartment last night with a passionate good-night kiss and a sweet smile, the memory of which had kept him tossing and turning for hours.

Well, he would keep his promise—after all, he was a man of his word—but from now on, he was going to do what he should have been doing since his arrival in Pittsburgh. And that was to stay away from Tara Brady.

If she had talked him into taking her side against his own family, it was anybody's guess as to what else she might be able to talk him into doing.

Like marrying her? that snide little voice in his head managed to taunt before Jed firmly blocked it out. He had other things to think about besides Tara Brady. It was time for him to begin to develop his social life here in Pittsburgh. The Ramseys had always managed to have a rip-roaring time on business trips, he reminded himself, and then frowned at the realization that he was the last rip-roaring Ramsey left. His sister was now respectably married, and his three brothers were hopelessly ensnared with those tenacious Brady sisters.

Well, *he* wasn't, and it was up to him to keep the Ramsey legend alive. He had a number of contacts to cultivate via the Southland Mall; a Ramsey never had trouble finding friends—or lovers.

Tara woke up in a sublime state of bliss. Last night had been a revelation to her. Jed Ramsey, her former nemesis, had been magically transformed into a man she *really* liked. A man she could talk to, a man who was caring and understanding and was willing to stand up for others, despite the cost to himself. She thought of how he had agreed to help Megan and Ricky, even though it meant defying a Ramsey edict. She well knew the amount of courage that kind of action required. And Jed had it.

A sensuous little shiver tingled along her spine as she thought about the kisses they had shared. The touches, the soft whispered words. The sexual chemistry between them was electric and exciting, but she was certain that their unfolding relationship held so much more. She wondered if she was falling in love with him. The thought didn't fill her with the horror such speculation would have spawned just one week ago. Instead, it made her sigh, dreamy-eyed.

She couldn't wait to see him tonight. Her heart jumped at the thought. She decided that she wanted to cook for him, to have a special dinner together that wasn't take-out pizza. Before she left for work, she filled her Crockpot slow-cooker with chunks of beef and an assortment of chopped vegetables for what she and her sisters called Brady's Irish Stew. Their mother had often fixed it, though there were inevitably more potatoes than meat in the stew back in those low-income days. When she arrived home after work, the stew would be cooked and ready to eat. She imagined herself and Jed having dinner together, talking, laughing, kissing . . .

Tara smiled her way through a frantic day at the station, thoughts of Jed keeping her afloat on a euphoric cloud. Colors seemed brighter, music sounded richer, even Vince Krajack's sexist jokes about his ex-wife didn't annoy her as they usually did.

Her apartment was filled with the stew's hearty aroma when she came home at the end of the day. Tara checked the Crockpot and was pleased with the results of the long slow cooking. She brushed her hair and reapplied her makeup, then changed from her rather serviceable pastel pinstripe dress into a pair of well-fitting gray slacks and a soft sweater of pink, yellow, and gray. She fixed a salad and set the table and waited, her nerves wired with a heart-pounding sense of urgency and anticipation.

Jed seemed to turn up around dinnertime, at least he had done so previously. She glanced at her watch and frowned. It was almost seven-thirty. Perhaps he hadn't returned from the Southland Mall or wherever else his business took him. She decided to go next door and find out.

Tara felt keyed up and nervous, as if butterflies were dive-bombing in her stomach. She was experiencing a strange sensation which alternated between elation and panic as she knocked at Jed's door. She knew he was home. She could hear music coming from within.

Moments later, he opened the door.

"Hi," she said in a rush, smiling up at him with shining brown eyes. "I wondered if you'd—"

Her words caught in her throat when she spotted the brunette sitting on the couch in the living room. Jed followed her gaze and watched the light abruptly fade from her eyes.

But she'd recovered herself before he could speak. "You have company," she said brightly with a brilliant false smile. "Sorry to disturb you. It was nothing important." She quickly turned to leave.

"Tara." He started after her, catching her arm.

Her traitorous body was already beginning to react to his nearness, his touch. Desire shuddered through her. It seemed that every time he touched her, her responses were quicker and more intense. And this time was no exception, even though she knew he had another woman waiting for him. The thought galvanized her to action. She tried to jerk away from him. "Let me go!"

"I just wanted to let you know that the so-called problem with your account is taken care of," Jed said, holding onto her despite her frantic attempts to break away. He couldn't seem to let her go. "I visited the bank this morning and used whatever it is we Ramseys use to get our way. Although you'll understand if I don't divulge the family's fail-safe tactics," he added with a devilishly winsome grin.

How dare he try to charm her? Tara seethed. To act as if that woman on the sofa were of no consequence? "If you expect me to be grateful for your intervention, I'm not," she snapped. "I could've managed it on my own. Now will you please let go of my arm?"

He didn't. She was so soft, he thought dizzily. She felt so delicate, so fragile. He caught his breath.

"I came here to, uh, borrow some salt," Tara stammered, praying that the small lie sounded credible. "But as you're obviously busy, I'll just get it from Les." If Jed knew that she'd prepared dinner for him, that she'd spent all day dreaming of a cozy evening with him, that she'd almost succumbed to the crazy delusion that she was in love with him . . .

"Jed?" The woman on the sofa rose and started walking toward the door. Tara took full advantage of the distraction to pull away from Jed and run up the steps.

Her face was flushed and her heart was pounding as she rang Leslie's doorbell. Part of her wanted to burst into tears, while the other part wanted to swear. Jed was entertaining another woman in his apartment. *Why should you expect anything different from a man with a reputation as a bona fide heartbreaker?* scolded the part of her that wanted to swear.

But I thought I would be different, that he might feel strongly enough to want to be only with me, wailed the part that wanted to cry.

Leslie answered the door, wearing his good blue suit and reeking of aftershave. "You're going out," Tara observed, trying to mask her disappointment. "I guess that means you won't be able to have dinner with me?"

Leslie's face was wreathed in smiles. "I'm taking Melissa to the new play at the Public Theatre. She suggested it, and I picked up the tickets today."

Tara hoped she sounded sufficiently enthusiastic as she wished him a good time. On impulse, she decided to invite Kayci to join her for dinner. She didn't want to face that stew alone, not after all the stupid fantasies she'd woven around it. Cooking for Jed, falling in love with him . . . Her face burned at her own foolishness.

"Stew?" Kayci echoed as she stared at Tara. "Tara, *puh-leeze!* I'm nauseous enough as it is. Don't make me any queasier by talking about things like *stew!*"

Tara studied the other woman's face. "You do look pale, Kayci. Do you think it's some kind of stomach bug?"

"A bug? I don't think so. Try a rat," Kayci said cryptically and closed the door.

Shot down on all fronts, Tara sighed, trudging back to her own apartment. The wholesome, hearty smell of the stew offended her. She scooped it into a plastic container and stuck it in the freezer, then fixed herself her old childhood favorite, a grilled peanut-butter sandwich.

The food's familiar taste and texture offered a modicum of comfort. Tara remembered all the times in the past when she'd sat in the dilapidated Brady kitchen, munching on grilled peanut-butter sandwiches, while her mother sipped tea and mourned the departure of the latest man in her life.

Oh, Mama, am I going to make a mess of it, too? she wondered glumly. For the first time in her life she'd been in danger of falling in love, and she'd chosen a man who didn't love her. Who didn't want to love her. Tara shivered. It was a classic Jerilyn Brady situation. And now her daughter Tara—that wise and confident child who'd made a vow to avoid her mother's pitfalls—had managed to make a frighteningly similar error in judgment.

The realization was enough to keep her awake for a long, long time that night. And then there was the distinct possibility that just across the hall, Jed Ramsey was bedded down with the pretty brunette who'd been draped so seductively across his couch.

Tara didn't get much sleep at all.

Neither did Jed. Even before Tara had arrived at his door, he'd been bored with pretty, sexy Andrea, the women's sportswear buyer he'd met at the Southland Mall that afternoon. He frowned. He couldn't seem to erase from his mind the image of Tara standing in his doorway. Her cheeks had been flushed, her eyes aglow, her smile sweet and warm and all for him. And then she'd seen Andrea.

She had been quick to hide the pain which had flashed in her eyes, but he had seen it. His mind kept running the scene through his brain like a never-ending newsreel. Tara, bright and happy, standing at his door, and seconds later, the hurt and betrayal in her big dark eyes, her smile gone.

He had hurt her, seeing Andrea had hurt her, and he felt like the kind of villainous scoundrel audiences pay to boo. Why should he feel that way, Jed wondered as he paced the floor in a fit of hyperactivity. He'd done nothing wrong. He was a bachelor who'd made no promises to anyone. He hadn't even hinted at a commitment to Tara Brady, yet somehow she made him feel as guilty as an adulterous husband caught in the act.

How in the world had she accomplished that? All he'd done was to kiss her a few times. Memories of Tara in his arms washed over him in a feverish hot flood. He'd touched her breasts, too, and his body grew taut at the recollection. He reminded himself that her clothes had always remained chastely in place and scowled at his own restraint. Lord, he'd gotten further with Marilee McBroom, his junior high school sweetheart, and he hadn't felt a moment's compunction about cheating on her!

Cheating? Jed groaned aloud at the direction his own thoughts had taken. There it was. He felt as if he were cheating on Tara by seeing another woman. A woman whom he'd dispatched from his apartment at nine o'clock without even a peck on the cheek. Because he hadn't wanted to touch her. He wanted to touch—to kiss, to be with, *to love?*—only one woman: Tara Brady.

His first impulse was pure Ramsey: To keep on fighting. To win. He almost managed to stifle that mature inner voice that asked him what he was fighting against, and why. And what he hoped to win. More nights like this one, pacing the floor, lonely and guilty and confused?

He finally admitted the depressing truth to himself. He hadn't won anything tonight. He'd lost. He, Jed Ramsey, was a loser. It was a bitter admission for a self-proclaimed master-of-his-fate. It took another full hour of pacing before he faced another irrefutable fact: He was in love.

The prospect of returning to her apartment, knowing that Jed undoubtedly had another woman stashed in his, held no appeal and Tara was determined to postpone it for as long as she could.

"Vinnie, do you feel like going out tonight?" she

asked Vince Krajack as they were preparing to leave the station after the six-o'clock newscast.

"With you?" Vince considered it. "Where?"

Tara shrugged. "Anywhere. Uh, Vin, we'll have to go dutch. I'd like to treat you, but I'm running a little short of funds." A call to the bank today had provided the maddening information that "the problem" with her account had not been resolved after all. Her rage at all things Ramsey had intensified.

"Honey, offering to pay your own way elevates you to mythical status in my book," said Vince, draping a casual arm around her shoulders. "After the three years with that blood-sucking, money-hungry troglodyte Serena, I—"

"Is Serena really as bad as you claim?" Tara interrupted curiously. "You make her sound like the female reincarnation of Attila the Hun."

"She's worse," Vince assured her. "My ex-wife makes Simon Legree look like Mother Teresa."

They had dinner in a new Pakistani restaurant, then went on to Station Square, the old city depot which had been converted into a covered mall of trendy shops, restaurants, and night spots.

They sat in the bar of a popular watering hole frequented by radio and TV reporters, and joined a group for a lively exchange of local media gossip. Several rounds of drinks were ordered and duly imbibed. Vince and a weekend TV anchorman challenged each other as to whose ex-wife was the worst and tried to prove their respective cases by regaling the others with marital horror stories. There was more drinking and lots of laughter.

The hours passed quickly and painlessly, with plenty of liquid refreshment, and by the time the group broke up around eleven, Tara found that she was having difficulty standing up.

"Vinnie, I think I might be drunk," she told him, wide-eyed. Her words were slurred and when she stumbled into an empty table, she giggled.

Vince heaved a sigh. "I'm sure of it, kid. I'll drive you home." He helped her into the front seat of his car, a ten-year-old Toyota. The back window had a long crack in it.

"I don't think it was such a good idea to have a sloe gin fizz and a margarita and a brandied apricot flip and a banana daiquiri on top of all that spicy Pakistani food," Tara concluded. "But I thought it would be interesting to try different drinks."

"That's what you were drinking?" Vince was appalled. "Ugh, it makes me sick just thinking about it. You aren't going to be sick, are you?" he asked nervously. "That bitch Serena puked in this car once and it took years to get rid of the odor. She made sure she took our new car when we split, natch."

Tara assured him that she wasn't going to be sick. But by the time they reached her apartment building, she wasn't so sure. "Everything is spinning, Vin," she murmured as he helped her to the front door of the building. "It feels as if the ground is dropping out from under me."

"Look, just don't get sick until we get you inside," Vince pleaded on a panicky note. "I can't promise you that I won't barf myself if I have to clean up a mess."

"I'm sorry, Vinnie. I guess I'm not the greatest drinking buddy, huh?"

"You're okay . . . as long as you don't get sick on me."

They heard a loud slam and the sound of footsteps. "Uh-oh!" There was genuine alarm in Vince's voice. "You didn't mention that you had a jealous lover at home, waiting to tear me apart limb by limb."

Through bleary eyes, Tara watched Jed Ramsey striding toward them.

"She—er—had a little too much to drink," Vince said as Jed stopped in front of them.

Jed folded his arms and glowered at the pair. "And you were planning on taking full advantage of her, weren't you?" he accused, his gray eyes glittering dangerously. He flexed his fingers, and Vince gulped.

"Hell, no," he said earnestly. "Not in her condition. She kamikazied her stomach with a revolting assortment of drinks. She's about to be sick. Here." Vince gave her a slight push forward, and Tara collided with Jed's frame. "She's all yours. You can have the pleasure of taking care of her." He gave Tara a pat on the shoulder. "Good luck, kid."

"You're so gallant, Vincent," Tara muttered crossly. "From now on, I'm on Serena's side."

Jed cupped Tara's shoulders with his hands. "I've been waiting for you for hours," he said tightly, "and you come staggering in close to midnight, half smashed. I ought to shake you until your teeth rattle."

"If you do, I'll be very, very sick," she promised shakily. "In fact, I might be anyway." An ear-ringing, throat-closing wave of nausea swept over her with violent force. She proceeded to be abysmally and ignominiously sick right then and there.

She could never remember being so utterly mortified in her entire life. Although Jed handled it better than Vince would have, Tara thought dizzily. He didn't get sick himself, but held onto her until the spasms had stopped shaking her body, then scooped her up into his arms and carried her inside. Unfortunately, he lectured her the entire time on her stupid and reckless behavior, and the follies of tangling with that old demon alcohol.

He hated her, she knew it, and Tara's eyes filled with tears. The urge to throw herself down and weep supplanted the urge to throw up her insides. She clutched the edge of her bathroom sink, desperately trying to do neither.

Jed turned on the taps and splashed cold water on her face, until she was spluttering and gasping. "You're going to have one killer headache tomorrow and I don't have an iota of sympathy for you," he said sternly. "You brought it all on yourself and—"

"Oh, go away and leave me alone." The cold water had strengthened her. She felt a bit better; the desire to either cry or lose her dinner had mercifully passed. She saw the displeasure cross Jed's face and it spurred her on. "As if *you*, a Ramsey, who's always bragged about drinking all night with the good ol' boys, should dare to give me a lecture on the evils of liquor."

"Yeah, yeah." Jed frowned thoughtfully. "I can't believe it myself. I cherished my reputation as a wild, high-living carouser. Who'd've ever dreamed I'd come to this? Lecturing you like some zealot from the temperance league."

She had to smile at the incredulity in his tone. "Can it be that beneath that playboy-cad exterior beats the heart of a morally upright good guy?" she teased.

"The ultimate cliché." Jed groaned. "No, I refuse to consider it."

She swayed backwards and he caught her around the waist and secured her firmly against him. "I'm putting you to bed. You can sleep it off," he said grimly and carried her into her bedroom.

He dropped her onto the bed and sat down beside her, then proceeded to strip off her jacket.

Tara protested mightily, particularly when he began to undo the buttons of her blouse. "Stop it, Jed." She slapped at his hands. "Just because I might be slightly in—intoxicated doesn't mean I don't know what you're trying to do. I won't go to bed with you. I won't!"

"Slightly intoxicated? Baby, you're totally juiced. Furthermore, I have absolutely no sexual intentions toward you."

He finished unbuttoning her blouse, despite her attempts to ward him off, and jerked it off her shoulders. His mouth went dry. Her brief bra of pale yellow satin and lace accentuated the rounded fullness of her beautifully shaped breasts. Under his intense gaze, her nipples peaked and pressed against the soft material. A sensual shudder shook him. He wanted to touch them, to see them bared for his eyes only. He wanted to put his mouth on her and taste those enticing small buds . . .

He swallowed hard. "Tonight," he added, qualifying his statement.

Tara flushed scarlet. She moved to snatch her blouse to hold in front of her, but her movements were jerky and uncoordinated, and Jed picked up the garment before she did. He continued to stare at her, then audaciously ran his knuckles over one hard-tipped crest.

Tara quivered. Her whole body was warm and tingling with sexual electricity. "You—You said you didn't have any sexual intentions toward me tonight," she reminded him breathlessly. It suddenly dawned on her what he had implied—that he would pursue his sexual intentions at some other time. He undoubtedly considered it a given that she would let him.

She grabbed her blouse away from him. "I'm sure you have some glamorous babe waiting for you in your apartment," she snapped as she fumbled with the blouse. To her unending frustration, she couldn't seem to get her arms into the sleeves. "Go and practice your sexual intentions on her."

"There isn't any glamorous babe waiting for me in my apartment," Jed said patiently. While she struggled with her blouse, he deftly unzipped her skirt.

"You mean you struck out with your cutie last night and you weren't able to find a replacement for tonight? You must be losing your touch, Jed." She tossed down her blouse to try to rezip her skirt.

It was too late. He had already lifted her hips and pulled it down, taking her half-slip with it. She tried to fight him, to no avail. "You have more hands than an octopus," she said accusingly.

"I'm quite experienced when it comes to undressing women," Jed agreed laconically. "And no, I didn't strike out last night. To stretch your baseball metaphor to the breaking point, I didn't even make it into the game. Because I didn't feel like playing, Tara."

Tara felt his gray eyes upon her and she scooted across the bed, away from him, blushing furiously. Her panties were very brief and very sheer. She caught the side of the bedspread and pulled it around her, then swayed dizzily as the room unexpectedly tilted.

Jed eased her back onto the mattress. "Lie down and keep still," he cautioned. "All that jerking around will make you sick again."

For a few moments, Tara obeyed. Her head was spinning and her stomach was roiling again. She watched in silence as Jed pulled off his shoes and socks. When he unbuckled his belt she felt obliged to speak up. "Jed, no, I—I can't."

"You're telling me," Jed said dryly. "You have nothing to worry about, Tara. Your virtue has never been safer. We're going to spend a totally nonsexual night together, with you in the role of patient and me in the role of—" he sighed as he held the small wastebasket up to her as spasm of nausea overtook her. "Janitor," he finished resignedly.

"You could've at least said 'nurse,' " Tara moaned as Jed wiped the perspiration from her brow with a cool washcloth. "I think I'm going to die."

"You're not going to die," he assured her. "But I'll wager that tonight is your first and last night as a hard-drinking reporter. You'll stick to ginger ale from now on. Where's your nightgown?"

She told him and he fetched it for her. She felt too weak to move when he removed her underwear with easy expertise, too lethargic to protest when his eyes swept over her, taking in her softly full breasts with their rosy pink nipples, the narrow indentation of her waist and firm flatness of her belly. Her hips flared gently, her legs were long and smooth and shapely. Jed drew in a sharp breath as he focused his gaze on the downy thatch shielding her femininity. It was the color of dark honey. No man had ever seen her, had ever touched her there . . .

Heat surged and thickened in his loins. No man but him. And suddenly he felt protective and possessive and a host of other emotions completely foreign to him. He helped her into her soft pale blue nightgown, pondering the situation as he tried to make her comfortable. He recognized the lust that was coursing through him, causing his body to harden with wanting. But those other feelings, the tenderness and the warm affection that helped him to temper his lust, made him put his own desires second to her needs . . . For the first time in ages Jed Ramsey, who'd seen and done it all, was experiencing something new.

And he liked it, it felt good. *He* felt good, and happier than he'd felt in a long, long time. He pulled off his shirt and jeans and slipped into bed beside her, wearing only his dark blue briefs. "Go to sleep," he ordered, pulling the covers around them both.

"I can't," she protested weakly. "I don't have anything on underneath my nightgown. I've never slept without any underpants on. And there's never been a man in my bed before, either."

"Things are tough all over, baby. I've never slept with underpants *on*. And I've never been in bed with a woman without laying her." He reached over and rubbed her arm. He didn't dare rub anything else. "Close your eyes, Tara. We'll make it through the night somehow."

"You're really staying here?" Tara whispered. "In my bed? All night?"

"I'm here in the role of a nurse, remember? Not as a janitor, not as a lover."

"But—but why?" Tara pressed her throbbing forehead with her fingertips. "You can't want to stay here with me. I might be sick again. You could be with any woman you wanted, doing whatever you wanted with her."

"Suppose I were to say that you're the woman I want to be with and simply lying beside you is what I want to do."

"I wouldn't believe you," Tara replied with a hint of her usual feistiness.

"Yeah, well, I can hardly believe it myself, but here I am. Now will you please shut up and let me get some sleep?"

Though Tara was certain she never would, she must have slept, for all too soon Jed was shaking her awake.

"Rise and shine, baby doll. Time to go to work."

His voice sounded louder than a boom box turned to full volume. Tara slitted one eye open and shuddered. Her head was pounding and there was a dreadful, sour taste in her mouth. Her stomach churned unpleasantly and her abdominal muscles were sore from last night's heaves. Had she ever felt this terrible in her life? Tara thought not. "I can't go to work today, Jed. I'm sick. I'll call in and—"

"You're not sick, you're hung over." Jed pulled back the covers and lifted her to her feet. "And since you brought it on yourself, you have to suffer the consequences, miserable though you may be. That means no calling in sick and spending the day recovering. You go about your everyday routine feeling like hell. It's a Ramsey rule."

"I always knew you Ramseys were crazy but this proves it." Tara sank down onto the edge of the bed. "Anyway, I'm not a Ramsey, so I don't have to follow your masochistic rules." She rolled over onto her stomach and buried her face in the pillow.

Jed picked her up and carried her into the bathroom. "Take a shower and get dressed," he ordered, setting her on her feet. "I'm driving you to the station today."

"I can't. I don't want to go. I feel awful." Her voice echoed in her head. She sounded perilously close to whining. Tara was horrified. She never whined. She cast a quick glance at Jed. He was watching her, his expression amused. But determined. She hadn't the slightest doubt that he would put her into the shower and dress her himself, if she continued to refuse.

He had undressed her last night. Her face flamed as she remembered lying naked and passive under his probing eyes. "I'll get ready now," she said swiftly and rushed into the bathroom.

"I thought you'd see it my way," Jed called after her. Laughter gleamed in his slate-gray eyes.

"You really don't have to drive me to the station," Tara said as Jed followed her from her apartment a half hour later. She was wearing an oyster-colored flared skirt which skimmed her knees, a matching jacket and a periwinkle blue blouse. Her mirror had assured her that she looked as normal and fit as she did every other workday. It was too bad that the interior riots going on in her head and stomach dispelled that myth. "I can get there myself."

"Your car didn't make it home last night, remember?" Jed took her arm and guided her up the street to the garage that housed his Lamborghini Countach. "Your good buddy Vince drove you back here."

Tara remembered. "Ohh, I feel like such a jerk." She groaned at the thought of last night's misadventures.

"The age-old morning-after lament." Jed grinned. "Everybody sings it at least once in their lives. Don't be too hard on yourself, Tara."

"You're so *cheerful,*" she grumbled. She squinted against the sun. Even her eyelids hurt. "I don't think the sun has ever shone this brightly before. Where is Pittsburgh's infamous sunless weather when you really need it?"

Jed laughed. It was true that he was feeling incredibly cheerful this morning. It made no sense, but there it was. He'd spent a sexless night, tending to Tara, yet when he'd awakened this morning he felt happier and more fulfilled than he did after a hot night of passion with his latest flame.

It was weird. He suspected that *he* was weird. Or was this what being in love was like? This eager sense of anticipation, these feelings of warmth and well-being toward the whole world and everyone in it—but most especially for Tara.

They entered the garage and he opened the car door for her.

"Jed?" she paused, gazing up at him with her velvety dark eyes. "Thanks for everything last night. And this morning too. I really do appreciate it."

He couldn't resist her. He caught her in his arms and brought her hard agaisnt his solid masculine frame. "Tara." He breathed her name raggedly as his mouth covered hers. It was the kind of kiss he'd never given before. The kiss of a man in love with the woman in his arms. It was passionate and deep, hot and tender, and it rapidly escalated out of control.

Neither wanted it to end. When they finally broke

apart a long time later, they gazed into each other's eyes, both of them trembling and breathless from the urgency and depth of their feelings.

Jed was the first to speak. "Tara," he began hesitantly, feeling uncertain in this new uncharted emotional terrain. "I don't want you seeing other men. That includes no more nights out with your pal Vince." He'd never made such a demand on a woman before and he was aware of its corollary. "And I'll stay away from other women," he added with a gulp. It was the first and only time he'd ever made that promise, either.

"You want us to date each other exclusively?" Tara repeated carefully. Elation bubbled in her veins, yet a wary caution caused her to hold back. She hadn't forgotten how crushed she'd been to find the brunette ensconced in his apartment the other night. She had a container of stew in her freezer that was a testament to her ability to misread him. "Why?"

"Why?" Clearly, he hadn't expected that question. "Because I don't want to be with anyone but you." There, it was out. He'd said it. Oddly, he felt a great relief. "And I think you feel the same way about me," he added, stroking her neck with his long, skilled fingers. "Am I right, Tara?"

Oh yes, he was right, Tara thought, quivering under the magic of his touch. Therein lay the danger. He could hurt her so much. Once again she thought of her mother, sobbing and broken, after the desertion of each of her lovers. And she remembered the pain she'd felt when she had knocked on his apartment door and seen the dark-haired woman inside.

Jed saw the apprehension in her dark eyes. "What is it?" he asked softly, drawing her back into his arms.

Tara melted against him. "I guess I'm scared that you'll only want me until you get me into bed," she confessed shakily. "And then you'll decide that you've had enough of exclusivity. You'll be telling me that we should see other people, that you—"

"No, baby," he interrupted fiercely. "That's not going to happen."

"Won't it? Your brother Slade dumped Shavonne, your brother Rad did the same to Erin. Sure, they eventually got back together but there were no guarantees that they would."

"And you want a guarantee that I won't dump you after I take you to bed?" Something along the lines of a wedding ring, he guessed, and heaved a sigh. The very fact that he didn't want to hop the next plane to Texas in order to escape was proof of how very much he'd come to care about her.

"Ah, Tara." He stroked her hair. "I'm not going to hurt you, honey. It looks like I've taken the bait and I'm on the hook. All that's left is for you to reel me in." It was humbling to liken oneself to a hapless fish, but quite apropos, he decided. And he was rewarded by Tara's sudden smile. He felt his heart take flight.

"I don't want to be with any man but you, Jed," she said huskily. "Let's give exclusivity a chance."

Nine

Jed was waiting to take her to dinner at the restaurant of her choice when Tara returned from work that night. She chose a restaurant on Mount Washington, less for the food, which was only average, than for the ride to it and its spectacular view of the city.

They drove to the incline at the foot of Mount Washington, where the restaurant was located high on the hill above. "What is this thing?" Jed asked warily, eyeing the steep railed track which scaled the tree-covered hill.

"It's the Mount Washington incline," explained Tara, taking his hand and guiding him to the station. "A ride on it is a must for everyone who visits Pittsburgh."

"It's a must I'd prefer to avoid," Jed muttered. Though a fearless Ramsey risk-taker, he didn't particularly care for heights. And he most certainly didn't care to step into the rickety cable car which pulled into the station. But he wasn't about to admit that to Tara, who blithely entered the car with nary a qualm.

She didn't cringe as the car started with a lurch that nearly threw the passengers off the narrow benches, although Jed did. She chatted brightly during the little car's perpendicular climb up the track. Jed kept his eyes glued to the window, wondering what were the chances of survival, should the wire cable snap.

That they safely reached the top unscathed was something of a miracle to him. He breathed a heartfelt sigh of relief. "Well, that was great," he said with credible enthusiasm. "I'm glad you suggested it."

Tara cast him a dry glance as they emerged into the upper station, where old photographs of the dark and smoggy Pittsburgh of yesteryear were framed and hanging on the walls. Before walking the short distance to the restaurant, they paused to admire the view from a vantage point designed specifically for that purpose. Pittsburgh sprawled below, and they observed the confluence of the three rivers, the Allegheny and the Monongahela meeting to form the Ohio.

The restaurant sported walls of glass in the cavernous dining room and Tara and Jed were seated at a window table with a magnificent view of the city below.

"The lights are starting to come on down there," Jed pointed out as he settled back into the comfortable upholstered chair and watched the city's nightly panorama begin to unfold. He ordered a drink and felt himself slowly begin to unwind.

"Feeling better?" Tara grinned at him. "I promise to keep you distracted on the incline ride down the hill."

He heaved a good-natured groan. "Was it obvious?"

"Only to me. It was the first time I'd ever seen stark terror in your eyes."

They grinned at each other. "So," Jed reached across the table and took her hand in his. "Tell me about your day. And then I'll bore you with a detailed description of how I spent hours on the phone trying to line up a mall's worth of discount stores . . ."

Neither one bored the other. They lingered at the restaurant for three hours, talking, laughing, enthralled with each other. Fortunately, it was a slow weeknight with no other customers waiting for their table, so the waiter did not feel compelled to hurry them out.

They strolled hand in hand back to the incline station. The cable car was empty and waiting and they sat down on one of the long wooden benches inside. A few moments later, the doors banged shut and the car began its descent.

Jed draped his arm around her shoulders and drew her closer. "You promised to distract me on the way down, remember?" he asked huskily. "What luck that we're the only passengers in the car."

His face was so very near that she needed only to lean forward a few inches to touch her lips to his cheek. Tara's pulse raced. The urge to touch him was a physical ache which throbbed deep in the most secret part of her.

His slate gray eyes held her dark velvet ones. "Jed," she whispered.

Sexual tension vibrated between them. Slowly, Tara slid her arms around his neck. Jed murmured her name and folded her deeply into his arms. With a lack of shyness that astonished her, she opened her mouth over his and slipped her tongue into the moist warmth of his mouth.

Jed took control of the kiss, deepening it with possessive mastery. His mouth was hot and hard and demanding, and she clung to him, a wild excitement burning inside her. Her senses were full of him, delighting in every intimate aspect of the warm weight of his hand spread across her stomach, of his stroking fingers on the nape of her neck, of the solid muscles of his chest against the burgeoning fullness of her breasts.

Far too soon, the cable car slid into the waiting platform at the bottom with a resounding bang. Tara and Jed slowly and reluctantly drew apart. For a moment, they stared at each other, dazed by the swift transformation from passion to reality.

Jed cleared his throat. "You did a first-class job of distracting me, honey. I wouldn't have noticed if they'd launched the damn car into outer space. Or cared," he added dryly. He smiled at her, then flung an arm around her waist and guided her out of the station toward the parking lot.

Tara glanced up at him. He was still smiling that rather bemused, lopsided grin. Impulsively, she wrapped her arm around his waist, and they walked in companionable silence to the gleaming Lamborghini.

They kissed good night at her door and he waited until she was safely inside her apartment before entering his own, establishing a pattern. The two of them had dinner in a different Pittsburgh restaurant each night. They held hands at the table and talked for hours about everything and anything, they fed each other samples of various dishes, they kidded and joked and laughed together.

And every night, they went to her apartment or his and indulged in an exciting, arousing, and exquisitely pleasurable necking session which always ended with a sweet good-night kiss at her door. And separate beds.

They spent the weekend, a rainy one, together. They went to the Southland Mall and to its bigger, grander new competitor. Tara listened intently as Jed outlined his plans for converting Southland into a total discount-store mall and got caught up in his enthusiasm. He found her stories of the Pittsburgh radio news scene just as fascinating.

They went to the movies and out to dinner. They watched the Steelers game, being played in Cleveland, on television in her apartment. They ordered pizza from Lucchino's, which Jed unconsciously referred to as "our" pizza place. Tara noted it and felt her heart swell with happiness. She was thinking in "our" these days, too. "Mine" and "yours" seemed to have naturally evolved into it.

She was sitting on his lap, late Sunday night, in the midst of a deep, torrid kiss, when the intrusive ring of the telephone caused them to surface with a mutual groan.

"Ignore it," commanded Jed, nibbling on her neck. His hands were on her breasts, caressing her, making her whimper with pleasure. She had no intention of leaving him.

But the phone kept ringing, insistently, persistently. Fifteen, eighteen, twenty rings.

"I'd better get it." Tara sighed regretfully and struggled to her feet. "It might be Megan. I've been trying to reach her at her dorm all week, but I kept missing her. I've left a million messages for her to call me back, collect. Maybe she finally has."

"You actually *want* to talk to her?" Jed leaned back against the cushions and ran his hand through his hair, tousling it. "I've been blessing my good fortune at not hearing from the Ramsey—Brady version of Romeo and Juliet."

Tara headed to answer the phone. Not very long ago, his comment would've prompted her to accuse him of being heartless and uncaring. Now she knew that was untrue. Jed had a penchant for making flippant remarks and wisecracks, but his actions belied his words. He had provided Megan and Ricky with an escape from their plight, however he might joke about them.

She herself was a case in point, Tara reflected dreamily. After all his disparaging jokes about her virginity, he hadn't tried to pressure or seduce her all week long.

"Tara, I don't know what I'm going to do. I can't go on like this!" Megan's voice, punctuated by sobs, came over the wire. "I haven't been able to get in touch with Ricky at all. They won't let me talk to him when I call him at home. They always say he's out with other girls, but I know he isn't. They won't let him call me, either. Oh, Tara, I just want to hear his voice! I miss him so much."

Tara swallowed. "Ricky hasn't called you at all?"

"They won't let him, Tara, I know it. Just like I know he's not out with any other girl. Ricky is suffering just like I am—maybe worse because he's being held prisoner there!"

Tara wasn't so sure. She could easily imagine Ricky

Ramsey deciding that his supposedly undying love for Megan was a hassle, that it was easier to give in to his parents' demands and date others. It had been difficult for her to imagine Megan falling for him in the first place. He'd always struck Tara as the quintessential spoiled brat.

"Megan, have you ever considered that maybe the Ramseys are telling the truth? Maybe Ricky is out with someone else."

"No!" cried Megan. "Oh, Tara, I can understand why you have doubts about him. You don't know him the way I do. He's not the shallow, self-indulgent, self-centered jerk we thought he was. He's shown me the sweet and thoughtful side of himself. Really, he's not a bit like that obnoxious, nasty Jed. He's more like Rad and Slade."

"Jed isn't obnoxious or nasty, Megan," Tara countered quickly, reflexively. "He sent you the plane tickets and the money, remember?"

"The note he sent along with them said that you'd blackmailed him into doing it." Megan paused. "You mean you didn't?"

"Of course not. Jed was quite concerned about Ricky. He wanted to help you both. Jed can be sweet and thoughtful, too, Megan. And understanding and generous. He's—different—from what we thought he was, Meg."

There was a brief silence. And then Megan's incredulous, apprehensive tones: "Tara, there isn't something going on between you and Jed Ramsey, is there?"

How was she going to answer that one? Tara wondered. She wasn't ready to drag both their families into her newfound relationship with Jed. "We've become good friends during the time he's been in Pittsburgh, Megan," she replied carefully.

"Good friends?" Megan emitted a shriek. "That's what all the celebrities say when they're having a hot fling with someone. Tara, tell me it isn't true! Tell me you aren't having an affair with Jed Ramsey!"

"I'm not having an affair with Jed Ramsey, Megan."

Megan was crying again. "I couldn't handle it if *you* defected to their side, too, Tara. I don't want another one of my sisters to marry another Ramsey!"

Tara found her sister's protests rather contradictory, given the fact that she was desperate to marry a Ramsey herself. And Megan had completely ignored the fact that Jed had been to one to provide her and Ricky with a means of escape from Ramsey domination. If Ricky actually wanted to escape . . .

Eventually, she managed to calm Megan down and even cheer her up a little by promising to call her again tomorrow. Frowning, Tara walked back to Jed, who was still sitting on the couch in her small living room. The television was on, turned to the all-news network.

Jed glanced up at her. "Yes, I preferred to hear about riots, famine, war, and pestilence instead of listening in on the latest about Megan and Ricky's romance," he said drolly.

Tara sat down beside him with a troubled sigh. "I think Ricky has dumped Megan, Jed. He hasn't called her once, and surely he has access to a telephone." Her eyes glittered with anger. "My poor little sister! She's heartbroken and that creep is out on the town with another girl."

Jed tensed. He picked up the remote control panel and turned off the TV. "Uh-oh, here it comes. You're going to lump me into the selfish-egotistical-fiend category, along with the rest of my family. You're going to accuse me of planning to use you. You're going to tell me to get lost right now because you want to dump me before I have the chance to dump you."

He stood up, his heart pounding, his face flushed, his whole being rejecting the scenario he had just described. He couldn't take it if Tara were to walk out of his life, he realized. Pain shot through him at the mere thought of such a fate.

Tara looked up at him in surprise. "You're wrong, Jed," she said quietly. "That never crossed my mind." She frowned thoughtfully. There was a time when she would've thought and done exactly what he'd suggested. But now . . . "I've learned to trust you, Jed. You've shown me a side of yourself I never knew existed."

Megan's words sprang to mind. They described the Jed she'd come to know. And to love, she was sure of that now. "You're not the shallow, self-indulgent, self-centered jerk I thought you were," she said, a sudden smile lighting her face. "You've shown me the sweet and thoughtful side of yourself."

Sweet? Thoughtful? Jed actually blushed. "I've never heard those words used to describe me before," he muttered.

"That's because you've never given anyone but me reason to use them."

"Yeah, well, I'm keeping it that way. I refuse to turn into one of those marshmallows who goes gooey with sentimentality whenever—"

"A marshmallow man?" She laughed and put her arms around him, hugging him tight. "I wonder if we can get you outfitted with a cute little sailor hat and coat?" Her laughter faded and she gazed up at him with dark liquid eyes, earnest and enormous in her small face. "I love you, Jed. I didn't realize how much until tonight, when I had to defend you to Megan."

She wasn't the first woman to tell him that she loved him, but this was the first time Jed was tempted to say it back. The adrenaline was still pumping through his system from his brief panic a few moments ago, when he had faced the intolerable notion that she might end it between them. But she hadn't. Instead, she had told him that she loved him.

He believed her. His pulse raced and his body, already taut and aroused from their tantalizing lovemaking earlier, demanded physical satisfaction. She was in love with him. The corners of his mouth twisted into a hungry smile. She wouldn't refuse the man she loved. Tonight was the night. They were going to consummate this relationship of theirs at last!

"And you love me," Tara continued confidently. "Oh,

Jed, I can't wait until we're married! I know we'll make each other happy!" She hugged him hard and cuddled close.

"M—married?" He remembered having the wind knocked out of him while playing football, but she seemed to have achieved the same effect with words. His thoughts were scrambled, and his only clear perception was how soft and warm and cuddly she felt in his arms. Of how good it felt to hold her. He could picture them sleeping together, her cuddling against him, drowsy and satiated from their lovemaking.

"We don't have to get married right away, of course," Tara added as Jed's silence lengthened. "I mean, we do have a lot of practical details to work out first. My career, for one. My contract with Double Q Radio runs for another year, so I'll be here in Pittsburgh for at least that long. And I'm glad. I don't especially want to live in Houston as a newlywed. Much as I love my family, I—"

"Wait a minute." Jed drew back slightly and stared down at her. If she'd shocked him before, she'd aptly succeeded in compounding it. "There's nothing to work out, baby. My wife will live with me in Houston, where my work is."

"I guess that means waiting until my contract is up then," Tara said slowly. "We could visit back and forth—"

"Visit, hell. I'll buy out your contract. You can work in radio in Houston. Or in TV there, if you prefer. Ramsey and Sons have holdings in both. One phone call from Dad and—"

"Never!" Tara declared, aghast. "The day I'd let Quentin Ramsey arrange my career will be the day that I—"

"Stop being so damn stubborn, Tara. There's nothing wrong with using contacts to land a job. That's the way the world operates, honey."

"I got the job at Double Q on my own, without any contacts," Tara reminded him. "I like knowing I was hired for my ability, not because of who happened to know me."

"And your ability will determine the course of your career in Houston, Tara," he assured her. "It will be up to you to make it at the station, once you're hired."

Tara shook her head. "I want to work out my contract at Double Q. If that means waiting to get married, then that's the way it'll have to be. At least I'll have some solid reporting and on-air experience to offer if I should have to resort to letting the Ramseys find me a job in Houston later on."

An idea struck her and she brightened. "Unless you want to get married sooner and have a commuter marriage for a while?" she suggested brightly. "With me in Pittsburgh and you in Houston. It's a very modern arrangement—and very practical in a case like ours."

"I will *not* tolerate a commuter marriage, not for any length of time," Jed exclaimed with a huff. "I don't want a modern, practical arrangement for a marriage. I want one of the old-fashioned kind. You know, where the husband and wife love each other too much to want to live apart."

"I do love you, Jed, but—"

"Forget the 'but,' Tara. Make it 'therefore.' "

She swallowed. "I love you, Jed, *therefore*, we'd better wait to get married."

"No, dammit! I want to marry you now!" he thundered. His words seemed to echo throughout the room. They stared at each other.

"How did you do it?" Jed blurted out, his gray eyes wide with astonishment. "I had no intention of proposing to you, but I just did. *I told you I wanted to marry you.* How did you get me to say it?"

"How did I do it?" Tara felt as if she'd been punched in the head. She stepped away from him, her dark eyes mirroring the psychic pain ripping through her. "I did it by telling you that I'd prefer to stay in Pittsburgh and work at Double Q Radio rather than jump at the chance to marry you and move back to Houston. Oh, it's exactly like I've always thought," she continued morosely. "A man wants a woman most when he thinks he can't have her. He's challenged and intrigued when she holds back."

She thought about her mother's tales. How Jerilyn's dark eyes would sparkle as she revealed the fun of playing hard to get, the thrill of the man's attentive chase! And then, inevitably, came Jerilyn's total and unconditional surrender, to be followed, just as inevitably, by the man's declining interest, his withdrawal, his desertion. Only the time frames differed in each affair. Tara remembered sitting worried and tense as she listened to her mother euphorically recite the details of a brand-new love interest. For she had learned, as Jerilyn never seemed to, exactly what would happen when a woman stopped playing games and started wanting a future with the man she loved.

Tara had always wondered how her mother could have been so blind, so utterly amnesic about the inevitable outcome. Well, she understood completely now. Love did that to you—made you blind and amnesic and stupidly optimistic.

She felt perilously close to tears. "As long as a man is unsure of a woman's feelings for him, he'll pursue her," she recited slowly, determined never to forget again. "His passion is linked with his uncertainty."

"I remember your reciting that particular bit of warped philosophy the day I arrived in Pittsburgh. It's both stupid and untrue, Tara."

"You just admitted that you had no intention of proposing to me. You accidentally blurted it out when you thought I was content to live without you." She gave her head a shake and her long, blond hair tumbled around her shoulders. "I almost blew it by telling you that I loved you, didn't I? You were about to beat a hasty retreat, but I managed to turn things around by throwing a roadblock in our mythical marriage plans. All of a sudden, you weren't so sure of me anymore, you weren't calling the shots, and all your romantic fervor blazed. I won and I didn't even know what I was doing. I didn't even realize we were playing a game."

"Tara, you're being ridiculous," he said, shifting uneasily. But was she? Hadn't she just recapped the whole scene with depressing accuracy?

Tara shrugged. "Maybe so." Her dark eyes shone with hurt and disillusionment. "But all these manipulations and strategies that masquerade as love and romance are ridiculous, too." She grasped a strand of her hair and nervously wound and rewound it around her fingers. "And it's so easy to get caught up in it, so easy. Even me. Knowing what I know—"

"Tara, for heaven's sakes, let's not make some sort of Greek tragedy out of this," Jed interrupted. He felt like a rat and he didn't like the feeling. No woman but Tara had ever been able to stir the deeper, finer feelings of his conscience. And now he had to contend with the fact that he had put that pain and disillusionment in her beautiful eyes. That moments before she had been happy and loving and in his arms, and he had ruined it all.

"You're right, it's no tragedy." She gave a sardonic little laugh. "It's a farce. The whole thing is a stupid waste of time. Mama and her cavalcade of lovers, Megan and Ricky, Kayci and the senator, you and me . . ." She paused and heaved a disgusted sigh. "What's the point? There's no happiness, no peace of mind—except maybe for Senator Saxon, and who wants to be like *him*?"

He hated hearing her talk this way. He hated having hurt her. Jed faced the inevitable. The moment of truth at last was here. He was going to do whatever it took to make her happy and loving again. To get her back in his arms.

"Tara, I love you," Jed heard himself say and was surprised that it was so easy. Because it was true, he reflected. "And I really do want to marry you." He smiled. He wasn't merely saying the words, he meant them, he admitted to himself. "I didn't accidentally blurt that out, Tara. It's what I really want."

He held open his arms to her, but she made no move toward him. "You're following the rules to the letter," she said, staring at him dispassionately. "I'm withdrawing myself from the game and that inspires you. We're back to the beginning again, and I just don't feel like playing anymore. I quit, Jed."

"Sweetheart, this isn't a game. We love each other and we're going to be married."

Tara scowled. "Oh, play another tune, Jed."

Play another tune? His first proposal of marriage and she replied with *that*? He was indignant. "Tara, I'm not going to beg you to marry me," he said testily.

"I know." She didn't look at him. "I don't expect you to."

"But you'd like me to, wouldn't you?" he pressed.

"I just want you to leave me alone," she said wearily. "I'm tired. I want to go to bed."

"Without me, of course." He was frowning fiercely. "Dammit, Tara, I'm tired of leaving you at the door every night. I haven't had a decent night's sleep since I arrived in this city. You keep me so wired, I can never wind down. I've never been so hung up on—so *obsessed* with—a woman before and it's driving me out of my mind."

She flashed a nasty smile. "What are you implying, Jed? That I should marry you so you can forget about me? So you can finally get a good night's sleep? Thanks, but no thanks."

He glowered at her. She was beginning to sound as malicious and sarcastic as any Ramsey. And he didn't like it, not one bit. "I don't want a sparring partner, Tara, I want—"

"You don't know what you want," Tara interrupted grimly. "But I do. And it's not a man who thinks I tricked him into proposing. It's not a man with whom I have to keep up a perpetual game of hard-to-get. I don't want to live my life that way. I want love and trust and loyalty, someone I have faith in and who has faith in me. If I can't have that, I'd rather be alone."

"You want *me*." Jed's voice rose. The more he persisted, the more she visibly withdrew from him. And the further she withdrew, the more desperately he pursued his suit, thus confirming her grim theory of male/female relations. He was struck by the futility of the situation, but saw no other course of action. His alternative was to leave. And what would that prove?

He took a deep breath. "I said I wouldn't beg, but if that's what it'll take to convince you, I'll do it, Tara. Please, please, don't do this to us. I don't want to waste my time pretending an interest in other women, and I don't want to watch and wait for you to come home with some other man."

Tara shivered at the grim scenes he'd depicted. She thought how much finding him with the brunette had hurt—she still hadn't the heart to defrost that stew, which had come to symbolize her misery that night. She thought of going out with Vinnie, pretending to laugh and have a good time, while hurting deep inside. No, she didn't want to endure any more of that, either.

"What do you suggest we do?" she asked warily, wishing she were strong enough to send him firmly on his way. Was she going to turn out to be her mother's daughter after all, despite her vows to live her life differently?

Jed breathed a silent sigh of relief. At least she didn't want to end it between them. It was the most he could hope for at this time. "Let's not do anything," he said. "Let's go on seeing each other, just as we have been. Let's forget we ever had this whole disastrous conversation."

Tara stared at the ground. She wanted to tell him that it was useless, that there had been profound changes during the past half hour which made picking up where they'd left off impossible. But if she were to do that . . . She thought of the time they'd spent together this past week, and her heart clenched. She wasn't ready to give him up. She couldn't do it. Maybe later, when she was stronger, but for now . . .

"All right," she said softly. "We'll try to pretend we didn't have this conversation."

It all seemed incredibly anticlimactic. They stood in

awkward silence for a few moments and then Tara said, "I guess you'd better go. It's late."

He nodded. And then leaned down to kiss her. She turned her head to avoid his mouth, and he ended up brushing her cheek with his lips.

"Good night, Jed," she said coolly, not meeting his eyes.

"Good night, Tara. Dinner tomorrow?"

"Unless one of us has to work late," she hedged politely.

He left her apartment, grim and dispirited. She might have agreed to pretend that they hadn't had tonight's conversation, but if it hadn't occurred, their good-night kiss would have long and intimate and they would have been happily and eagerly making plans for tomorrow night.

Ten

They continued to see each other, but it wasn't the same. Tara was polite and pleasant, but reserved, and though Jed tried—he was absolutely at his most charming, the epitome of warm, funny and attentive—he couldn't breech the wall she'd erected between them. He knew she was on her guard . . . waiting for him to what? To leave her because she'd confessed to loving him?

That was it in the proverbial nutshell, he knew. She didn't trust him to stay. By midweek, he decided that he'd had it. He was a Ramsey and he didn't have to put up with this! He was doing all the work in this relationship while she acted as if she didn't care if he was around or not. She wouldn't hold his hand; it was as though his touch repulsed her. And, of course, there was no more kissing. If he moved quickly enough, he was able to sneak in a quick peck on her cheek as he said good night, but that was it.

He didn't need this, Jed told himself righteously. A Ramsey deserved an adoring and ardent lover who stroked his ego while ignoring her own. It would be better for both of them if they called it quits right now.

But he somehow never got around to telling her that. How could he? He loved her too much. His flashes of indignation were always replaced by that irrefutable fact. There was nothing he could do but to stick around and convince her just how serious he was about their future together.

They both groaned when Leslie Polk called to remind them of his cousin's party on Saturday night. They offered lame excuses, but Les was having none of it. He and Melissa arrived promptly at eight o'clock to drive them to the party.

Tara and Jed were consigned to the backseat while Les confidently slid behind the wheel of Melissa's car. There had been a remarkable transformation in the quiet young couple who had been too shy to speak during that first dinner at Tara's apartment. In addition to seeing each other every day at work, Les and Melissa had spent almost every evening together since their first arranged date and were now completely comfortable together. They had their own conversation, their own private jokes, many with scientific nuances that were lost on Jed and Tara.

It seemed that the tables had truly turned. Melissa and Les talked and laughed easily in the front while Jed and Tara alternated between awkward silence and stiltedly polite conversation in the back.

They kept casting covert glances at each other. Although Tara had been careful to move close to the window, Jed slid to the middle of the seat with no compunction. He sat close to her, so close that their shoulders were touching. Tara felt his thigh press against hers and tried to inch away. Unfortunately, the unyielding presence of the car door prevented her from going any farther. She hadn't been this physically close to him since their falling-out on Sunday night, and her deprived senses seemed determined to make up for what had been missing. She reeled from the feel of his body next to hers. His heady masculine scent filled her nostrils. She could conjure up the taste of his mouth without even trying. Hot arrows of sexual awareness and sharp sexual tension pierced her every nerve.

Tara's dark eyes slid hungrily over him. He looked

particularly handsome tonight in an elegant charcoal gray suit, white shirt and eye-catching yellow tie. She had chosen to wear the one truly smashing dress she owned, bought last spring to wear to the Pittsburgh Media Awards party. It was a strapless dark purple mini with leaves of gold embroidered on the tight-fitting bodice. The cut and style of the dress showed off her figure to alluring advantage. She'd created quite a stir at the awards party.

But she'd worn the dress tonight strictly to stir Jed.

"You look beautiful tonight, Tara," Jed murmured in a sexy growl which made her squirm in her seat in an effort to control the liquid heat cascading through her.

"Thank you," she replied stiffly. She wanted to cast off her cloak of reserve, but she couldn't seem to do it. It was wrapped around her too tightly to remove casually . . . or even formally.

There was silence between them once more.

"Did you talk to Megan today?" asked Jed with commendable interest.

"I've talked to her every day this week. Her situation hasn't changed." Tara's lips tightened. "She's heart-broken and she still hasn't heard a word from Ricky. According to your parents, his life in Houston is one perpetual date. Megan, of course, doesn't believe it, although I'm afraid she's soon going to have to."

He'd certainly made the wrong choice of subject, Jed thought with an inward groan. He could almost hear Tara's thoughts about faithless, game-playing Ramseys. Naturally, she considered him one of them.

The silence between them grew so tense that even Les and Melissa noticed. They tried to bring Tara and Jed into their own conversation, a sort of ironic replay of that Saturday night when Les and Melissa had been the mute ones.

Leslie's cousin, Fred Polk, lived in a big old house in the Point Breeze section of the city. The four entered the imposing hallway, which was ablaze with lights.

"So this is a swankenda, huh?" Jed murmured to Tara.

Tara couldn't suppress a smile. This Pittsburgh "swankenda" was little more than a cottage, compared to the Ramsey manse in River Oaks, Texas. "I just hope the Seen columnist isn't here," she murmured fervently. "If my name were to turn up in that column, I'd never live it down at work. Vince and Bob would have a field day with it."

A tall, rather manic man in a tux, bearing a marked physical resemblance to Leslie, bounded over to them to greet Les effusively. Les introduced Melissa, Tara, and Jed to his cousin.

"This is great. I'm so glad you could come. We have a wonderful buffet in the dining room," Fred gestured expansively toward the grand, chandeliered room to the left. "There's dancing. We have a great little dance band, and upstairs . . ."

He continued on, his voice brimming with enthusiasm. Tara tuned him out. Though she tried, she couldn't seem to concentrate on anything but Jed, who was standing beside her, lightly cupping her elbow in his hand. She knew she should move away. She hadn't let him touch her all week, but she was starved for his touch. She was starved for *him*.

What was she going to do? she wondered, her mind swirling in confusion. She was trying to protect herself by staying aloof, but she knew it was a losing battle. If only she could fathom why he kept hanging around her. Because she was challenging him by playing hard to get?

But she wasn't exactly acting hard to get, she reminded herself. She wasn't using all the manipulative little tricks her mother had told her were essential in capturing a man's interest. She was seeing Jed regularly, he—

"Tara, want to dance?"

Leslie's invitation stunned her so much, it took her a few seconds to nod in agreement. This confident young man, fully in command of himself socially, was not the Leslie Polk she had met a year ago. He had come into his own, thanks to his relationship with Melissa.

The two of them left Melissa and Jed talking to Fred and headed into the room where the band pounded out their version of that sentimental classic, "Feelings."

At least somebody's romance had worked out, Tara thought, as she and Les began a slow dance. She was happy for him and Melissa, and told him so.

"Melissa and I both know how much we owe you and Jed," Les said seriously. "We laugh about how you two dragged us out of our shells. The truth is, we might've never had the courage to start dating if it hadn't been for that dinner party you and Jed engineered."

Tara eyes misted. "I'm glad everything is going so well for you two, Les."

"And Melissa and I want things to work out for you and Jed, too, Tara. I guess we just want everybody to be as happy as we are. And you and Jed aren't." He gazed into her sad brown eyes. "What happened, Tara? Is there anything we can do to help "

Tara shrugged. "Try summoning Chad Cherrington back from Russia." It was a weak joke and she knew it. She heaved a gloomy sigh. "Oh, Les, I'm so confused. It's as though I want to drive Jed away because I know he's eventually going to leave, anyway. I've been awful this week—stiff and stilted and even sulky, I guess. I don't know why Jed is still around."

"Because he's as crazy about you as I am about Melissa," Les concluded with a smile. "Sounds like you two have a bit of a communication problem. You need to talk things out without the threat of either one of you leaving if your discussion should escalate into a quarrel."

Tara gave her head a wry shake. A few weeks ago, she'd had to suggest that he share a Twinkie with his secret heartthrob. Now he was dispensing advice like Dear Abby. Love was strange business indeed.

Jed and Melissa danced by, and Les jovially insisted on changing partners. He and Melissa disappeared into the throng, leaving Jed and Tara facing each other. The band struck up another slow song.

"Shall we?" Jed didn't give her time to refuse. He

pulled her into his arms and held her close. So close she could hardly move without her body rubbing provocatively against his. She felt his virile response and desire, swift and sharp, slice through her. Her breasts swelled, wanting the touch of his hands, and her legs trembled against the hard columns of his thighs. There was an aching emptiness in her that cried out to be filled.

"I missed you this week," he murmured, nuzzling the soft, scented hollow of her neck. It felt so good to hold her, he felt almost dazed with wanting. She fit into his arms as though she had been designed just for him. She fit him as no other woman in the world ever had.

"You missed me?" Tara managed a stilted little laugh. "You've seen me every day."

"I've seen the prim, polite and socially correct Tara Brady every day," he amended. He nipped erotically at the soft lobe of her ear. "I miss my own private Tara. The one I was just getting to know until I—"

"Jed, don't." The sexy huskiness of his voice, and the warmth of his hard, muscular frame, were having a sensually devastating effect upon her. It was impossible to maintain any semblance of distance—physical, emotional or intellectual—with the rushes of intense pleasure surging through her. She found herself wondering why she should even bother to try.

His thumb traced a slow circle on her palm and when he made a subtle, thrusting movement against her hips, a hungry little moan escaped from her throat. Instinctively, she arched into him.

Jed was too experienced, of course, to miss her voluptuous response to him. "Talk to me, Tara," he said softly, rubbing his big hand slowly, sensuously over her back. He caressed the bare skin of her shoulders, tracing erotic little patterns with his fingertips. His lips moved in her hair and his breath was warm against her cheek.

Tara could only cling to him, feeling suddenly weightless, mindless, and helpless against the wild needs coursing through her. She loved him; that was the only fact her brain seemed capable of assimilating at this point.

"Don't keep shutting me out," Jed said hoarsely. "I love you, Tara. If I'd ever doubted it, this week has been the ultimate proof of how much I really do care."

"It has?" She stared up at him with puzzled brown eyes. "But—"

"I learned beyond a shadow of doubt that I'd rather be with you," he interrupted. "Even when you're mad at me, even when you're treating me like a suspicious parole officer treats his most untrustworthy parolee, I'd rather be with you than with any other woman, no matter how accommodating she might try to be."

A sudden streak of white hot jealousy tore through her. "And what other woman was trying to be accommodating?" she demanded.

"Honey, it's not important. What I'm trying to tell you is that—"

"It was that brunette bombshell from the mall, wasn't it?" It was Tara's turn to interrupt. "Has she been making a play for you all week?"

What a question, she thought, gazing at Jed. The man was gorgeous, he was smart and sexy, he was the most exciting, attractive, *lovable* man in the world. Of course the brunette bombshell was after him. But she couldn't have him, Tara vowed with sudden, fierce determination. Jed was *hers*. For better or worse, they belonged together. She had no doubts about that now.

"Tara, forget about anyone else. I have," Jed interjected quickly.

"You're mine, Jed Ramsey," Tara said, her dark eyes blazing. "I don't care how much our families want us to get together, we're going to be together because it's what *we* want. And I do want to be with you, Jed," she added in a fervid whisper. "So very much."

His face broke into a smile so joyous that it brought emotional tears to her eyes. "You're the only woman in the world for me, Tara, the woman I love and want to marry and have kids with—" he paused to stare thoughtfully into her eyes. "Do you want to have kids, Tara? We've never talked about it."

She smiled. "You're asking a Brady if she wants children? That's like asking a politician if he wants votes. But, if you wouldn't mind, I'd like to wait until I'm at least twenty-five to get pregnant. I'd like to have a couple of years alone with you."

"Does this mean that you trust me, Tara?" he asked, obviously deeply moved. "That you believe that I love you and are willing to take a chance on me? With me?"

"I love you, Jed. I just needed to be reminded how much." She lifted her face for his kiss. "And how irrevocably."

His mouth descended toward hers and they gazed into each other's eyes, feeling all the love and hope and promise reflected there. And then—

"Hey, folks, here at Freddie Polk's parties, we always have something new, something different, something out of the ordinary!"

The loud, piercing voice of Fred Polk made both Jed and Tara visibly start.

"And tonight," continued Fred in his machine-gun delivery, "it's *this!*"

Before Jed and Tara could move, speak, or react in any way, Fred Polk had snapped a pair of handcuffs on the two of them, chaining them together.

Tara stared down at the shiny steel cuff which physically bound her to Jed. She gave her wrist a jerk. Jed's arm jerked, too. They stared at each other in horror.

"Hey!" Jed found his voice. "Get these things off us— now!"

Fred gave a bizarre laugh which was remarkable similar to the manic cartoon woodpecker's, and was on his way. For a few shocked moments, they watched him handcuff other unsuspecting couples together.

"This is crazy!" Jed gave his wrist a shake. Tara's arm shook, too. He scowled. "Don't worry, honey, I'll make that little jerk unlock these cuffs and then we'll get out of here."

"Well, well, here you two are, together at last." A very satisfied Leslie Polk, his arm around a smiling Melissa, joined them. "There's no getting away from each other now. You're going to have to stay together and talk out your differences."

"Les used his influence with Fred to have you two handcuffed together," Melissa said proudly. "Fred's plan is to handcuff strangers to each other, but he relented and made an exception for you two when Les explained your situation."

Tara glanced around the room. Fred and a few of his loyal henchmen were zooming around snapping handcuffs on startled pairs of guests. "You mean those people don't know each other?" she asked incredulously.

"No!" Les and Melissa laughed with delight. "Isn't it great?" Melissa added happily.

"Great?" Jed echoed. "For men and women to be randomly paired off and handcuffed together for an evening?" He was embarrassed to realize that such a stunt would've won a hearty endorsement from him in his wild bachelor days which, he recognized with surprising relief, were finally past him.

"No, it's not great, Melissa," he continued, proud of his newfound maturity. "It reaches the critical mass of lunacy! Leslie, tell your maniacal cousin to unlock these damned cuffs!"

"Sorry, Jed," said Les with a shrug. "You and Tara are going to have to stay together and talk everything out, without the threat of one of you storming off."

"We've already talked things out!" Jed raged. "We're two mature adults who love each other and who don't need to resort to stupid *gadgets* to make things right between us!" He held up his cuffed wrist and shook it back and forth. Tara's arm went back and forth, too.

"Leslie, we appreciate your efforts on our behalf," Tara put in tactfully, "but we'd really like to get out of these cuffs and go home."

"We want to be alone, and we don't need these *things* to keep us together," Jed added, glowering at the cuffs.

"Oh." Leslie looked somewhat discomfited. "I'll ask Fred for the key."

But Fred Polk had other plans. Apparently, a number of disgruntled guests in handcuffs were also badgering him for the keys to their freedom. "Hey, folks," Fred announced, his voice booming over the amplifier. "How can we have fun tonight if everybody is obsessed with keys? Let's just cast our fates to the wind—and these keys out the window!"

With that he tossed a loose handful of tiny keys out an open window onto the ground below. A few of the guests laughed, but most of them were horrified. There was a sudden stampede out the doors.

Jed and Tara were part of the crowd on the lawn, searching through the grass, picking up keys, trying them in the locks, and then discarding them as they continued their hunt for the right key to free them.

"We could search for hours and still never find the key," Jed exclaimed in disgust. "Let's go home and call a locksmith. They make emergency calls. It'll cost a fortune, but it will be worth every cent."

"I don't even want to ask how you happen to know about locksmiths making emergency calls to unlock handcuffs," Tara said archly, then obliterated her forbidding demeanor by grinning. She felt euphoric, floating on air. The handcuffs were an irritant that couldn't spoil her happiness.

Jed put his free arm around her and hugged her close. "Let's call a taxi and get out of this loony bin, honey. I can't wait to be alone with you."

They kissed and cuddled, whispered and laughed in the back of the taxi, and the driver was tactful enough not to mention the handcuffs on their wrists. Jed rewarded him with a generous tip.

They went to Jed's apartment and Jed located a locksmith in the phone book, who promised to come within the next few hours. It was, the man explained, a very busy night.

"I bet all his calls are from hysterical people who were guests at Fred Polk's party," Tara said. "Imagine being handcuffed to someone you didn't know, someone you didn't find at all attractive, and then watching Fred throw those keys out the window."

"Fred sure is different from his cousin Les," Jed observed cryptically, and then they looked at each other and burst into laughter.

It was no hardship to spend the next two and a half hours handcuffed together. They spent them on Jed's couch, kissing, petting, loving with touches and words. When the doorbell rang, they were reluctant to move.

"I think I'll send the locksmith home," Jed murmured huskily, smiling into Tara's passion-clouded eyes. "I like being permanently attached to you."

She gave him a dreamy smile and crossed the room with him in a love-sweet daze. Jed pulled open the door and prepared to greet the locksmith.

But it wasn't the locksmith who stood in the doorway. Tara drew in a sharp, shocked breath. It was Carling Templeton, the senator's daughter, the woman who had sent Jed fleeing from Houston. Because she'd wanted to get married and he hadn't.

One look at Jed's appalled expression assured Tara that he harbored no secret doubts or regrets about leaving his former girlfriend. "What are you doing here, Carling?" he asked. His voice was as unwelcoming as his expression.

Carling gaped from Jed to Tara, and her wide blue eyes missed nothing. Not their love-mussed clothes or their tousled hair or their lips, swollen and moist from hours of kissing. And then she spied the handcuffs.

She emitted a horrified gasp. "I'll never forgive you for this, Jed Ramsey," she cried shrilly. "To think I came all the way from Houston to give you another chance, only to find you playing kinky sex games with—with—"

"Tara is my fiancée," Jed interjected coldly and his steel gray eyes held a dangerous glitter. "So choose your words very carefully, Carling."

"Fiancée?" Carling's voice rose to a squeak. "You're going to marry *her?*"

"Yes." Jed drew Tara close and the chain between the handcuffs jangled. "Tara and I plan to be married as soon as possible." He touched his lips to Tara's forehead.

"I hope you don't expect me to offer my congratulations!" snapped Carling.

Jed shrugged. "It would be a classy thing to do, Carling. Just remind yourself that ours was hardly the love affair of the century. In fact, we didn't have an affair at all. If you'll remember, I told you that you came with too many strings attached for me."

He looked lovingly at Tara. "As it happened, Tara here has more strings than a twenty-meter sloop, but it's my pleasure to be caught and tied and—"

"Oh, shut up," Carling said sourly.

Tara found her voice and quickly stepped into the fray. "I know this must've come as a surprise to you, Carling, and—"

"Surprise?" Carling snarled. "That's an understatement. This is by far the most humiliating, mortifying, demeaning moment of my entire life!"

Tara and Jed exchanged glances. He interlocked the fingers of his cuffed hand with Tara's. "I don't suppose it would help if I were to give you some well-meaning spiel about moments like this building character," he remarked to Carling. "So why don't you display some of that famous Templeton class and character and wish us well? And then go home," he added firmly.

Carling's face turned scarlet. "Congratulations," she said tightly. "I—I wish you both much happiness in your marriage." She turned and started down the small set of stairs leading to the vestibule.

Tara gave her full marks for class and character. She was proud of Jed, too. She squeezed his fingers as she gazed up to him.

He rolled his eyes heavenward. "What a night." He groaned. "First Wild Fred's party, now Carling on our doorstep. Makes you wonder what's going to happen next, doesn't it?"

They had only seconds to wait to find out. For, as Carling was pulling open the heavy front door to leave the building, Kayci Cann came barreling through it and nearly knocked the other girl against the wall. Kayci hardly noticed; she was crying too hard. And right on her heels was Senator Glenn Saxon.

"Holy smoke," Jed said to Tara. "Now it's all going to hit the fan. Senator Templeton is one of President Lipton's oldest and closest cronies. And you know the kind of attacks Saxon's been mounting on Lipton. Templeton's livid; he loathes Saxon. Wait till Carling recognizes him."

Which Carling did, within a split second. "Glenn Saxon," she said with acid sweetness. "What a surprise to meet you here."

"Saxon's doomed," Jed muttered. He almost felt sorry for the man. Almost, but not quite. "Carling's in a rotten mood and gunning for a target. Saxon—*with Kayci!*—is tailor-made for her."

Tara watched the drama unfold before her with a kind of alarmed fascination. Her eyes kept darting from Saxon to Carling to Kayci, who was still sobbing as she leaned against the iron railing of the stairs.

Glenn Saxon obviously couldn't quite place Carling Templeton, which only added insult to injury on what must be a truly wretched night for her. Tara, who had had a few wretched nights of her own recently, felt a pang of empathy.

"Darling, you're so darned beautiful, and I'm so damned ashamed of myself," Senator Saxon said to Carling in dulcet tones, his eyes sliding lustily over her shapely figure. "But it seems your name has just slipped my mind. Maybe you could help me out a little?"

Carling's face was a mask of indignant rage. But before she could speak, Kayci stepped forward. "Who are you?" she asked Carling. "Another one of his women? Are you fool enough to be carrying his baby, too?"

Carling recoiled in shock. Saxon reached over and slapped Kayci's cheek with the full palm of his hand. The sound reverberated painfully throughout the small hallway.

"Why, you—you big bully!" Tara was incensed. She started toward Saxon, and as Jed was chained to her, he came right along.

Kayci clutched her reddened cheek and wept uncontrollably.

"You're pregnant?" Carling asked her, a gleam lighting her blue eyes. "And it's Saxon's child? I wonder if he happened to offer you money, for one reason or another?"

"Oh, yes, he offered me money," Kayci said bitterly. She fumbled in her coat pocket and pulled out a crumbled check which she thrust into Carling's hand. "I told him I was having his baby and he gave me *this* and told me to get rid of it!"

"Why, I'm outraged!" Carling exclaimed. "And after all those profamily speeches he's always giving! How dare he treat the mother of his unborn child this way! My daddy, Senator Clayton Templeton, was recently named honorary chairman of an antiabortion group, you know. Oh, just wait till he and Uncle Bradford hear about this!"

Tara put her free arm around Kayci. "Kayci, I want you to know that Jed and I will help you in any way we can."

"Oh, so will Daddy and I," Carling agreed sweetly. "May I show him this check as evidence?"

"I think it would be a good idea if Kayci first showed the check to my friend Anne Linaberger who works for our local television station," Tara suggested. "That's a network affiliate," she added succinctly.

Anne had said to wait until the line between private indiscretion and potential scandal had been crossed, and in Tara's opinion, Senator Glenn Saxon had finally crossed it. She was glad to hand the story over. Not only was Anne the more experienced newswoman, but her breaking the story would spare Christine Logston the embarrassment of having Tara do it at Double Q. Tara was savvy enough to realize that working with Christine would be incredibly difficult were she the one to expose Saxon.

"A television reporter." Carling was all smiles. "Of course."

Glenn Saxon had turned pale. He slumped against the wall, staring glumly at the ground.

"I'd punch your lights out for smacking Kayci, but I think they have a much more effective way of fixing you, dude," Jed said to the senator. "I'm not one for making political analyses, but I'd have to predict that as far as politics go, you're history."

"Locksmith here." A plump, graying man carrying a tool box joined the assembly in the foyer. "Who needs handcuffs removed?"

Jed and Tara held up their hands. Kayci stared at them, wide-eyed. *Little Tara?* she managed to gasp. "Why, whoever would've thought it. You always seemed so wholesome, so sweet! And you're into *handcuffs?*"

Tara blushed. She could try to explain, she supposed. But they probably wouldn't believe her anyway.

"Tara is a very clever and very sexy girl to have landed Jed Ramsey," Carling said with grudging respect. "Obviously, you and I could take lessons from her, Kayci."

Kayci sniffled sadly, and Carling gave her arm an encouraging squeeze. She seemed to have cheered up considerably; apparently the prospect of wrecking her father's political enemy had redeemed the evening for her.

"Let's go inside," Jed suggested. Listening to Kayci and Carling express admiration for Tara's matrimonial machinations was making him uncomfortable. After all, he hadn't been manipulated into marrying Tara. He'd fallen in love and marriage was the natural culmination of that love. He knew that now. He congratulated himself on his mature acceptance of the situation.

Jed headed for his apartment, Tara chained and following faithfully, The locksmith, Kayci, and Carling followed them while Glenn Saxon slunk out the door.

"As soon as these are off, I'll call Anne," Tara promised the two women. "I"m sure she'll want to come over and interview Kayci right away."

Jed looked at the group and heaved a sigh. "This isn't exactly the way I'd planned to spend the night I got engaged, sweetheart."

But he was resigned to his fate. He and Tara had a lifetime of nights to spend together. Tomorrow . . . his blood thickened as a surge of pure loving lust coursed through him. Tomorrow he and Tara would make love, he was sure of it. He absolutely couldn't wait any longer to make her his own.

Eleven

When Tara called Jed the next morning to ask if he wanted to go to church with her, his first inclination was to decline. But then he remembered that other Sunday morning, when he'd seen Tara and Les return from church, sharing an umbrella and talking as they walked in the rain.

It was raining this morning. *He* could be the man sharing the umbrella with Tara, the one to talk and laugh with her as they tramped through the rain. It was an irresistible prospect. Besides, since he and Tara were going to be married, he'd better get used to doing things like attending church on Sunday mornings. A few months ago, he would have blanched at the notion. Now, he rather liked it. It sounded so committed, so upright, so *married*. Just what he wanted to be.

And he had a great time. The Jed Ramsey of old would have found the concept of church as a great time incomprehensible, but the newly engaged Jed thoroughly enjoyed himself. He sat next to Tara in the church and when she smiled at him and slipped her hand in his, the swell of pure happiness that flowed through him was like nothing he had never known.

Sharing the umbrella, they walked to a small coffee shop near the church and had breakfast. And as they walked home together, they talked and laughed and stopped to kiss, ignoring the raindrops that pelted against the umbrella.

"Being with you like this was my fantasy," Jed said huskily as he pulled Tara closer. "And I have some other much more explicit fantasies, to act out when we're back in your apartmant."

"It's my fantasy, too," Tara said softly. "I want to make love with you, Jed."

She thought of her dream, to be married to the man she was making love with, and gently put it aside. Jed needed her now, and she wanted to please him, to give and give to him, without any self-imposed rules, restrictions or conditions. She would have liked a gold band on her finger when Jed took her to bed but she wouldn't demand it. Wasn't it enough, knowing that he loved her?

Her heart was pounding with anticipation as they entered the vestibule of the apartment building. She turned to give Jed a tremulous smile and he leaned down to touch his lips to hers.

"So there is something going on between you two! I told Ricky so!" came the triumphant sound of Megan Brady's voice.

Tara and Jed broke apart and stared in shock at the young couple rushing toward them.

"Megan!" Tara exclaimed with astonishment.

"Ricky!" Jed's astonishment was mixed equally with chagrin.

Megan threw her arms around Tara. "Are you surprised? We arrived about an hour ago and we've been sitting on the steps, waiting for you."

"Surprised is putting it mildly. Talk about timing . . ." Jed muttered as his younger brother heartily shook his hand in greeting.

"We have so much to tell you!" cried Megan, linking one arm with Tara's and the other with Ricky's. "But, first, will you drive us to Rhode Island today? According to Ricky's research, since we've already had our blood tests, we can be married there right away."

"Ricky researched it, huh?" Jed drawled.

Ricky nodded proudly. "While I was stuck in Houston, listening to Dad tell Megan over the phone that I was out with other girls. I wasn't, of course. I was spending every minute making plans to marry her."

Megan gave him a quick, affectionate kiss. "And today he arrived on campus to get me, and here we are! Oh, Tara, I'm so happy. I didn't doubt for one minute that Ricky loved me."

"I know you didn't, Megan," Tara said thoughtfully. She herself certainly had, and she felt ashamed of her lack of faith in the Ramsey her youngest sister loved.

"Well, I guess we're going to have to hear the whole story," Jed said resignedly as he ushered them all inside his apartment. "How did you manage to escape from the Ramsey gulag, Rick?"

"Vanessa engineered the whole thing," Ricky said happily.

"Vanessa?" echoed Tara. "Your sister Vanessa?"

Megan nodded. "Vanessa isn't the scary witch we thought she was, Tara. Not anymore, anyway. She talked to Ricky, and when he told her what their folks were doing to us, she was solidly on our side."

Ricky grinned. "She said it was wrong of Mama and Daddy to completely take over our lives, that we deserved the chance to make our own decisions and mistakes and not waste years of our lives rebelling against Ramsey manipulations."

"That sounds like Vanessa, all right," Jed said. "So how did she spirit you two out of the state?"

"It wasn't easy." Ricky's smile faded. "Dad assigned one of his lackeys to stick to me like a cocklebur. I couldn't even make a phone call without intervention. So when Vanessa said she wanted to take me to visit with her and Linc over at their place, Dad said okay, but the stooge had to go along."

Megan began to bounce excitedly on the sofa. "Wait till you hear how Vanessa got rid of that—that gumshoe, Tara! She drove him way out of town, and then she and Ricky made him get out of the car, took his wallet, and left him on a deserted country road! Then they drove to Austin to pick me up at school."

"Whew! And you don't think Vanessa is scary?" Jed arched his brows. "She's a one-woman commando raid. What did her husband think of all this? Or didn't she bother to inform him?"

Ricky beamed. "Linc was behind her all the way. Literally. He followed us out to that old country road where we ditched the goon. His presence definitely convinced the guy to do what we said. Have you ever seen the muscles on Linc's arms, Jed? Wow! When he rolled up his sleeves and flexed his fingers, Dad's lackey turned pale! Linc didn't have to do another thing or even say a word!"

"Vanessa and Linc drove us to the airport and we flew into Pittsburgh because we promised you that we wouldn't get married until we talked to you first, Tara," Megan added.

"So now we're supposed to lecture you on things like responsibility, and conscientious decision-making, et cetera, et cetera," Jed drawled laconically. "Damn, I feel like we've been cast as the second leads in a Molly Ringwald teen flick. What have we done to deserve that fate?"

Tara slipped onto his lap and linked her arms around his neck. "All I know is that if Ricky and Megan feel about each other the way I feel about you, I have no arguments to offer against their marriage. I love you so much, Jed. I couldn't bear to be apart from you."

Megan and Ricky cheered.

Jed ignored them. "What about a commuter marriage?" he asked Tara, watching her intently. "I remember you mentioning how modern and practical they are."

"They *are* modern and practical." Tara touched her forehead to his and gently rubbed his nose with hers, Eskimo style. "But it's not for me, Jed. Not for us. I want to live with you all the time."

"I feel the same way, sweetheart," Jed murmured.

"So you two are going to get married, huh?" Ricky smiled at them. "We're real happy for you, aren't we, Megan?"

Megan nodded. "And Quentin and Nola will be thrilled. It'll make up for Ricky and me running off." Her big, dark eyes grew serious. "You know how Quentin Ramsey loves to have things his own way—as much as he hates *not* having his own way. We're lucky he won with Jed and Tara, even though Ricky and I thwarted him."

"Dad had nothing to do with Tara and me getting together. He had no expectations as far as either of us were concerned," countered Jed.

Megan and Ricky looked at each other and laughed. "Are you kidding?" exclaimed Ricky. "You two were set up by our daddy, Jed. He's taking bets as to when your wedding will be!"

Jed stared at his younger brother. "Of course we weren't set up, Rick. Tara and I discovered each other all on our own."

Ricky chuckled. "Not according to Daddy. He's been bragging how he used something called inverse logic on you two. He let you both think he'd given up trying to get you together and that he believed Tara's tale about her imaginary boyfriend."

"How did he know that Chad didn't exist?" asked Tara, aghast.

Ricky shrugged. "He had it checked out. And then there was the matter of Carling Templeton—Daddy said he did *not* want to be related to Clayton Templeton, even though they were old friends. So he had to seem enthusiastic about Jed and Carling, so Jed would worry about being trapped into marriage by the two fathers."

"It worked!" Jed gasped. "I was sure those two old connivers were conspiring to marry me off to Carling."

"Daddy's biggest obstacle was getting you and Tara in the same city," continued Ricky, "but he came up with some tale about wanting to save the Southland Mall and sent you up here, supposedly to study the situation, Jed."

Jed stiffened. "Supposedly?" he repeated carefully. "I've *been* studying the situation, I've spent hours putting together a plan to convert Southland to a discount mall, I have chain stores willing to come in and—"

"It was all a ploy, Jed," said Ricky. "Dad went along with your ideas because he wanted an excuse to keep you in Pittsburgh, close to Tara. As soon as you marry her, he'll sell the mall, as he planned to do all along."

"Sell it?" Jed stared at him, staggered. "But Southland Mall is a sentimental favorite of Dad's. He wanted to salvage it and keep it viable and productive because—"

"That's just a tale he spun for you, Jed," Ricky said patiently.

"I can't believe you bought it," Megan added. "Everybody knows that Quentin Ramsey doesn't mix business with sentiment."

"Why, that scheming, conniving snake!" Tara cried, hopping to her feet. "How dare he treat Jed this way? Jed has some terrific plans worked out for the mall. He can make it work as an all discount-store mall. He—"

"I fell right into his trap," Jed said, a flush creeping from his neck to his face. "What a naive idiot I've been to think that Quentin Ramsey actually valued my input on anything, that he would ever take a suggestion of mine and go with it. All the plans I've made, all the calls and contacts . . . and he's planned to sell out all along."

"I love Daddy, and I know he loves us, but he can be an overbearing bully and a genuine creep at times," Ricky said quietly. "It's lucky that we brothers and Vanessa are married—or are *going to be married*—" he added, squeezing Megan's hand, "to people who are strong enough to help us keep Quentin Ramsey from trying to run our lives."

"And speaking of *going to be married*," Megan interjected. "Are you two going to give us a lecture on how we're too young to get married? And why we should play the field and date lots of other people so that someday we *might* find someone else that we love as much as we love each other now?"

Tara hardly heard her. She hadn't taken her eyes from **Jed since** he'd heard Ricky's bald pronouncement about selling the mall. He was staring moodily into space, and she could guess what he was thinking. Her heart began to sink into the roiling pit of her stomach. She had a terrible premonition that she was the pawn in a newly declared Ramsey civil war. And as anyone with even rudimentary knowledge of chess knows, pawns are inevitably discarded and cast aside.

Ricky Ramsey seemed unaware of the effect his revelation had had on his older brother. He was clearly more interested in his own fate. "Megan and I have everything all planned," he offered eagerly in rebuttal to the anticipated lecture that had yet to be delivered. "I'll graduate in the spring and we're going to stay in Austin for the next few years, till Megan gets her degree. We've decided to wait for a few years to have kids, at least until after Megan graduates. And then—"

"Okay, let's go," Jed said decisively, rising to his feet. "Get your stuff, kids, you're eloping to Rhode Island."

Ricky's eyes widened. "Just like that? Don't you want to hear how we plan to manage if Daddy gets ugly and tries to cut off all our money?"

"I don't need to because it'll never happen," Jed said brusquely. "The minute the folks hear you're married, they'll act as if it was their idea all along. They'll buy you a cute little house in Austin and pay a decorator to fix it up for you. They'll throw a gigantic reception in your honor and shower you with gifts. Dad will find Rick a job in Austin so Megan can continue at the university. And if you have a baby a little earlier than planned, no sweat. Dad will hire the best baby nurse money can buy."

"Do you really think so, Jed?" Ricky asked wistfully.

"How can you be so sure?" demanded Megan, her dark eyes shadowed with doubt.

"Because Quentin Ramsey never loses," Jed said tersely. "And if he were to rail against your marriage after you'd eloped, it would prove that he'd lost. So he'll play it like a winner. The fact that Vanessa helped you first gives you a huge advantage. You know the Ramsey family: we can't stand to be outdone or outsmarted by anyone, not even one of our own. Dad can't let Vanessa one-up him on accepting your marriage, so he'll have to outdo her contribution."

Megan and Ricky looked pleased and hugged each other in triumph. Tara wished she could share the young couple's joy, but her heart felt like lead in her chest. She'd heard the unspoken words in Jed's cynical analysis of his father's reaction to the kids' marriage.

"Can't stand to be outdone or outsmarted by anyone, not even one of our own," he'd said. And Tara was certain that to Jed's way of thinking, he'd been both professionally and personally bested by Quentin Ramsey. Now he would retaliate like the fiercely proud, competitive Ramsey that he was.

There was nothing he could do to sabotage his father's plans to sell the Southland Mall—as chairman of the board and principle stockholder Quentin Ramsey held the final say in corporate decisions. But when it came to Quentin's marriage plans for his son . . . why, Jed could efficiently put an end to them by leaving town and Tara Brady.

He was going to drop her, she knew it.

They decided to take Tara's trusty Cougar because it afforded them more room than Jed's made-for-two Lamborghini Countach. Jed hardly said a word during the drive to Providence, Rhode Island. Megan and Ricky happily snuggled in the cramped backseat, where they kissed and snacked on pretzels and soda and listened to tapes on their headsets. They were too wrapped up in each other to notice the silence up front. But Tara was all too aware of it. She sat, taut and rigid, fighting to control the treacherous tears which seemed on the verge of escaping the moment she let down her guard. Jed was making plans, she was certain of it. Plans that did not include her.

Once in Providence, Jed found the justice of the peace without any trouble. Tara and Jed watched

Megan and Ricky complete the paperwork necessary for a marriage license. There was a small fee required and Ricky pulled a few bills from his pocket and paid it, his other hand clutching Megan's.

Tara felt tears fill her eyes. Her baby sister was getting married! This—this isn't the way it should be," she said in a choked whisper, more to herself than to Jed, who hadn't said a word since their arrival. "They should be having a big wedding in a church filled with flowers. Megan should be wearing a beautiful white satin-and-lace dress, not a miniskirt and sweater from Neiman-Marcus. And all our family should be here, our sisters and our nieces and little Connor."

"Is that the kind of wedding you'd like for yourself or for Megan?" Jed asked. "Because it sounds like a nightmare to me, but if that's what you've always dreamed of, I'll put on a monkey suit and we'll have any kind of extravaganza you want."

Tara froze. "Please don't, Jed. I know you don't want to say anything while Megan and Ricky are with us, but you don't have to pretend—"

She tried to swallow the huge boulder that was lodged in her throat, to no avail. When she tried to talk, it blocked her words and when she tried to take a breath, it sounded suspiciously like a sob.

Jed put his hands on her shoulders and turned her around, forcing her to face him. "Don't have to pretend?" he repeated. "Pretend what?" He sounded angry.

"Jed, I know how you feel about being tricked by your father." Her voice trembled. "You're furious with him and—and with me, too."

"Sure, I'm mad at Dad," he agreed. "But why should I be angry with you? You're as much a victim of his manipulations as I am."

She drew a deep breath and summoned every bit of her Brady pride. It was every bit as sustaining as the Ramsey pride, and sometimes just as prickly. "Jed, I know you're not going to marry me," she said swiftly, urgently, before she lost her courage and pleaded with him to do it anyway. "You're not going to give your father the satisfaction of falling in with his plans, especially not after the mall—"

"What are you talking about?" Jed's fingers tightened. "Do you really think I'd drop you just to spite my father? Dammit, Tara, I love you. I thought I'd convinced you of that."

"You've hardly said a word to me or to anyone, since Ricky told you about your father's schemes," she said, gulping back a sob. "You haven't looked at me, you—" She lost the battle with the tears she'd been fighting to suppress, and they gushed from her eyes.

"You're a stupid little fool," Jed said, but his tone made those harsh words sound like an endearment. He pulled her into his arms and threaded his fingers through her hair, caressing her, comforting her. "I'm never going to give you up, Tara. The thought didn't cross my mind once. What did come to mind—and what I've been preoccupied with—are my plans for the Southland Mall. I've never enjoyed a project more and I'm not going to quit and return to Houston when my daddy snaps his fingers."

Tara slowly raised her head. "You're not?"

"No. I have it all worked out. You and I are going to stay in Pittsburgh, at least until your contract with the station is up. Meanwhile, I'll be working on changing the mall. You see, I'm going to offer, or maybe threaten is the better word, to buy Southland from Ramsey and Sons. I know Vanessa will agree to help finance me, and maybe Rad and Slade will, too. It won't really matter. Dad won't be able to stand the prospect of any Ramsey infighting. He'll scrap his plans to sell and insist that I stay and finish the job. *Then* we'll make a decision on whether to keep or sell the mall."

As Tara gazed at him, relief so sharp it was almost physical in intensity surged through her. She'd been right. Just like a true Ramsey, he had been plotting revenge. But she wasn't a part of it. The Southland Mall was. She clutched him and clung to him, burying her head in his chest.

"You deserve to be turned over my knee and spanked for having so little faith in me," Jed continued severely. "But I'll forgive you because until very recently, I didn't deserve any woman's faith or trust. Or love."

They were about to kiss when an excited Megan and Ricky rushed over to them. "We're all ready," Ricky exclaimed. "I have the ring and everything. We need you two to sign the paper as our witnesses and then the J.P. will marry us."

"You're a lucky guy, Rick," Jed said, clapping his brother on the back. "I wish Tara and I were getting married this afternoon. We could be each other's witnesses, have a double wedding. Not to mention a wedding night tonight."

Megan blushed. "Well, why don't you?" she suggested.

"Tara wants a big wed—" Jed began.

"No, I don't," Tara interrupted. "I thought a big, traditional wedding would be nice for Megan, not for me. Now I think it'll be perfect for Colleen."

A huge grin spread slowly across Jed's face. "Then you'd consider marrying me today? Here? Right now?"

"I don't have to consider it for a second." Tara flung her arms around him. "Oh, Jed, I'd love to marry you today. Here. Right now."

A short while later, the justice of the peace performed the double ceremony, shook hands with the grooms, kissed the cheeks of the brides and wished both couples the best of luck.

"I have a surprise for you two, a wedding present from Tara and me," Jed announced to the younger Ramsey couple during the happy drive back to Pittsburgh. "We're treating you to an all-expense-paid honeymoon in the Caribbean resort of your choice. We'll call the travel agent as soon as we get back to the apartment and you can leave tonight."

Ricky was ecstatic, and Megan cried with joy. They both proclaimed Jed the most generous, most understanding brother in the whole world and promised to make him godfather of their first child.

In the front seat, Tara cuddled even closer and whispered lovingly in his ear, "You're also the craftiest brother in the whole world."

"Ah, you've seen through my plot to get rid of them," he said with a positively wicked grin. "How well you know me, my beautiful bride."

A few hours later, Megan and Ricky were dispatched to an exclusive resort in Jamaica, and Tara and Jed toasted the younger newlyweds and each other with a bottle of chilled champagne. Tara, recalling the last memorable time she'd tangled with alcohol, limited herself to one small glass.

"And now, my love," Jed took the empty glass from her and scooped her up into his arms. "My sweet bride, who has miraculously managed to remain a virgin during a Ramsey courtship, *at last* it's time for us to have a good old-fashioned wedding night."

Her arms encircled his neck and she laid her head against his shoulder as he carried her to his bedroom. She was excited and expectant and trembling with arousal. "Oh, Jed, I feel as if I've been waiting all my life for you," she said with a soft sigh.

"I know, sweetheart, I feel the same way," he said, setting her gently, carefully, down on the bed.

He began to undress her, kissing her and whispering words of love and reassurance as he deftly removed each garment. Her blue, beige, and rose dress, her stockings, her lacy blue slip and matching bra and panties all landed in a colorful heap at her feet. He pulled off his own clothing just as quickly, and they joined Tara's in the growing pile on the floor beside the bed.

"You're so beautiful," he murmured, staring down at her. With a deep sigh, he touched her breasts. They fit perfectly in his palms and he leaned down and kissed first one tight, tingling pink nipple, then the other.

Hot streaks of sensation flamed through her and she reached out to touch the furred thickness of his chest. Her eyes swept shyly over him, from his wide, hard chest to his taut stomach and narrow hips, the long, muscular legs, and—her eyes widened and she blushed. He was so big, so strong and hard. For the first time, Tara felt a qualm of unease.

Jed watched her; he was staring just as intently at her. "It's going to be all right, baby," he said softly, drawing her into his arms for a long, lingering kiss. Slowly, he eased her back onto the mattress, lying close beside her. "I love you so much, my precious, my wife."

She touched his mouth, the smooth-shaven curve of his jaw, the tanned column of his throat with her fingers. "I love you, Jed," she whispered. And he loved her; she was his wife. Her confidence returned in full measure. This was her wedding night and she was going to do her part to make it a dream come true for both her and her husband.

Her hands moved over his shoulders, his back, learning him, loving him. And while her fingers continued their sensual exploration, Jed caressed the slender hollow of her waist, the enticing curve of her hips, then cupped and fondled her breasts in a slow, sensuous massage.

Tara moaned and arched voluptuously against his hands. Her eyes drifted languidly to Jed's face and she saw the desire burning in the blue-gray depths of his eyes. He smiled a slow, sexy smile that took her breath away, then lowered his head to take one pink-tipped crest into his mouth.

Tara could hardly breathe. She strained closer, craving more of him, *needing* him with an urgency she had never known. When he began to sensuously suck her sensitive nipples, she cried out at the intensity of the pleasure.

"Oh, Jed, it feels so good," she told him, holding nothing back, sighing and whispering her pleasure as they kissed and caressed. "You feel so good," she said, daring to touch the bold masculine shaft.

She felt a shudder convulse his body and a thrill of sheer feminine power raced through her. She stroked him, experimenting, playing, learning until Jed was breathless and fighting for control.

"You're so responsive, my darling, so passionate, so incredibly exciting," he murmured unsteadily. His hand closed possessively over the moist softness of her femininity.

Tara moaned as his fingers rubbed and caressed and probed, sending her spiraling to sensual heights she never dreamed existed. She felt so sexy, so wild, and so deeply in love with him.

Her hips arched in a primitive, erotic rhythm entirely beyond her control. Her heart thudded violently against her ribs and she felt herself slipping over some unknown invisible edge as every one of her nerves drew tight to focus on the hot pulsing deep within her.

"Let go, baby, let it happen," Jed commanded, his voice husky and thick with passion. "Don't hold back, Tara. Come to me."

White hot flames of sensation seemed to engulf her; she felt as if she were flying apart. And then she was convulsed with paroxysms of rapturous pleasure so consuming that she was hardly aware of him moving over her and settling himself between her legs.

He merged their bodies with one masterful stroke. "You're inside me," Tara gasped and clung tightly to him. She'd never dreamed it could be like this, that it would feel so natural and right to open herself to a man, to envelop him intimately. She blushed hotly. She'd never thought she would enjoy it so much, but she loved this full feeling of her husband inside her. She loved the way he was moving within her, deep, slow strokes which accelerated and made her move with him, for him, until the ever-tightening coil of tension mounting and building within her suddenly snapped.

Tara cried his name as incredible waves of pleasure lashed through her. The sensual force of her climax catapulted Jed into the same tempestuous whirlwind which had claimed her, and together they rode the impassioned storm until it subsided into a blissful, languorous glow.

"Oh, Jed, it was wonderful," Tara said softly. "You're

wonderful." She was curled up next to him, her head on his shoulder, her hands caressing him lightly, lovingly. She'd never felt more comfortable or content in her life. "I love you so much."

"I love you even more now than I did before we went to bed," Jed said wondrously. "I didn't think—I never knew—that you could use sex to create more and more love." He seemed awed by the concept, as if he'd discovered one of life's great truths.

"I believe it's called sexual bonding," Tara said with a drowsy sigh. "You're not the only one who occasionally catches Oprah Winfrey's show," she added, smiling languidly.

"Sexual bonding." Jed grinned. "Well, honey, ours is as explosive and as strong as nuclear fission. We're together forever." He cupped her cheek in his big hand and leaned down to tenderly kiss her lips. "I like knowing that my lover is my wife," he murmured softly, giving her an affectionate, playful squeeze. "And all the fooling around we did before we were married made tonight that much more exciting and satisfying."

She slipped her smooth, slender leg between his hard, hair-roughened ones, savoring the differing textures between them. "If I'd known all that fooling around would lead to something as fantastic as this . . ." Her voice trailed off on a blissful sigh. "I think I would've gone to bed with you the first time you tried to get me there."

"This is going to sound strange, coming from a smooth operator like me, but it wouldn't have been as good, Tara." Jed stroked her hair with loving tenderness. "It's our love, our marriage, that made it so much more than great sex."

She smiled into his eyes. "So, speaking as a *reformed* smooth operator, you think that being in love and married makes for the best sex?" She'd known that all along, of course.

"Absolutely," Jed said. His gray eyes gleamed. "And I didn't come by that information on any TV talk show,

Tara. I learned it myself here tonight. From you. With you."

"I've learned a lot tonight, too, Jed." She moved sinuously against him. "But there's so much more I want to learn." Her voice was seductively sweet. She moved to lie on top of him, stringing sensuous little kisses along his neck. "With you and from you. Will you teach me?"

Jed groaned as a fierce wave of pleasure whipped through him. "Tara, there isn't anything I'd rather do," he assured her, taking her mouth in a possessive kiss.

Epilogue

Both the combined Ramsey and Brady families were delighted with Tara and Jed's marriage, and they accepted and supported Ricky and Megan's marriage, just as Jed had predicted.

He'd also correctly assessed his father's reaction to his intention of buying the Southland Mall in a financial alliance with his sister and brothers. After a brief board meeting, Jed received word to stay on in Pittsburgh and complete Southland's transition from dying, outdated mall to thriving discount-store mall. Tara was pleased to be able to work out her contract at Double Q Radio, and the happy couple rented a condo and settled in for their year in Pittsburgh.

Anne Linaberger's effective interview with Kayci Cann was picked up by all the networks and earned her national exposure. She was hired away by a rival network affiliate in New York City.

Along with the inevitable barrage of media jokes—*Saxon Was Canned*, read one of the many tasteless headlines—Kayci was inundated with letters of sympathy and money, along with book offers from a host of publishers. Her staunchest supporters were Senator Clayton Templeton and his daughter Carling, who kept in touch with her throughout her pregnancy. When

Kayci's baby boy was born, the child was anonymously adopted by a couple who, as Senator Templeton poignantly related, "wept with joy when the infant was placed in their arms."

Melissa Minger and Leslie Polk were married a few months after Tara and Jed's wedding and jointly carried on their research at CMU.

Fred Polk's parties continued to be noted in the Seen column, although Tara and Jed never attended another one.

The voters of Pennsylvania voted overwhelmingly against Glenn Saxon in his reelection bid to the senate. His opponent, Nancy Auer, who'd been nominated as a sacrificial candidate against the seemingly unbeatable Saxon, found herself on the way to Washington as a United States senator. Saxon's presidential campaign ended before it began, and he moved to California where he dropped from the public eye. Saxon's wife, after divorcing him and winning a large settlement and custody of the children, became the spokesperson for a national group of displaced homemakers. Her story was also optioned by several publishing houses.

Erin and Rad Ramsey's son Christopher was born, prompting Quentin Ramsey to jovially consider changing the name of the family firm to Ramsey and Sons and Grandsons. He was only half kidding.

With all his children married, Quentin turned his full attention back to his business, as his children and their spouses made it quite clear that any interference in their respective marriages would not be tolerated. He traveled with his wife and doted on his grandchildren and occasionally found himself worrying about the remaining single Brady sister, Colleen. He was very fond of her and knew she would be much happier if she were married. . . .

THE EDITOR'S CORNER

A critic once wrote that LOVESWEPT books have "the most off-the-wall titles" of any romance line. And recently, I got a letter from a reader asking me who is responsible for the "unusual titles" of our books. (Our fans are so polite; I'll bet she wanted to substitute "strange" for unusual!) Whether off-the-wall or unusual—I prefer to think of them as memorable—our titles are dreamed up by authors as well as editors. (We editors must take the responsibility for the most outrageous titles, though.) Next month you can look forward to six wonderful LOVESWEPTs that are as original, strong, amusing—yes, even as off-the-wall—as their titles.

First, **McKNIGHT IN SHINING ARMOR,** LOVESWEPT #276, by Tami Hoag, is an utterly heartwarming story of a young divorced woman, Kelsie Connors, who has two children to raise while holding down two *very* unusual jobs. She's trying to be the complete Superwoman when she meets hero Alec McKnight. Their first encounter, while hilarious, holds the potential for disaster . . . as black lace lingerie flies through the air of the conservative advertising executive's office. But Alec is enchanted, not enraged—and then Kelsie has to wonder if the "disaster" isn't what he's done to her heart. A joyous reading experience.

SHOWDOWN AT LIZARD ROCK, LOVESWEPT #277, by Sandra Chastain, features one of the most gorgeous and exciting pairs of lovers ever. Kaylyn Smith has the body of Wonder Woman and the face of Helen of Troy, and handsome hunk King Vandergriff realizes the

(continued)

moment he sets eyes on her that he's met his match. She is standing on top of Lizard Rock, protesting his construction company's building of a private club on the town's landmark. King just climbs right up there and carries her down . . . but she doesn't surrender. (Well, not immediately.) You'll delight in the feisty shenanigans of this marvelous couple.

CALIFORNIA ROYALE, LOVESWEPT #278, by Deborah Smith, is one of the most heart-stoppingly beautiful of love stories. Shea Somerton is elegant and glamorous just like the resort she runs; Duke Araiza is sexy and fast just like the Thoroughbreds he raises and trains. Both have heartbreaking pain in their pasts. And each has the fire and the understanding that the other needs. But their goals put them at cross-purposes, and neither of them can bend . . . until a shadow from Shea's early days falls over their lives. A thrilling romance.

Get out the box of tissues when you settle down to enjoy **WINTER'S DAUGHTER,** LOVESWEPT #279, by Kathleen Creighton, because you're bound to get a good laugh and a good cry from this marvelous love story. Tannis Winter, disguised as a bag-lady, has gone out onto the streets to learn about the plight of the homeless and to search for cures for their ills. But so has town councilman Dillon James, a "derelict" with mysterious attractions for the unknowing Tannis. Dillon is instantly bewitched by her courage and compassion . . . by the scent of summer on her skin and the brilliance of winter in her eyes. Their hunger for each other grows quickly . . . and to ravenous proportions. Only a risky confrontation can clear up the misunderstandings they face, so that they can finally have it all. We think you're going to treasure this very rich and very dramatic love story.

Completing the celebration of her fifth year as a published writer, the originator of continuing character romances, Iris Johansen, gives us the breathlessly emotional love story of the Sheik you met this month, exciting Damon El Karim, in **STRONG, HOT WINDS,** LOVESWEPT #280. Damon has vowed to punish the lovely Cory Brandel, the mother of his son, whom she's kept secret from him. To do so, he has her kidnapped with the

(continued)

boy and brought to Kasmara. But in his desert palace, as they set each other off, his sense of barbaric justice and her fury at his betrayal quickly turn into quite different emotions. Bewildered by the tenderness and the wild need he feels for her, Damon fears he can never have Cory's love. But at last, Cory has begun to understand what makes this complex and charismatic man tick—and she fears she isn't strong enough to give him the enduring love he so much deserves! Crème de la crème from Iris Johansen. I'm sure you join all of us at Bantam in wishing her not five, but *fifty* more years of creating great love stories!

Closing out the month in a very big way is **PARADISE CAFE**, LOVESWEPT #281, by Adrienne Staff. And what a magnificent tale this is. Beautiful Abby Clarke is rescued by ruggedly handsome outdoorsman Jack Gallagher—a man of few words and fast moves, especially when trying to haul in the lady whom destiny has put in his path. But Abby is not a risk taker. She's an earnest, hardworking young woman who's always put her family first . . . but Jack is an impossible man to walk away from with his sweet, wild passion that makes her yearn to forget about being safe. And Jack is definitely *not* safe for Abby . . . he's a man with wandering feet. You'll relish the way the stay-at-home and the vagabond find that each has a home in the center of the other's heart. A true delight.

I trust that you'll agree with me that the six LOVE-SWEPTs next month are as memorable as their off-the-wall titles!

Enjoy!

Carolyn Nichols

Carolyn Nichols
  Editor
LOVESWEPT
Bantam Books
666 Fifth Avenue
New York, NY 10103

THE HOMETOWN HUNK CONTEST

FOR EVERY WOMAN WHO HAS EVER SAID—
"I know a man who looks just like the hero of this book"
—HAVE WE GOT A CONTEST FOR YOU!

To help celebrate our fifth year of publishing LOVESWEPT we are having a fabulous, fun-filled event called THE HOMETOWN HUNK contest. We are going to reissue six classic early titles by six of your favorite authors.

> *DARLING OBSTACLES* by Barbara Boswell
> *IN A CLASS BY ITSELF* by Sandra Brown
> *C.J.'S FATE* by Kay Hooper
> *THE LADY AND THE UNICORN* by Iris Johansen
> *CHARADE* by Joan Elliott Pickart
> *FOR THE LOVE OF SAMI* by Fayrene Preston

Here, as in the backs of all July, August, and September 1988 LOVESWEPTS you will find "cover notes" just like the ones we prepare at Bantam as the background for our art director to create our covers. These notes will describe the hero and heroine, give a teaser on the plot, and suggest a scene for the cover. Your part in the contest will be to see if a great looking local man—or men, if your hometown is so blessed—fits our description of one of the heroes of the six books we will reissue.

THE HOMETOWN HUNK who is selected (one for each of the six titles) will be flown to New York via United Airlines and will stay at the Loews Summit Hotel—the ideal hotel for business or pleasure in midtown Manhattan—for two nights. All travel arrangements made by Reliable Travel International, Incorporated. He will be the model for the new cover of the book which will be released in mid-1989. The six people who send in the winning photos of their HOMETOWN HUNK will receive a pre-selected assortment of LOVESWEPT books free for one year. Please see the Official Rules above the Official Entry Form for full details and restrictions.

We can't wait to start judging those pictures! Oh, and you must let the man you've chosen know that you're entering him in the contest. After all, if he wins he'll have to come to New York.

Have fun. Here's your chance to get the cover-lover of your dreams!

Carolyn Nichols

Carolyn Nichols
Editor
LOVESWEPT
Bantam Books
666 Fifth Avenue
New York, NY 10102–0023

THE HOMETOWN HUNK CONTEST

DARLING OBSTACLES
(Originally Published as LOVESWEPT #95)
By Barbara Boswell

COVER NOTES

The Characters:

Hero:
GREG WILDER's gorgeous body and "to-die-for" good looks
haven't hurt him in the dating department, but when
most women discover he's a widower with four kids, they
head for the hills! Greg has the hard, muscular build of an
athlete, and his light brown hair, which he wears neatly
parted on the side, is streaked blond by the sun. Add to
that his aquamarine blue eyes that sparkle when he laughs,
and his sensual mouth and generous lower lip, and you're
probably wondering what woman in her right mind
wouldn't want Greg's strong, capable surgeon's hands working their magic on her—kids or no kids!

Personality Traits:
An acclaimed neurosurgeon, Greg Wilder is a celebrity of
sorts in the planned community of Woodland, Maryland.
Authoritative, debonair, self-confident, his reputation for
engaging in one casual relationship after another almost
overshadows his prowess as a doctor. In reality, Greg
dates more out of necessity than anything else, since he
has to attend one social function after another. He considers most of the events boring and wishes he could
spend more time with his children. But his profession is a
difficult and demanding one—and being both father and
mother to four kids isn't any less so. A thoughtful, generous, sometimes befuddled father, Greg tries to do it all.
Cerebral, he uses his intellect and skill rather than physical
strength to win his victories. However, he never expected
to come up against one Mary Magdalene May!

Heroine:
MARY MAGDALENE MAY, called Maggie by her friends, is the thirty-two-year-old mother of three children. She has shoulder-length auburn hair, and green eyes that shout her Irish heritage. With high cheekbones and an upturned nose covered with a smattering of freckles, Maggie thinks of herself more as the girl-next-door type. Certainly, she believes, she could never be one of Greg Wilder's beautiful escorts.

Setting: The small town of Woodland, Maryland

The Story:
Surgeon Greg Wilder wanted to court the feisty and beautiful widow who'd been caring for his four kids, but she just wouldn't let him past her doorstep! Sure that his interest was only casual, and that he preferred more sophisticated women, Maggie May vowed to keep Greg at arm's length. But he wouldn't take no for an answer. And once he'd crashed through her defenses and pulled her into his arms, he was tireless—and reckless—in his campaign to win her over. Maggie had found it tough enough to resist one determined doctor; now he threatened to call in his kids and hers as reinforcements—seven rowdy snags to romance!

Cover scene:
As if romancing Maggie weren't hard enough, Greg can't seem to find time to spend with her without their children around. Stealing a private moment on the stairs in Maggie's house, Greg and Maggie embrace. She is standing one step above him, but she still has to look up at him to see into his eyes. Greg's hands are on her hips, and her hands are resting on his shoulders. Maggie is wearing a very sheer, short pink nightgown, and Greg has on wheat-colored jeans and a navy and yellow striped rugby shirt. Do they have time to kiss?

THE HOMETOWN HUNK CONTEST

IN A CLASS BY ITSELF
(Originally Published as LOVESWEPT #66)
By Sandra Brown

COVER NOTES

The Characters:

Hero:
LOGAN WEBSTER would have no trouble posing for a Scandinavian travel poster. His wheat-colored hair always seems to be tousled, defying attempts to control it, and falls across his wide forehead. Thick eyebrows one shade darker than his hair accentuate his crystal blue eyes. He has a slender nose that flairs slightly over a mouth that testifies to both sensitivity and strength. The faint lines around his eyes and alongside his mouth give the impression that reaching the ripe age of 30 wasn't all fun and games for him. Logan's square, determined jaw is punctuated by a vertical cleft. His broad shoulders and narrow waist add to his tall, lean appearance.

Personality traits:
Logan Webster has had to scrape and save and fight for everything he's gotten. Born into a poor farm family, he was driven to succeed and overcome his "wrong side of the tracks" image. His businesses include cattle, real estate, and natural gas. Now a pillar of the community, Logan's life has been a true rags-to-riches story. Only Sandra Brown's own words can describe why he is masculinity epitomized: "Logan had 'the walk,' that saddle-tramp saunter that was inherent to native Texan men, passed down through generations of cowboys. It was, without even trying to be, sexy. The unconscious roll of the hips, the slow strut, the flexed knees, the slouching stance, the deceptive laziness that hid a latent aggressiveness." Wow! And not only does he have "the walk," but he's fun

and generous and kind. Even with his wealth, he feels at home living in his small hometown with simple, hard-working, middle-class, backbone-of-America folks. A born leader, people automatically gravitate toward him.

Heroine:
DANI QUINN is a sophisticated twenty-eight-year-old woman. Dainty, her body compact, she is utterly feminine. Dani's pale, lustrous hair is moonlight and honey spun together, and because it is very straight, she usually wears it in a chignon. With golden eyes to match her golden hair, Dani is the one woman Logan hasn't been able to get off his mind for the ten years they've been apart.

Setting: Primarily on Logan's ranch in East Texas.

The Story:
Ten years had passed since Dani Quinn had graduated from high school in the small Texas town, ten years since the night her elopement with Logan Webster had ended in disaster. Now Dani approached her tenth reunion with uncertainty. Logan would be there . . . Logan, the only man who'd ever made her shiver with desire and need, but would she have the courage to face the fury in his eyes? She couldn't defend herself against his anger and hurt—to do so would demand she reveal the secret sorrow she shared with no one. Logan's touch had made her his so long ago. Could he reach past the pain to make her his for all time?

Cover Scene:
It's sunset, and Logan and Dani are standing beside the swimming pool on his ranch, embracing. The pool is surrounded by semitropical plants and lush flower beds. In the distance, acres of rolling pasture land resembling a green lake undulate into dense, piney woods. Dani is wearing a strapless, peacock blue bikini and sandals with leather ties that wrap around her ankles. Her hair is straight and loose, falling to the middle of her back. Logan has on a light-colored pair of corduroy shorts and a short-sleeved designer knit shirt in a pale shade of yellow.

THE HOMETOWN HUNK CONTEST

C.J.'S FATE
(Originally Published as LOVESWEPT #32)
By Kay Hooper

COVER NOTES

The Characters:

Hero:
FATE WESTON easily could have walked straight off an
Indian reservation. His raven black hair and strong, well-
molded features testify to his heritage. But somewhere
along the line genetics threw Fate a curve—his eyes are
the deepest, darkest blue imaginable! Above those blue
eyes are dark slanted eyebrows, and fanning out from
those eyes are faint laugh lines—the only sign of the fact
that he's thirty-four years old. Tall, Fate moves with easy,
loose-limbed grace. Although he isn't an athlete, Fate takes
very good care of himself, and it shows in his strong
physique. Striking at first glance and fascinating with
each succeeding glance, the serious expressions on his
face make him look older than his years, but with one
smile he looks boyish again.

Personality traits:
Fate possesses a keen sense of humor. His heavy-lidded,
intelligent eyes are capable of concealment, but there is a
shrewdness in them that reveals the man hadn't needed
college or a law degree to be considered intelligent. The set
of his head tells you that he is proud—perhaps even a bit
arrogant. He is attractive and perfectly well aware of that
fact. Unconventional, paradoxical, tender, silly, lusty, gentle, comical, serious, absurd, and endearing are all words
that come to mind when you think of Fate. He is not
ashamed to be everything a man can be. A defense attorney by profession, one can detect a bit of frustrated actor
in his character. More than anything else, though, it's the

impression of humor about him—reinforced by the elusive dimple in his cheek—that makes Fate Weston a scrumptious hero!

Heroine:
C.J. ADAMS is a twenty-six-year-old research librarian. Unaware of her own attractiveness, C.J. tends to play down her pixylike figure and tawny gold eyes. But once she meets Fate, she no longer feels that her short, burnished copper curls and the sprinkling of freckles on her nose make her unappealing. He brings out the vixen in her, and changes the smart, bookish woman who professed to have no interest in men into the beautiful, sexy woman she really was all along. Now, if only he could get her to tell him what C.J. stands for!

Setting: Ski lodge in Aspen, Colorado

The Story:
C.J. Adams had been teased enough about her seeming lack of interest in the opposite sex. On a ski trip with her five best friends, she impulsively embraced a handsome stranger, pretending they were secret lovers—and the delighted lawyer who joined in her impetuous charade seized the moment to deepen the kiss. Astonished at his reaction, C.J. tried to nip their romance in the bud—but found herself nipping at his neck instead! She had met her match in a man who could answer her witty remarks with clever ripostes of his own, and a lover whose caresses aroused in her a passionate need she'd never suspected that she could feel. Had destiny somehow tossed them together?

Cover Scene:
C.J. and Fate virtually have the ski slopes to themselves early one morning, and they take advantage of it! Frolicking in a snow drift, Fate is covering C.J. with snow—and kisses! They are flushed from the cold weather and from the excitement of being in love. C.J. is wearing a sky-blue, one-piece, tight-fitting ski outfit that zips down the front. Fate is wearing a navy blue parka and matching ski pants.

THE HOMETOWN HUNK CONTEST

THE LADY AND THE UNICORN
(Originally Published as LOVESWEPT #29)
By Iris Johansen

COVER NOTES

The Characters:

Hero:
Not classically handsome, RAFE SANTINE's blunt, craggy features reinforce the quality of overpowering virility about him. He has wide, Slavic cheekbones and a bold, thrusting chin, which give the impression of strength and authority. Thick black eyebrows are set over piercing dark eyes. He wears his heavy, dark hair long. His large frame measures in at almost six feet four inches, and it's hard to believe that a man with such brawny shoulders and strong thighs could exhibit the pantherlike grace which characterizes Rafe's movements. Rafe Santine is definitely a man to be reckoned with, and heroine Janna Cannon does just that!

Personality traits:
Our hero is a man who radiates an aura of power and danger, and women find him intriguing and irresistible. Rafe Santine is a self-made billionaire at the age of thirty-eight. Almost entirely self-educated, he left school at sixteen to work on his first construction job, and by the time he was twenty-three, he owned the company. From there he branched out into real estate, computers, and oil. Rafe reportedly changes mistresses as often as he changes shirts. His reputation for ruthless brilliance has been earned over years of fighting to the top of the economic ladder from the slums of New York. His gruff manner and hard personality hide the tender, vulnerable side of him. Rafe also possesses an insatiable thirst for knowledge that is a passion with him. Oddly enough, he has a wry sense of

humor that surfaces unexpectedly from time to time. And, though cynical to the extreme, he never lets his natural skepticism interfere with his innate sense of justice.

Heroine:
JANNA CANNON, a game warden for a small wildlife preserve, is a very dedicated lady. She is tall at five feet nine inches and carries herself in a stately way. Her long hair is dark brown and is usually twisted into a single thick braid in back. Of course, Rafe never lets her keep her hair braided when they make love! Janna is one quarter Cherokee Indian by heritage, and she possesses the dark eyes and skin of her ancestors.

Setting: Rafe's estate in Carmel, California

The Story:
Janna Cannon scaled the high walls of Rafe Santine's private estate, afraid of nothing and determined to appeal to the powerful man who could save her beloved animal preserve. She bewitched his guard dogs, then cast a spell of enchantment over him as well. Janna's profound grace, her caring nature, made the tough and proud Rafe grow mercurial in her presence. She offered him a gift he'd never risked reaching out for before—but could he trust his own emotions enough to open himself to her love?

Cover Scene:
In the gazebo overlooking the rugged cliffs at the edge of the Pacific Ocean, Rafe and Janna share a passionate moment together. The gazebo is made of redwood and the interior is small and cozy. Scarlet cushions cover the benches, and matching scarlet curtains hang from the eaves, caught back by tasseled sashes to permit the sea breeze to whip through the enclosure. Rafe is wearing black suede pants and a charcoal gray crew-neck sweater. Janna is wearing a safari-style khaki shirt-and-slacks outfit and suede desert boots. They embrace against the breathtaking backdrop of wild, crashing, white-crested waves pounding the rocks and cliffs below.

THE HOMETOWN HUNK CONTEST

CHARADE
(Originally Published as LOVESWEPT #74)
By Joan Elliott Pickart

COVER NOTES

The Characters:

Hero:
The phrase tall, dark, and handsome was coined to describe TENNES WHITNEY. His coal black hair reaches past his collar in back, and his fathomless steel gray eyes are framed by the kind of thick, dark lashes that a woman would kill to have. Darkly tanned, Tennes has a straight nose and a square chin, with—you guessed it!—a Kirk Douglas cleft. Tennes oozes masculinity and virility. He's a handsome son-of-a-gun!

Personality traits:
A shrewd, ruthless business tycoon, Tennes is a man of strength and principle. He's perfected the art of buying floundering companies and turning them around financially, then selling them at a profit. He possesses a sixth sense about business—in short, he's a winner! But there are two sides to his personality. Always in cool command, Tennes, who fears no man or challenge, is rendered emotionally vulnerable when faced with his elderly aunt's illness. His deep devotion to the woman who raised him clearly casts him as a warm, compassionate guy—not at all like the tough-as-nails executive image he presents. Leave it to heroine Whitney Jordan to discover the real man behind the complicated enigma.

Heroine:
WHITNEY JORDAN's russet-colored hair floats past her shoulders in glorious waves. Her emerald green eyes, full breasts, and long, slender legs—not to mention her peaches-

and-cream complexion—make her eye-poppingly attractive. How can Tennes resist the twenty-six-year-old beauty? And how can Whitney consider becoming serious with him? If their romance flourishes, she may end up being Whitney Whitney!

Setting: Los Angeles, California

The Story:
One moment writer Whitney Jordan was strolling the aisles of McNeil's Department Store, plotting the untimely demise of a soap opera heartthrob; the next, she was nearly knocked over by a real-life stunner who implored her to be his fiancée! The ailing little gray-haired aunt who'd raised him had one final wish, he said—to see her dear nephew Tennes married to the wonderful girl he'd described in his letters . . . only that girl hadn't existed—until now! Tennes promised the masquerade would last only through lunch, but Whitney gave such an inspired performance that Aunt Olive refused to let her go. And what began as a playful romantic deception grew more breathlessly real by the minute. . . .

Cover Scene:
Whitney's living room is bright and cheerful. The gray carpeting and blue sofa with green and blue throw pillows gives the apartment a cool but welcoming appearance. Sitting on the sofa next to Tennes, Whitney is wearing a black crepe dress that is simply cut but stunning. It is cut low over her breasts and held at the shoulders by thin straps. The skirt falls to her knees in soft folds and the bodice is nipped in at the waist with a matching belt. She has on black high heels, but prefers not to wear any jewelry to spoil the simplicity of the dress. Tennes is dressed in a black suit with a white silk shirt and a deep red tie.

THE HOMETOWN HUNK CONTEST

FOR THE LOVE OF SAMI
(Originally Published as LOVESWEPT #34)
By Fayrene Preston

COVER NOTES

Hero:
DANIEL PARKER-ST. JAMES is every woman's dream come true. With glossy black hair and warm, reassuring blue eyes, he makes our heroine melt with just a glance. Daniel's lean face is chiseled into assertive planes. His lips are full and firmly sculptured, and his chin has the determined and arrogant thrust to it only a man who's sure of himself can carry off. Daniel has a lot in common with Clark Kent. Both wear glasses, and when Daniel removes them to make love to Sami, she thinks he really is Superman!

Personality traits:
Daniel Parker-St. James is one of the Twin Cities' most respected attorneys. He's always in the news, either in the society columns with his latest society lady, or on the front page with his headline cases. He's brilliant and takes on only the toughest cases—usually those that involve millions of dollars. Daniel has a reputation for being a deadly opponent in the courtroom. Because he's from a socially prominent family and is a Harvard graduate, it's expected that he'll run for the Senate one day. Distinguished-looking and always distinctively dressed—he's fastidious about his appearance—Daniel gives off an unassailable air of authority and absolute control.

Heroine:
SAMUELINA (SAMI) ADKINSON is secretly a wealthy heiress. No one would guess. She lives in a converted warehouse loft, dresses to suit no one but herself, and dabbles in the creative arts. Sami is twenty-six years old, with

long, honey-colored hair. She wears soft, wispy bangs and has very thick brown lashes framing her golden eyes. Of medium height, Sami has to look up to gaze into Daniel's deep blue eyes.

Setting: St. Paul, Minnesota

The Story:
Unpredictable heiress Sami Adkinson had endeared herself to the most surprising people—from the bag ladies in the park she protected . . . to the mobster who appointed himself her guardian . . . to her exasperated but loving friends. Then Sami was arrested while demonstrating to save baby seals, and it took powerful attorney Daniel Parker-St. James to bail her out. Daniel was smitten, soon cherishing Sami and protecting her from her night fears. Sami reveled in his love—and resisted it too. And holding on to Sami, Daniel discovered, was like trying to hug quicksilver. . . .

Cover Scene:
The interior of Daniel's house is very grand and supremely formal, the decor sophisticated, refined, and quietly tasteful, just like Daniel himself. Rich traditional fabrics cover plush oversized custom sofas and Regency wing chairs. Queen Anne furniture is mixed with Chippendale and is subtly complemented with Oriental accent pieces. In the library, floor-to-ceiling bookcases filled with rare books provide the backdrop for Sami and Daniel's embrace. Sami is wearing a gold satin sheath gown. The dress has a high neckline, but in back is cut provocatively to the waist. Her jewels are exquisite. The necklace is made up of clusters of flowers created by large, flawless diamonds. From every cluster a huge, perfectly matched teardrop emerald hangs. The earrings are composed of an even larger flower cluster, and an equally huge teardrop-shaped emerald hangs from each one. Daniel is wearing a classic, elegant tuxedo.

LOVESWEPT® HOMETOWN HUNK CONTEST

OFFICIAL RULES

> IN A CLASS BY ITSELF by Sandra Brown
> FOR THE LOVE OF SAMI by Fayrene Preston
> C.J.'S FATE by Kay Hooper
> THE LADY AND THE UNICORN by Iris Johansen
> CHARADE by Joan Elliott Pickart
> DARLING OBSTACLES by Barbara Boswell

1. NO PURCHASE NECESSARY. Enter the HOMETOWN HUNK contest by completing the Official Entry Form below and enclosing a sharp color full-length photograph (easy to see details, with the photo being no smaller than 2½″ × 3½″) of the man you think perfectly represents one of the heroes from the above-listed books which are described in the accompanying Loveswept cover notes. Please be sure to fill out the Official Entry Form completely, and also be sure to clearly print on the back of the man's photograph the man's name, address, city, state, zip code, telephone number, date of birth, your name, address, city, state, zip code, telephone number, your relationship, if any, to the man (e.g. wife, girlfriend) as well as the title of the Loveswept book for which you are entering the man. If you do not have an Official Entry Form, you can print all of the required information on a 3″ × 5″ card and attach it to the photograph with all the necessary information printed on the back of the photograph as well. YOUR HERO MUST SIGN BOTH THE BACK OF THE OFFICIAL ENTRY FORM (OR 3″ × 5″ CARD) AND THE PHOTOGRAPH TO SIGNIFY HIS CONSENT TO BEING ENTERED IN THE CONTEST. Completed entries should be sent to:

> BANTAM BOOKS
> HOMETOWN HUNK CONTEST
> Department CN
> 666 Fifth Avenue
> New York, New York 10102–0023

All photographs and entries become the property of Bantam Books and will not be returned under any circumstances.

2. Six men will be chosen by the Loveswept authors as a HOMETOWN HUNK (one HUNK per Loveswept title). By entering the contest, each winner and each person who enters a winner agrees to abide by Bantam Books' rules and to be subject to Bantam Books' eligibility requirements. Each winning HUNK and each person who enters a winner will be required to sign all papers deemed necessary by Bantam Books before receiving any prize. Each winning HUNK will be flown via **United Airlines** from his closest United Airlines-serviced city to New York City and will stay at the ▪▪ S▪SS▪▪▪ Hotel—the ideal hotel for business or pleasure in midtown Manhattan—for two nights. Winning HUNKS' meals and hotel transfers will be provided by Bantam Books. Travel and hotel arrangements are made by *▪▪▪▪▪▪ TRAVEL▪▪▪▪▪▪▪▪* and are subject to availability and to Bantam Books' date requirements. Each winning HUNK will pose with a female model at a photographer's studio for a photograph that will serve as the basis of a Loveswept front cover. Each winning HUNK will receive a $150.00 modeling fee. Each winning HUNK will be required to sign an Affidavit of Eligibility and Model's Release supplied by Bantam Books. (Approximate retail value of HOMETOWN HUNK'S PRIZE: $900.00.) The six people who send in a winning HOMETOWN HUNK photograph that is used by Bantam will receive free for one year each, LOVESWEPT romance paperback books published by Bantam during that year. (Approximate retail value: $180.00.) Each person who submits a winning photograph

will also be required to sign an Affidavit of Eligibility and Promotional Release supplied by Bantam Books. All winning HUNKS' (as well as the people who submit the winning photographs) names, addresses, biographical data and likenesses may be used by Bantam Books for publicity and promotional purposes without any additional compensation. There will be no prize substitutions or cash equivalents made.

3. All completed entries must be received by Bantam Books no later than September 15, 1988. Bantam Books is not responsible for lost or misdirected entries. The finalists will be selected by Loveswept editors and the six winning HOMETOWN HUNKS will be selected by the six authors of the participating Loveswept books. Winners will be selected on the basis of how closely the judges believe they reflect the descriptions of the books' heroes. Winners will be notified on or about October 31, 1988. If there are insufficient entries or if in the judges' opinions, no entry is suitable or adequately reflects the descriptions of the hero(s) in the book(s), Bantam may decide not to award a prize for the applicable book(s) and may reissue the book(s) at its discretion.

4. The contest is open to residents of the U.S. and Canada, except the Province of Quebec, and is void where prohibited by law. All federal and local regulations apply. Employees of Reliable Travel International, Inc., United Airlines, the Summit Hotel, and the Bantam Doubleday Dell Publishing Group, Inc., their subsidiaries and affiliates, and their immediate families are ineligible to enter.

5. For an extra copy of the Official Rules, the Official Entry Form, and the accompanying Loveswept cover notes, send your request and a self-addressed stamped envelope (Vermont and Washington State residents need not affix postage) before August 20, 1988 to the address listed in Paragraph 1 above.

LOVESWEPT® HOMETOWN HUNK OFFICIAL ENTRY FORM

BANTAM BOOKS
HOMETOWN HUNK CONTEST
Dept. CN
666 Fifth Avenue
New York, New York 10102–0023

HOMETOWN HUNK CONTEST

YOUR NAME_____

YOUR ADDRESS_____

CITY_____ STATE_____ ZIP_____

THE NAME OF THE LOVESWEPT BOOK FOR WHICH YOU ARE ENTERING THIS PHOTO

_____by_____

YOUR RELATIONSHIP TO YOUR HERO_____

YOUR HERO'S NAME_____

YOUR HERO'S ADDRESS_____

CITY_____ STATE_____ ZIP_____

YOUR HERO'S TELEPHONE #_____

YOUR HERO'S DATE OF BIRTH_____

YOUR HERO'S SIGNATURE CONSENTING TO HIS PHOTOGRAPH ENTRY

_____

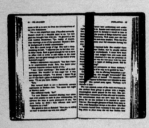

THE DELANEY DYNASTY

Men and women whose loves and passions are so glorious it takes many great romance novels by three bestselling authors to tell their tempestuous stories.

THE SHAMROCK TRINITY